WITHDRAWN

MOTHER was
a LOVELY
BEAST

MOTHER was a LOVELY BEAST

A Feral Man Anthology
Fiction and Fact About
Humans Raised by Animals
Edited by

Philip José Farmer

Chilton Book Company
Radnor, Pennsylvania

Library of Congress Cataloging in Publication Data

Farmer, Phillip Jose, comp.
 Mother was a lovely beast.

 CONTENTS: Burroughs, E. R. The God of Tarzan.—
Farmer, P. J. Extracts from the memoirs of "Lord
Greystoke".—Wolfe, G. Tarzan of the grapes. [etc.]
  1. Wolf children—Fiction. 2. Wolf children.
I. Title.
PZ1.F24Mo [PS648.W58] 813'.01 74-11117
ISBN 0-8019-5964-0

Acknowledgments

The God of Tarzan (from *Jungle Tales of Tarzan*) by Edgar Rice Bur-
    roughs is reprinted with the permission of Edgar Rice Burroughs,
    Inc., Copyright by Story Press Corporation, 1916, 1917.
Extracts From *The Memoirs of Lord Greystoke* is published with the
    permission of "John Clayton." Copyright © 1974, by Philip
    José Farmer.
Tarzan of the Grapes by Gene Wolfe. Copyright © 1972 by Mercury
    Press, Inc., reprinted by permission of the author and his agent,
    Virginia Kidd.
Relic by Mack Reynolds, Copyright © 1966 by Mercury Press, Inc.,
    reprinted by permission of the author and his agents, Scott Mere-
    dith Literary Agency, Inc., 580 Fifth Avenue, New York, N.Y.,
    10036.
One Against a Wilderness by William L. Chester. Copyright 1937 by
    The McCall Company.
Shasta of the Wolves (chapters II, III, V, XVIII) by Olaf Baker, re-
    printed by permission of Dodd, Mead and Company, Inc., from
    Shasta of the Wolves, by Olaf Baker. Copyright 1919 by Dodd,
    Mead and Company, Inc. Copyright renewed 1947 by Olaf Baker.
Scream of the Condor by George Bruce, first printed in *George Bruce's
    Sky Fighters*.
The Man Who Really Was . . . Tarzan by Thomas Llewellan Jones, first
    printed in *Man's Adventures*, March 1959, Stanley Publications,
    Inc., 261 Fifth Avenue, New York, N.Y., 10016.

Come on, poor babe,
Some powerful spirit instruct the kites
        and the ravens
To be thy nurses! Wolves and bears, they say,
Casting their savageness aside, have done
Like offices of pity.

The Winter's Tale

Contents

Introduction   ix
Foreword   2
THE GOD OF TARZAN   4
     Edgar Rice Burroughs
Foreword   23
EXTRACTS FROM THE MEMOIRS OF "LORD GREYSTOKE"   26
     Philip José Farmer (editor)
Foreword   76
TARZAN OF THE GRAPES   77
     Gene Wolfe
Foreword   86
RELIC   87
     Mack Reynolds
Foreword   109
ONE AGAINST A WILDERNESS   111
     William L. Chester
Foreword   136
SHASTA OF THE WOLVES   138
     Olaf Baker
Foreword   162
SCREAM OF THE CONDOR   163
     George Bruce
Foreword   216
THE MAN WHO REALLY WAS . . . TARZAN   217
     Thomas Llewellan Jones
Afterword   228
THE FERAL HUMAN IN MYTHOLOGY AND FICTION   231
     Philip José Farmer
Bibliography   244

Introduction

A FERAL man is a human being, male or female, who has been raised from an early age by wild animals or who has survived by himself since infancy in wild country.

The feral man theme has been popular since very early times, perhaps since the days of the cave man. Many heroes and heroines of classical myths were adopted by animals after their human parents had abandoned them. Wolves, lions, and bears were the favorite beast-parents of mythology, though goats often figured. These are also prominent in modern feral-man fiction, though the apes have become the most popular foster parents. This can be attributed to the fact that apes are closer to man in anatomy and intelligence than any other creature and are closely associated with the world-famous character of Tarzan.

The feral man theme has always had a strong appeal for several reasons. He is the only truly free man. Or at least he seems to be. He is especially liked by children and romanticists, who resent the strictures, tabus, vexations, and insecurities of civilization. He appeals to the desire to be close to Mother Nature. He is usually a heroic type or a superman and so vicariously satisfies the wish to be superior to others. Lastly, he appeals to realists when he is used in fiction to satirize the hypocrisies, stupidities, cruelties, and inhumanities of civilization. As the Noble Savage, the Outsider, the feral man looks objectively at the discrepancy between the ideal and the real in society.

Jonathan Swift did this when he depicted the Yahoos and the Houyhnhnms. He was deliberately paradoxical in making the all-too-human, truly feral Yahoos civilized man as he is and the sentient horses civilized man as he ought to be. Swift, of course, gave only half the truth. In the Yahoo, he left out those elements of compassion, tenderness, and striving-for-the-ideal that do exist in humanity. But in portraying the Houyhnhnms, he completed the painting. Man is both Yahoo and Houyhnhnm. Unfortunately, the Yahoo too often dominates.

Edgar Rice Burroughs' Tarzan books sometimes have this satiric element. Tarzan is the two-legged Houyhnhnm from the jungle, the Outsider, and we are the Yahoos. This use of satire in the Tarzan books has been overlooked by most literary critics, who regard Tarzan as a two-dimensional character in a comic book-type adventure series. But then they have never taken the trouble to study the Tarzan books. They base their misconceptions on the movies, which have little to do with the books. It is true that the Tarzan stories are largely "just adventure," but Tarzan is also a Candide wearing a leopard loincloth and is armed not only with a knife but an objective view of mankind. Burroughs, however, laughs gently, whereas Swift's mockery is savage and bitter.

The selections here are mainly items not previously available to the general public. Most are stories which have been out of print. Two, *Relic* and *Tarzan of the Grapes*, appeared in the *Magazine of Fantasy and Science-Fiction* a few years ago. The former is a satirical pastiche of the Tarzan legend and a prophecy of things to come. Wolfe's story is an example of modern myth derived from another modern myth which is itself a contemporization of an ancient myth. Myth, according to Marshall McLuhan, is the contraction, or implosion, of any process, the instant vision of a complex process that usually extends over a long period. In both Burroughs and Wolfe, the vision arises from one of the universal dreams that have existed since the Stone Age—the arrival of the hero, the demigod, as savior. Only the setting differs from that of the ancient myth; it is in our time.

Burroughs generally acts as the spokesman for the masses, who like their myths converted into folktales which deal, on the surface, with physical events. *The God of Tarzan* is an exception. *Tarzan of the Grapes* contains all the sociological relevance which critics find so important. But its essential relevance does not depend on ephemeral situations. At the same time, it could not have existed if the mythical figure of Burroughs' Tarzan had not existed. And Burroughs' hero is the extension of what Joseph Campbell says is the survival of the heroes and deeds and unconscious logic of myth. The two greatest psychologists of the twentieth century, Freud and Jung, he says, have irrefutably demonstrated this.

When I use "mythical" in connection with Tarzan, I do not mean that he is only a character created by Burroughs to embody modern myth. There are two elements in the Tarzan stories. One is that of romance, the fictional feral man who represents an important *persona* in the collective unconscious of humanity, an archetype overlooked by Carl Jung. The second is the very real element, since Tarzan is based on a man who actually existed.

A French writer, Lucien Malson, has written a thesis about fifty-two seemingly authenticated cases of European wild children. This appeared in 1966 in an issue of the Paris daily newspaper *Le Monde*. The French film director, Francois Truffaut, was so struck by this that he made a movie about "Victor," a child discovered living alone in the forests of Aveyron in 1798. He based the film on the newspaper accounts of that time and the reports of a Dr. Itard, a famous eye-ear-nose-and-throat specialist. Itard took the child into his house to study him and to develop the latent human characteristics of Victor. Itard had some success, though Victor was only able to utter a few words imperfectly; and he could not associate a word with the referent object unless it was actually in his hands.

Truffaut concluded that man is no more than an animal if he has been isolated from human society from an early age. Without going into the implications of "nothing but an animal," I can state that the feral children who became case histories were unable to use language. They had passed through a certain necessary stage in their development without encountering human speech, and the neural centers controlling language could no longer function. The child has to learn to speak at an early age. It is presumed that Victor did know language when he was left for dead by his parents, since he must have been about three or four at that time. But he had forgotten French; and in his seven to eight years of solitude, he had passed the critical stage of linguistic development. The potential for speech exists in every normal child, but the child without any society sinks into a state equal to that of a beast. I recommend, for those interested in Victor's case, *The Wild Child* by Francois Truffaut.

I also highly recommend *Wolf Child and Human Child, The Life History of Kamala the Wolf Girl*, by the distinguished child psychologist Arnold Gesell. This is an account of two girls apparently raised by some wolves in India. It includes photographs and excerpts from the diary of Reverend J. Singh (and his wife), who raised Kamala and Amala in their orphanage after the two were dug out of the wolves' den. Gesell was convinced that the case histories were authentic. However, in 1951 (after the death of Singh), the sociologist W. F. Ogburn and the anthropologist N. K. Bose personally investigated this case. They were unable to find the village that was supposed to have been near the den where the girls were captured. They did find some witnesses who said that the girls had been brought to Singh. They gave the reverend a good character, but others stated that Singh was a well-known liar. These, however, were natives whose faith made them hostile to Singh's Episcopalianism. Nor is it unlikely that the very small village of Godamuri, isolated in the jungle, could have disappeared between 1930 and 1951.

I've read the extracts and am convinced that it's either true or Singh had missed his calling as a novelist. There are too many realistic details which one would expect only from actual observation or from a writer gifted with superb extrapolative powers.

The nonfiction at the end of this volume consists of an article which may be a hoax or a semihoax and my informal essay on feral man in mythology and fiction. I would have liked to have included Malson's thesis, but it did not arrive from France in time. But if a sequel is published, it will contain his translated article.

Also, while I was preparing this collection, I received two stories which will be the brightest items in a sequel. These are *Twish of the Kofas,* by a new writer, Tincrowdor, and *Karhun Tytär (The Bear's Daughter)* by a Finnish woman, Liisa Jalava. These are the only good stories I've ever read about feral females. Unfortunately, the great majority of feral human stories are about males. I suppose that this is because most of the readers of such stories are males. Another reason is that the feral environment is so demanding that it is presumed only a rugged male could survive. This is ridiculous, since it has been established that the female of the species is as deadly as the male and somewhat more rugged. Moreover, the record of authentic cases of feral humans describes many females who thrived in animal society or survived through their own efforts in solitude.

The God of Tarzan is the only item herein readily available to the public. It can be obtained in the Ballantine Books edition of *Jungle Tales of Tarzan.* I have included it for several reasons. It is a fascinating account of how Tarzan taught himself to read and write English without having heard a word of English. It is a narrative of the dawning of the consciousness of God in a child raised in a society with no concept of cosmology or eschatology. And it helps illuminate some references in the autobiographical account which follows it, *Extracts from the Memoirs of "Lord Greystoke."*

MOTHER was a LOVELY BEAST

FOREWORD to
The God of Tarzan

The best feral human stories try to illuminate the
mind of the man or woman who has been raised in a
dark world, the nonhuman world. The nervous system of
the child is cast into a human mold by reason of its
heredity, but the environment has shaped it otherwise.
The mind has two parallel world-lines which, in a
Lobachevskian fashion, never quite meet. In
Lobachevsky's geometry, parallel lines don't meet;
but they do approach each other asymptotically. The
distance between them becomes less as they are extended.
Just so, the feral human's mind has adopted a
half-animal world view and may keep this unchanged
unless it encounters the human world. Then it becomes
more human. But it never becomes all human.

Throughout his Tarzan stories, Edgar Rice Burroughs
was more concerned with adventure than with
psychology. But every once in a while he would try
to extrapolate the feral human mind. He came closest
to success in the first novel, Tarzan of the Apes, and
in a collection of short stories, Jungle Tales of Tarzan.
The latter describes in physical and psychological
detail the ape man when he was nineteen, just before
he met white Westerners and shortly after he had
encountered black Africans of an isolated community.
In a sense, Tarzan had previously encountered the
Western world, since he had taught himself to read
English and had gained some fluency in reading

2

the books in the cabin of his long-dead parents. So he was not altogether the innocent. But his knowledge of the Western world was necessarily confused and vague. He had no referents.

My favorite among the Jungle Tales of Tarzan is The God of Tarzan. In this we see the ingenious method by which he taught himself to pronounce words he had never heard. He comes across references to God, the Creator, a concept unknown to the subhumans he grew up among. He becomes obsessed with eschatology, ontology, and cosmogony without, of course, having as yet come across these philosophical and theological terms. Like George Bernard Shaw's heroine in Adventures of the Black Girl in Her Search for God and Amos Tutuola's heroine of Simbi and the Satyr of the Dark Jungle, Tarzan goes forth to track down the Creator.

He fails in this quest, of course. But he discovers something in him that at least brings him closer to his Creator and, hence, to humanity. He discovers compassion.

The God of Tarzan

BY EDGAR RICE BURROUGHS

MONG the books of his dead father in the little cabin by the land-locked harbor, Tarzan of the Apes found many things to puzzle his young head. By much labor and through the medium of infinite patience as well, he had, without assistance, discovered the purpose of the little bugs which ran riot upon the printed pages. He had learned that in the many combinations in which he found them they spoke in a silent language, spoke in a strange tongue, spoke of wonderful things which a little ape-boy could not by any chance fully understand, arousing his curiosity, stimulating his imagination and filling his soul with a mighty longing for further knowledge.

A dictionary had proven itself a wonderful storehouse of information, when, after several years of tireless endeavor, he had solved the mystery of its purpose and the manner of its use. He had learned to make a species of game out of it, following up the spoor of a new thought through the mazes of the many definitions which each new word required him to consult. It was like following a quarry through the jungle—it was hunting, and Tarzan of the Apes was an indefatigable huntsman.

There were, of course, certain words which aroused his curiosity to a greater extent than others, words which, for one reason or another, excited his imagination. There was one, for example, the meaning of which was rather difficult to grasp. It was the word *God*. Tarzan first had been attracted to it by the fact that it was very short and that it commenced with a larger g-bug than those about it—a male g-bug it was to Tarzan, the lower-case letters being females. Another fact which attracted him to this word was the number of he-bugs which figured in its definition—Supreme Deity, Creator or Upholder of the Universe. This must be a very important word indeed, he would have to look into it, and he did, though it still baffled him after many months of thought and study.

However, Tarzan counted no time wasted which he devoted to these strange hunting expeditions into the game preserves of knowledge, for each word and each definition led on and on into strange places, into new worlds where, with increasing frequency, he met old, familiar faces. And always he added to his store of knowledge.

But of the meaning of *God* he was yet in doubt. Once he thought he had grasped it—that God was a mighty chieftain, king of all the Mangani. He was not quite sure, however, since that would mean that God was mightier than Tarzan—a point which Tarzan of the Apes, who acknowledged no equal in the jungle, was loath to concede.

But in all the books he had there was no picture of God, though he found much to confirm his belief that God was a great, an all-powerful individual. He saw pictures of places where God was worshiped; but never any sign of God. Finally he began to wonder if God were not of a different form than he, and at last he determined to set out in search of Him.

He commenced by questioning Mumga, who was very old and had seen many strange things in her long life; but Mumga, being an ape, had a faculty for recalling the trivial. That time when Gunto mistook a sting-bug for an edible beetle had made more impression upon Mumga than all the innumerable manifestations of the greatness of God which she had witnessed, and which, of course, she had not understood.

Numgo, overhearing Tarzan's questions, managed to

wrest his attention long enough from the diversion of
flea hunting to advance the theory that the power which
made the lightning and the rain and the thunder came
from Goro, the moon. He knew this, he said, because the
Dum-Dum always was danced in the light of Goro. This
reasoning, though entirely satisfactory to Numgo and
Mumga, failed fully to convince Tarzan. However, it
gave him a basis for further investigation along a new
line. He would investigate the moon.

That night he clambered to the loftiest pinnacle of
the tallest jungle giant. The moon was full, a great, glori-
ous, equatorial moon. The ape-man, upright upon a
slender, swaying limb, raised his bronzed face to the silver
orb. Now that he had clambered to the highest point
within his reach, he discovered, to his surprise, that Goro
was as far away as when he viewed him from the ground.
He thought that Goro was attempting to elude him.

"Come, Goro!" he cried, "Tarzan of the Apes will not
harm you!" But still the moon held aloof.

"Tell me," he continued, "if you be the great king
who sends Ara, the lightning; who makes the great noise
and the mighty winds, and sends the waters down upon
the jungle people when the days are dark and it is cold.
Tell me, Goro, are you God?"

Of course, he did not pronounce God as you or I
would pronounce His name, for Tarzan knew naught of
the spoken language of his English forbears; but he had
a name of his own invention for each of the little bugs
which constituted the alphabet. Unlike the apes he was
not satisfied merely to have a mental picture of the things
he knew, he must have a word descriptive of each. In
reading he grasped a word in its entirety; but when he
spoke the words he had learned from the books of his
father, he pronounced each according to the names he
had given the various little bugs which occurred in it,
usually giving the gender prefix for each.

Thus it was an imposing word which Tarzan made of
God. The masculine prefix of the apes is *bu*, the feminine

mu; g Tarzan had named *la*, o he pronounced *tu*, and d was *mo*. So the word *God* evolved itself into *Bulamutumumo*, or, in English, he-g-she-o-she-d.

Similarly he had arrived at a strange and wonderful spelling of his own name. Tarzan is derived from the two ape words *tar* and *zan*, meaning white skin. It was given him by his foster mother, Kala, the great she-ape. When Tarzan first put it into the written language of his own people he had not yet chanced upon either *white* or *skin* in the dictionary; but in a primer he had seen the picture of a little white boy and so he wrote his name *bumudomutomuro*, or he-boy.

To follow Tarzan's strange system of spelling would be laborious as well as futile, and so we shall in the future, as we have in the past, adhere to the more familiar forms of our grammar school copybooks. It would tire you to remember that *do* meant b, *tu* o, and *ro* y, and that to say he-boy you must prefix the ape masculine gender sound *bu* before the entire word and the feminine gender sound *mu* before each of the lower-case letters which go to make up boy—it would tire you and it would bring me to the nineteenth hole several strokes under par.

And so Tarzan harangued the moon, and when Goro did not reply, Tarzan of the Apes waxed wroth. He swelled his giant chest and bared his fighting fangs, and hurled into the teeth of the dead satellite the challenge of the bull ape.

"You are not Bulamutumumo," he cried. "You are not king of the jungle folk. You are not so great as Tarzan, mighty fighter, mighty hunter. None there is so great as Tarzan. If there be a Bulamutumumo, Tarzan can kill him. Come down, Goro, great coward, and fight with Tarzan. Tarzan will kill you. I am Tarzan, the killer."

But the moon made no answer to the boasting of the ape-man, and when a cloud came and obscured her face, Tarzan thought that Goro was indeed afraid, and was hiding from him, so he came down out of the trees and awoke Numgo and told him how great was Tarzan—how he had frightened Goro out of the sky and made him tremble. Tarzan spoke of the moon as *he*, for all things large or awe inspiring are male to the ape folk.

Numgo was not much impressed; but he was very sleepy, so he told Tarzan to go away and leave his betters alone.

"But where shall I find God?" insisted Tarzan. "You are very old; if there is a God you must have seen Him. What does He look like? Where does He live?"

"I am God," replied Numgo. "Now sleep and disturb me no more."

Tarzan looked at Numgo steadily for several minutes, his shapely head sank just a trifle between his great shoulders, his square chin shot forward and his short upper lip drew back, exposing his white teeth. Then, with a low growl he leaped upon the ape and buried his fangs in the other's hairy shoulder, clutching the great neck in his mighty fingers. Twice he shook the old ape, then he released his tooth-hold.

"Are you God?" he demanded.

"No," wailed Numgo. "I am only a poor, old ape. Leave me alone. Go ask the Gomangani where God is. They are hairless like yourself and very wise, too. They should know."

Tarzan released Numgo and turned away· The suggestion that he consult the blacks appealed to him, and though his relations with the people of Mbonga, the chief, were the antithesis of friendly, he could at least spy upon his hated enemies and discover if they had intercourse with God.

So it was that Tarzan set forth through the trees toward the village of the blacks, all excitement at the prospect of discovering the Supreme Being, the Creator of all things. As he traveled he reviewed, mentally, his armament—the condition of his hunting knife, the number of his arrows, the newness of the gut which strung his bow—he hefted the war spear which had once been the pride of some black warrior of Mbonga's tribe.

If he met God, Tarzan would be prepared. One could

never tell whether a grass rope, a war spear, or a poisoned arrow would be most efficacious against an unfamiliar foe. Tarzan of the Apes was quite content—if God wished to fight, the ape-man had no doubt as to the outcome of the struggle. There were many questions Tarzan wished to put to the Creator of the Universe and so he hoped that God would not prove a belligerent God; but his experience of life and the ways of living things had taught him that any creature with the means for offense and defense was quite likely to provoke attack if in the proper mood.

It was dark when Tarzan came to the village of Mbonga. As silently as the silent shadows of the night he sought his accustomed place among the branches of the great tree which overhung the palisade. Below him, in the village street, he saw men and women. The men were hideously painted—more hideously than usual. Among them moved a weird and grotesque figure, a tall figure that went upon the two legs of a man and yet had the head of a buffalo. A tail dangled to his ankles behind him, and in one hand he carried a zebra's tail while the other clutched a bunch of small arrows.

Tarzan was electrified. Could it be that chance had given him thus early an opportunity to look upon God? Surely this thing was neither man nor beast, so what could it be then other than the Creator of the Universe! The ape-man watched the every move of the strange creature. He saw the black men and women fall back at its approach as though they stood in terror of its mysterious powers.

Presently he discovered that the deity was speaking and that all listened in silence to his words. Tarzan was sure that none other than God could inspire such awe in the hearts of the Gomangani, or stop their mouths so effectually without recourse to arrows or spears. Tarzan had come to look with contempt upon the blacks, principally because of their garrulity. The small apes talked a great deal and ran away from an enemy. The big, old bulls of Kerchak talked but little and fought upon the slightest provocation. Numa, the lion, was not given to loquacity, yet of all the jungle folk there were few who fought more often than he.

Tarzan witnessed strange things that night, none of which he understood, and, perhaps because they were strange, he thought that they must have to do with the God he could not understand. He saw three youths receive their first war spears in a weird ceremony which the grotesque witch-doctor strove successfully to render uncanny and awesome.

Hugely interested, he watched the slashing of the three brown arms and the exchange of blood with Mbonga, the chief, in the rites of the ceremony of blood brotherhood. He saw the zebra's tail dipped into a caldron of water above which the witch-doctor had made magical passes the while he danced and leaped about it, and he saw the breasts and foreheads of each of the three novitiates sprinkled with the charmed liquid. Could the ape-man have known the purpose of this act, that it was intended to render the recipient invulnerable to the attacks of his enemies and fearless in the face of any danger, he would doubtless have leaped into the village street and appropriated the zebra's tail and a portion of the contents of the caldron.

But he did not know, and so he only wondered, not alone at what he saw but at the strange sensations which played up and down his naked spine, sensations induced, doubtless, by the same hypnotic influence which held the black spectators in tense awe upon the verge of a hysteric upheaval.

The longer Tarzan watched, the more convinced he became that his eyes were upon God, and with the conviction came determination to have word with the deity. With Tarzan of the Apes, to think was to act.

The people of Mbonga were keyed to the highest pitch of hysterical excitement. They needed little to release the accumulated pressure of static nerve force which the terrorizing mummery of the witch-doctor had induced.

A lion roared, suddenly and loud, close without the palisade. The blacks started nervously, dropping into utter silence as they listened for a repetition of that all-too-familiar and always terrorizing voice. Even the witch-doctor paused in the midst of an intricate step, remaining momentarily rigid and statuesque as he plumbed his cunning mind for a suggestion as how best he might take advantage of the condition of his audience and the timely interruption.

Already the evening had been vastly profitable to him. There would be three goats for the initiation of the three youths into full-fledged warriorship, and besides these he had received several gifts of grain and beads, together with a piece of copper wire from admiring and terrified members of his audience.

Numa's roar still reverberated along taut nerves when a woman's laugh, shrill and piercing, shattered the silence of the village. It was this moment that Tarzan chose to drop lightly from his tree into the village street. Fearless among his blood enemies he stood, taller by a full head than many of Mbonga's warriors, straight as their straightest arrow, muscled like Numa, the lion.

For a moment Tarzan stood looking straight at the witch-doctor. Every eye was upon him, yet no one had moved—a paralysis of terror held them, to be broken a moment later as the ape-man, with a toss of head, stepped straight toward the hideous figure beneath the buffalo head.

Then the nerves of the blacks could stand no more. For months the terror of the strange, white, jungle god had been upon them. Their arrows had been stolen from the very center of the village; their warriors had been silently slain upon the jungle trails and their dead bodies dropped mysteriously and by night into the village street as from the heavens above.

One or two there were who had glimpsed the strange figure of the new demon and it was from their oft-repeated descriptions that the entire village now recognized Tarzan as the author of many of their ills. Upon another occasion and by daylight, the warriors would doubtless have leaped to attack him, but at night, and

this night of all others, when they were wrought to such
a pitch of nervous dread by the uncanny artistry of their
witch-doctor, they were helpless with terror. As one man
they turned and fled, scattering for their huts, as Tarzan
advanced. For a moment one and one only held his
ground. It was the witch-doctor. More than half self-
hypnotized into a belief in his own charlatanry he faced
this new demon who threatened to undermine his ancient and lucrative profession.

"Are you God?" asked Tarzan.

The witch-doctor, having no idea of the meaning of the
other's words, danced a few strange steps, leaped high in
the air, turning completely around and alighting in a
stooping posture with feet far outspread and head thrust
out toward the ape-man. Thus he remained for an instant
before he uttered a loud "Boo!" which was evidently intended to frighten Tarzan away; but in reality had no
such effect.

Tarzan did not pause. He had set out to approach and
examine God and nothing upon earth might now stay his
feet. Seeing that his antics had no potency with the visitor, the witch-doctor tried some new medicine. Spitting
upon the zebra's tail, which he still clutched in one hand,
he made circles above it with the arrows in the other
hand, meanwhile backing cautiously away from Tarzan
and speaking confidentially to the bushy end of the tail·

This medicine must be short medicine, however, for
the creature, god or demon, was steadily closing up the
distance which had separated them. The circles therefore
were few and rapid, and when they were completed, the
witch-doctor struck an attitude which was intended to be
awe inspiring and waving the zebra's tail before him, drew
an imaginary line between himself and Tarzan.

"Beyond this line you cannot pass, for my medicine is
strong medicine," he cried. "Stop, or you will fall dead as
your foot touches this spot. My mother was a voodoo, my
father was a snake; I live upon lions' hearts and the en-
trails of the panther; I eat young babies for breakfast and
the demons of the jungle are my slaves. I am the most

powerful witch-doctor in the world; I fear nothing, for I cannot die. I—" But he got no further; instead he turned and fled as Tarzan of the Apes crossed the magical dead line and still lived.

As the witch-doctor ran, Tarzan almost lost his temper. This was no way for God to act, at least not in accordance with the conception Tarzan had come to have of God.

"Come back!" he cried. "Come back, God, I will not harm you." But the witch-doctor was in full retreat by this time, stepping high as he leaped over cooking pots and the smoldering embers of small fires that had burned before the huts of villagers. Straight for his own hut ran the witch-doctor, terror-spurred to unwonted speed; but futile was his effort—the ape-man bore down upon him with the speed of Bara, the deer.

Just at the entrance to his hut the witch-doctor was overhauled. A heavy hand fell upon his shoulder to drag him back. It seized upon a portion of the buffalo hide, dragging the disguise from him. It was a naked black man that Tarzan saw dodge into the darkness of the hut's interior.

So this was what he had thought was God! Tarzan's lip curled in an angry snarl as he leaped into the hut after the terror-stricken witch-doctor. In the blackness within he found the man huddled at the far side and dragged him forth into the comparative lightness of the moonlit night.

The witch-doctor bit and scratched in an attempt to escape; but a few cuffs across the head brought him to a better realization of the futility of resistance. Beneath the moon Tarzan held the cringing figure upon its shaking feet.

"So you are God!" he cried. "If you be God, then Tarzan is greater than God," and so the ape-man thought. "I am Tarzan," he shouted into the ear of the black. "In all the jungle, or above it, or upon the running waters, or the sleeping waters, or upon the big water, or the little water, there is none so great as Tarzan. Tarzan is greater than the Mangani; he is greater than the Gomangani.

With his own hands he has slain Numa, the lion, and
Sheeta, the panther; there is none so great as Tarzan.
Tarzan is greater than God. See!" and with a sudden
wrench he twisted the black's neck until the fellow
shrieked in pain and then slumped to the earth in a
swoon.

Placing his foot upon the neck of the fallen witch-
doctor, the ape-man raised his face to the moon and
uttered the long, shrill scream of the victorious bull ape.
Then he stooped and snatched the zebra's tail from the
nerveless fingers of the unconscious man and without a
backward glance retraced his footsteps across the village.

From several hut doorways frightened eyes watched
him. Mbonga, the chief, was one of those who had seen
what passed before the hut of the witch-doctor. Mbonga
was greatly concerned. Wise old patriarch that he was,
he never had more than half believed in witch-doctors,
at least not since greater wisdom had come with age; but
as a chief he was well convinced of the power of the
witch-doctor as an arm of government, and often it was
that Mbonga used the superstitious fears of his people to
his own ends through the medium of the medicine-man.

Mbonga and the witch-doctor had worked together and
divided the spoils, and now the "face" of the witch-doctor
would be lost forever if any saw what Mbonga had seen;
nor would this generation again have as much faith in any
future witch-doctor.

Mbonga must do something to counteract the evil influence of the forest demon's victory over the witch-doctor. He raised his heavy spear and crept silently from his
hut in the wake of the retreating ape-man. Down the
village street walked Tarzan, as unconcerned and as deliberate as though only the friendly apes of Kerchak
surrounded him instead of a village full of armed enemies.

Seeming only was the indifference of Tarzan, for alert
and watchful was every well-trained sense. Mbonga, wily
stalker of keen-eared jungle creatures, moved now in utter
silence. Not even Bara, the deer, with his great ears could
have guessed from any sound that Mbonga was near; but

the black was not stalking Bara; he was stalking man, and so he sought only to avoid noise.

Closer and closer to the slowly moving ape-man he came. Now he raised his war spear, throwing his spear-hand far back above his right shoulder. Once and for all would Mbonga, the chief, rid himself and his people of the menace of this terrifying enemy. He would make no poor cast; he would take pains, and he would hurl his weapon with such great force as would finish the demon forever.

But Mbonga, sure as he thought himself, erred in his calculations. He might believe that he was stalking a man —he did not know, however, that it was a man with the delicate sense perception of the lower orders. Tarzan, when he had turned his back upon his enemies, had noted what Mbonga never would have thought of considering in the hunting of man—the wind. It was blowing in the same direction that Tarzan was proceeding, carrying to his delicate nostrils the odors which arose behind him. Thus it was that Tarzan knew that he was being followed, for even among the many stenches of an African village, the ape-man's uncanny faculty was equal to the task of differentiating one stench from another and locating with remarkable precision the source from whence it came.

He knew that a man was following him and coming closer, and his judgment warned him of the purpose of the stalker. When Mbonga, therefore, came within spear range of the ape-man, the latter suddenly wheeled upon him, so suddenly that the poised spear was shot a fraction of a second before Mbonga had intended. It went a trifle high and Tarzan stooped to let it pass over his head; then he sprang toward the chief. But Mbonga did not wait to receive him. Instead, he turned and fled for the dark door-way of the nearest hut, calling as he went for his warriors to fall upon the stranger and slay him.

Well indeed might Mbonga scream for help, for Tarzan, young and fleet-footed, covered the distance between them in great leaps, at the speed of a charging lion. He was growling, too, not at all unlike Numa himself. Mbonga heard and his blood ran cold. He could feel the wool stiffen upon his pate and a prickly chill run up his spine, as though Death had come and run his cold finger along Mbonga's back.

Others heard, too, and saw, from the darkness of their huts—bold warriors, hideously painted, grasping heavy war spears in nerveless fingers. Against Numa, the lion, they would have charged fearlessly. Against many times their own number of black warriors would they have raced to the protection of their chief; but this weird jungle demon filled them with terror. There was nothing human in the bestial growls that rumbled up from his deep chest; there was nothing human in the bared fangs, or the cat-like leaps. Mbonga's warriors were terrified—too terrified to leave the seeming security of their huts while they watched the beast-man spring full upon the back of their old chieftain.

Mbonga went down with a scream of terror. He was too frightened even to attempt to defend himself. He just lay beneath his antagonist in a paralysis of fear, screaming at the top of his lungs. Tarzan half rose and kneeled above the black. He turned Mbonga over and looked him in the face, exposing the man's throat, then he drew his long, keen knife, the knife that John Clayton, Lord Greystoke, had brought from England many years before. He raised it close above Mbonga's neck. The old black whimpered with terror. He pleaded for his life in a tongue which Tarzan could not understand.

For the first time the ape-man had a close view of the chief. He saw an old man, a very old man with scrawny neck and wrinkled face—a dried, parchment-like face which resembled some of the little monkeys Tarzan knew so well. He saw the terror in the man's eyes—never before had Tarzan seen such terror in the eyes of any animal, or such a piteous appeal for mercy upon the face of any creature.

Something stayed the ape-man's hand for an instant. He wondered why it was that he hesitated to make the kill; never before had he thus delayed. The old man seemed to wither and shrink to a bag of puny bones beneath his eyes. So weak and helpless and terror-stricken he appeared that the ape-man was filled with a great contempt; but another sensation also claimed him—something new to Tarzan of the Apes in relation to an enemy. It was pity—pity for a poor, frightened, old man.

Tarzan rose and turned away, leaving Mbonga, the chief, unharmed. With head held high the ape-man walked through the village, swung himself into the branches of the tree which overhung the palisade and disappeared from the sight of the villagers.

All the way back to the stamping ground of the apes, Tarzan sought for an explanation of the strange power which had stayed his hand and prevented him from slaying Mbonga. It was as though someone greater than he had commanded him to spare the life of the old man. Tarzan could not understand, for he could conceive of nothing, or no one, with the authority to dictate to him what he should do, or what he should refrain from doing.

It was late when Tarzan sought a swaying couch among the trees beneath which slept the apes of Kerchak, and he was still absorbed in the solution of his strange problem when he fell asleep.

The sun was well up in the heavens when he awoke. The apes were astir in search of food. Tarzan watched them lazily from above as they scratched in the rotting loam for bugs and beetles and grubworms, or sought among the branches of the trees for eggs and young birds, or luscious caterpillars.

An orchid, dangling close beside his head, opened slowly, unfolding its delicate petals to the warmth and light of the sun which but recently had penetrated to its shady retreat. A thousand times had Tarzan of the Apes witnessed the beauteous miracle; but now it aroused a keener interest, for the ape-man was just commencing to ask himself questions about all the myriad wonders which heretofore he had but taken for granted.

What made the flower open? What made it grow from

a tiny bud to a full-blown bloom? Why was it at all? Why
was he? Where did Numa, the lion, come from? Who
planted the first tree? How did Goro get way up into the
darkness of the night sky to cast his welcome light upon
the fearsome nocturnal jungle? And the sun! Did the sun
merely happen there?

Why were all the peoples of the jungle not trees? Why
were the trees not something else? Why was Tarzan different from Taug, and Taug different from Bara, the deer,
and Bara different from Sheeta, the panther, and why was
not Sheeta like Buto, the rhinoceros? Where and how,
anyway, did they all come from—the trees, the flowers,
the insects, the countless creatures of the jungle?

Quite unexpectedly an idea popped into Tarzan's head.
In following out the many ramifications of the dictionary
definition of God he had come upon the word *create*—
"to cause to come into existence; to form out of nothing."

Tarzan almost had arrived at something tangible when
a distant wail startled him from his preoccupation into
sensibility of the present and the real. The wail came
from the jungle at some little distance from Tarzan's swaying couch. It was the wail of a tiny balu. Tarzan recognized it at once as the voice of Gazan, Teeka's baby. They
had called it Gazan because its soft, baby hair had been
unusually red, and *Gazan* in the language of the great
apes, means red skin.

The wail was immediately followed by a real scream
of terror from the small lungs. Tarzan was electrified into
instant action. Like an arrow from a bow he shot through
the trees in the direction of the sound. Ahead of him he
heard the savage snarling of an adult she-ape. It was
Teeka to the rescue. The danger must be very real. Tarzan could tell that by the note of rage mingled with fear
in the voice of the she.

Running along bending limbs, swinging from one tree
to another, the ape-man raced through the middle ter-
races toward the sounds which now had risen in volume
to deafening proportions. From all directions the apes of
Kerchak were hurrying in response to the appeal in the

tones of the balu and its mother, and as they came, their roars reverberated through the forest.

But Tarzan, swifter than his heavy fellows, distanced them all. It was he who was first upon the scene. What he saw sent a cold chill through his giant frame, for the enemy was the most hated and loathed of all the jungle creatures.

Twined in a great tree was Histah, the snake—huge, ponderous, slimy—and in the folds of its deadly embrace was Teeka's little balu, Gazan. Nothing in the jungle inspired within the breast of Tarzan so near a semblance to fear as did the hideous Histah. The apes, too, loathed the terrifying reptile and feared him even more than they did Sheeta, the panther, or Numa, the lion. Of all their enemies there was none they gave a wider berth than they gave Histah, the snake.

Tarzan knew that Teeka was peculiarly fearful of this silent, repulsive foe, and as the scene broke upon his vision, it was the action of Teeka which filled him with the greatest wonder, for at the moment that he saw her, the she-ape leaped upon the glistening body of the snake, and as the mighty folds encircled her as well as her offspring, she made no effort to escape, but instead grasped the writhing body in a futile effort to tear it from her screaming balu.

Tarzan knew all too well how deep-rooted was Teeka's terror of Histah. He scarce could believe the testimony of his own eyes then, when they told him that she had voluntarily rushed into that deadly embrace. Nor was Teeka's innate dread of the monster much greater than Tarzan's own. Never, willingly, had he touched a snake. Why, he could not say, for he would admit fear of nothing; nor was it fear, but rather an inherent repulsion bequeathed to him by many generations of civilized ancestors, and back of them, perhaps, by countless myriads of such as Teeka, in the breasts of each of which had lurked the same nameless terror of the slimy reptile.

Yet Tarzan did not hesitate more than had Teeka, but leaped upon Histah with all the speed and impetuosity

that he would have shown had he been springing upon
Bara, the deer, to make a kill for food. Thus beset the
snake writhed and twisted horribly; but not for an instant
did it loose its hold upon any of its intended victims, for
it had included the ape-man in its cold embrace the
minute that he had fallen upon it.

Still clinging to the tree, the mighty reptile held the
three as though they had been without weight, the while
it sought to crush the life from them. Tarzan had drawn
his knife and this he now plunged rapidly into the body
of the enemy; but the encircling folds promised to sap
his life before he had inflicted a death wound upon the
snake. Yet on he fought, nor once did he seek to escape
the horrid death that confronted him—his sole aim was
to slay Histah and thus free Teeka and her balu.

The great, wide-gaping jaws of the snake turned and
hovered above him. The elastic maw, which could accom-
modate a rabbit or a horned buck with equal facility,
yawned for him; but Histah, in turning his attention upon
the ape-man, brought his head within reach of Tarzan's
blade. Instantly a brown hand leaped forth and seized
the mottled neck, and another drove the heavy hunting
knife to the hilt into the little brain.

Convulsively Histah shuddered and relaxed, tensed and
relaxed again, whipping and striking with his great body;
but no longer sentient or sensible. Histah was dead, but
in his death throes he might easily dispatch a dozen apes
or men.

Quickly Tarzan seized Teeka and dragged her from the
loosened embrace, dropping her to the ground beneath,
then he extricated the balu and tossed it to its mother.
Still Histah whipped about, clinging to the ape-man; but
after a dozen efforts Tarzan succeeded in wriggling free
and leaping to the ground out of range of the mighty
battering of the dying snake.

A circle of apes surrounded the scene of the battle; but
the moment that Tarzan broke safely from the enemy
they turned silently away to resume their interrupted
feeding, and Teeka turned with them, apparently forget-

ful of all but her balu and the fact that when the interruption had occurred she just had discovered an ingeniously hidden nest containing three perfectly good eggs.

Tarzan, equally indifferent to a battle that was over, merely cast a parting glance at the still writhing body of Histah and wandered off toward the little pool which served to water the tribe at this point. Strangely, he did not give the victory cry over the vanquished Histah. Why, he could not have told you, other than that to him Histah was not an animal. He differed in some peculiar way from the other denizens of the jungle. Tarzan only knew that he hated him.

At the pool Tarzan drank his fill and lay stretched upon the soft grass beneath the shade of a tree. His mind reverted to the battle with Histah, the snake. It seemed strange to him that Teeka should have placed herself within the folds of the horrid monster. Why had she done it? Why, indeed, had he? Teeka did not belong to him, nor did Teeka's balu. They were both Taug's. Why then had he done this thing? Histah was not food for him when he was dead. There seemed to Tarzan, now that he gave the matter thought, no reason in the world why he should have done the thing he did, and presently it occurred to him that he had acted almost involuntarily, just as he had acted when he had released the old Gomangani the previous evening.

What made him do such things? Somebody more powerful than he must force him to act at times. "All-powerful," thought Tarzan. "The little bugs say that God is all-powerful. It must be that God made me do these things, for I never did them by myself. It was God made Teeka rush upon Histah. Teeka would never go near Histah of her own volition. It was God who held my knife from the throat of the old Gomangani. God accomplishes strange things for he is 'all-powerful.' I cannot see Him; but I know that it must be God who does these things. No Mangani, no Gomangani, no Tarmangani could do them."

And the flowers—who made them grow? Ah, now it

was all explained—the flowers, the trees, the moon, the sun, himself, every living creature in the jungle—they were all made by God out of nothing.

And what was God? What did God look like? Of that he had no conception; but he was sure that everything that was good came from God. His good act in refraining from slaying the poor, defenseless old Gomangani; Teeka's love that had hurled her into the embrace of death; his own loyalty to Teeka which had jeopardized his life that she might live. The flowers and the trees were good and beautiful. God had made them. He made the other creatures, too, that each might have food upon which to live. He had made Sheeta, the panther, with his beautiful coat; and Numa, the lion, with his noble head and his shaggy mane. He had made Bara, the deer, lovely and graceful.

Yes, Tarzan had found God, and he spent the whole day in attributing to Him all of the good and beautiful things of nature; but there was one thing which troubled him. He could not quite reconcile it to his conception of his new-found God.

Who made Histah, the snake?

FOREWORD to
Extracts from the
Memoirs of "Lord Greystoke"

The items in this book are divided into three classes. One
contains fictional accounts of feral human beings. A
second, by far the smallest, is the terminal essay. The
third is the only valid example of first-person reporting by
a feral man himself, and it is presented here.

This is composed of selections from memoirs written
by a man who was raised from the age of one by beings
halfway on the scale of evolution between the great apes
and modern man. His parents, English aristocrats, were
marooned on the coast of Gabon, then French Equatorial
Africa, in 1888. His mother died a year after he was born,
and his father was killed the same day. Fortunately, he
was taken from the cradle and raised by a female
"anthropoid" whose own baby had just died.

In 1909, "Lord Greystoke" made his first contact with
whites and was taken to France. After a series of
adventures, he assumed his British inheritance, which
included a title. He also married an American woman of
an old Virginia and Maryland family. In 1912 an
American writer, Edgar Rice Burroughs, heard some
garbled accounts of "Greystoke" and used these as the
basis for a novel which now ranks among the world
classics of literature. This was Tarzan of the Apes, a highly
fictionalized narrative which nevertheless was essentially
true.

In 1968 I was able to ascertain the true identity of
"Lord Greystoke" and to track him down. I did this

23

through a close study of Burke's Peerage and another
source I am not free to divulge. I got in contact with
"Greystoke," and he agreed to give me a fifteen-minute
interview. An abridged version of this was printed in the
Esquire magazine of September 1972. The meeting
supposedly took place in Libreville, Gabon. But I have
now been given permission by "Greystoke" to reveal that
this actually occurred in a motel near Chicago.

The interview was so short that I was not able to ask
nearly all the questions I had hoped to. "Greystoke,"
however, promised that he would send me some portions
of his memoirs and that I could publish them. He did not
say when he would send them or from where. But in May
1973, I received a package mailed from San Francisco.
Part of it is printed herein.

I was happy to learn just how "Greystoke" managed to
come into his inheritance and title. Burroughs, referred to
as "B" in these memoirs, wrote that "Greystoke" was
revealed as the true heir after his cousin died. I knew that
this could not be true. Such a spectacular event would
have been widely publicized, and the world would know
exactly who "Greystoke" was. The account here explains
how "Greystoke" managed to avoid all publicity and
exposure. I had suspected that something such as he
describes had occurred, and I am glad that my suspicions
were valid. The beauty of this revelation is that even now,
without a certain clue which I discovered quite by
accident, the identity of "Greystoke" remains a secret.

I was also happy because this is the only account that I
have ever read which gives an insight into what it is like to
be a feral man. It tells in authentic detail just how he was
raised; it gives the mundane details, in short, the days in
the life of a truly wild man. It also offers some insight into
the psychology of a human raised by nonhumans. Or, to
be exact, a human raised by creatures as close to beasts as
to humans.

In one sense, "Greystoke" is not a true feral man. The
beings among whom he grew up were language-users, and
this differentiates him from all the other authentic cases

of feral men. *He was not linguistically, and hence
mentally, retarded. He grew up in a society which was less
than human but which had enough human elements to
enable him to adjust to the culture of Homo sapiens.*

*The wording herein is not always that of "Greystoke."
It is frank enough as it is, but I have substituted Latinisms
for his "Anglo-Saxonisms" in his references to sexual and
excretory matters. "Greystoke" has no emotional
reactions to the use of "tabu" words and felt free to use
them in his memoirs. I have made the substitutions
necessitated by the recent Supreme Court ruling on
obscenity and pornography, which is a step backwards
toward Victorian darkness and idiocy.*

*The order of the sections here is not necessarily as
arranged by "Greystoke."*

Extracts from the
Memoirs of "Lord Greystoke"

EDITED BY PHILIP JOSÉ FARMER

HOW IT WAS WITH J

I LOOKED out of the cabin window, and there was the ship.

I'd seen ships in pictures. But this was a real sailing ship, an enormous thing of beauty and awe.

I knew it was artificial, but I never thought of it as such. It was a living being, as much alive as an elephant and even stranger than my first sight of an elephant. I never was to get over that deeply ingrained assumption that anything that moved was alive. I've traveled on a hundred ships, driven dozens of automobiles, and piloted scores of airplanes, and I always feel that I am on or in a living being.

And so I waited for the great creature to come to a stop and let the smaller creatures, human beings, from its back. My heart was thudding, I was dry-skinned, my mouth was dry, and I was quivering. At last! To see, not pictures, but the flesh! To face, to talk with, beings of my own kind!

Still, I did not run out to greet them. My experiences with the blacks had taught me that humans might be hostile no matter how friendly I was. I retreated from the cabin to the bush, and there I spied on them. Presently, a longboat was let down off the davits (I was proud because I knew what *davits* were, though I couldn't pronounce the word, of course).

After a while, the boat beached, and some men got out onto the sand. A few minutes later, one of them was murdered during a quarrel.

26

I was wise to hide in the bush. They were dangerous.

When I saw J* step out of the boat, I was thrilled. I had never seen anything so beautiful except for my foster mother, and that was a completely different kind of beauty, of course. I also got an erection.

This was the normal response of a twenty-year-old human male and of an adult male n'k. B never mentioned this in his novel for several reasons. One, he did not know of it. Two, if he had guessed that it did occur, he could not have described it. Such references were forbidden. He might have said that I was "inflamed with lust," but then the literary conventions required that the hero be "pure in thought and deed." "Purity" required that his mind and body be unconnected with his genitals. Every adult reader knew, of course, that the hero would have an erection, but this was ignored. Or perhaps every adult reader did not know this. The ignorance of sexual matters among the female population of English speakers circa 1909 was amazing. And often tragic.

I did know, from my reading, that the characters in the novels were never described as having genitals nor was the sexual act described except by the most circuitous route. And only the villains were ever "inflamed with lust."

I knew that if I were to display myself to the woman, she would be shocked and repelled. But even if I had done so, I was wearing an antelope-skin loincloth. This was one I'd taken from a black and habitually wore because I knew that humans did not expose their genitals. I was mistaken in this, since a number of preliterates, various Sudanese blacks, and Australian aborigines, etc., go completely naked. Or did so at that time.

The males who had first landed seemed to be in control of the woman and her party, so I did not venture

* I don't know if this stands for Jane, Jean, Jill, June, or some other name. "Greystoke" has the annoying, but necessary, habit of using initials only to designate individuals whose identity needs shielding.

out. I was afraid, rightly, that the sailors would try to
kill me if I revealed myself. I intended to watch until I
got a chance to rescue the woman and her party. I wasn't
sure whether or not the sailors intended to butcher their
prisoners and eat them. Though none of the novels or
histories I'd read had said anything about cannibalism
being accepted in human civilization, I assumed that it
was tabu. The article on cannibalism in the encyclopedia
stated that the custom was prevalent among certain
groups of African blacks, and I knew that the blacks near
the n'k territory were cannibals. Perhaps the practice
existed among some groups of whites.

In any event, I did know that rape was common among
all groups of men, and I was determined that the woman
was not going to be raped. Not unless, of course, she
accepted it. I understood that there were certain women,
prostitutes or whores, who sold their bodies for use by
men. The woman did not seem to be one of those, but
then I did not know exactly how one recognized a whore.

I kept a close watch on the tall beautiful blonde with
the large grey eyes. Events for the next few days occurred
somewhat as B described them, including my posting
a warning note on the door of the cabin after it had been
ransacked by the mutineers. I was capable by then of
writing simple English sentences. Contrary to what B
wrote, however, I did not sign my n'k name. This would
have been impossible, since I did not know the correla-
tion of n'k sounds with the Latin alphabet. I printed the
English translation of one of my n'k names: WHITE
BOY. Rather, I gave the translation I preferred. As I've
said elsewhere, my name could be translated as Worm,
Hairless Boy, and others even more derogatory.

B was also correct when he described me as breaking
the neck of a big cat with a full nelson when it tried to
get into the cabin window after J and E.* However, the
cat was a leopard, not a lioness, and it was an old male.

---

* J's black mother surrogate, the servant of J's father. J's mother died
at J's birth, and E raised her. E was J's chaperone on the treasure-
hunting expedition.

One of the extraordinarily large leopards that existed in that area, it had become a man-eater, preying on the village of blacks. Actually, it was my fault that it was a man-eater, since I had thrown the body of one of the blacks I'd killed to it and so enabled it to acquire a taste for human meat.

On that day when J and E bathed in a pool and J was carried off by Tks, I heard her screaming and tracked the two down. Tks had become king of the tribe after I'd abdicated, but he had been driven out because of his cruelty and his disdain of the tribal laws. He was, I believe, a psychopath. His aberrations may have been caused by being dropped on his head when he was an infant. In any event, he was wandering around when he saw J bathing. He grabbed her and ran off. He did not swing through the trees with her as B described. He was too heavy to have progressed in monkey fashion even if he had been alone. He ran with her in his arms until he got winded and then pushed her ahead of him.

I arrived before he could rape her, and I killed him with my knife. This would have happened sooner or later, since Tks hated me, and I was happy to have it over with. Besides, it made me look good in J's eyes.

She, however, had a short-lived relief. I scooped her up and kissed her all over, as was the n'k custom when making love. This panicked her, and she fought and screamed. I stopped, since I did not want to offend her, though I did not understand why she was so frightened. After I released her, she insisted that we return to the pool so she could put her clothes on. I did not understand her words or gestures, though the gestures were plain enough. I think now that I did not want to understand her. I wanted to keep her for my own, and I was sure that in a short time she would get over her fright.

As B said, I did not return her to the cabin until the next day. She got over her fright somewhat, though my evident tumescent state ensured that she could not relax completely. When night came, I tried to hold her in my arms to keep her warm (also hoping by this to overcome her objections). But she would have none of that. She preferred to sit against the trunk of a tree and shiver all night.

Our relations were not quite as idyllic or as innocent as B portrayed.

Next day, I took her back to the pool, where she donned her clothes. I wanted to watch her, but she made it evident that I must not do so. After a while, I got the idea and turned my back. I did not understand why she was so embarrassed by covering her nakedness. After all, she had been completely naked for twenty-four hours.

Now that I look back on it, I am surprised that J did not become so disgusted with me that she found it impossible to love me. My eating habits must have repulsed her, and my lack of Western toilet training horrified her. But she understood that I was a feral man and that I was in no way responsible for my behavior. She also understood that I was restraining myself from making love to her and so I got some credit as being a basically decent human being.

I wonder what she would have thought if she had known that I'd mated quite often with some of the n'k females? I was unable to tell her about this at that time, and it was just as well. Though she was a liberal-minded woman despite her Victorian conditioning, she might not ever have forgiven me for having three wives. Having had, I should say. When I abdicated the kingship and left the tribe, I also divorced the three females, since I did not want them as companions.

Some years later, I told her about them, and her only response was to laugh and to ask me if I had had any children by them. I answered, truthfully, that I had not.

Since these females had babies by n'k males after I'd left them, it was evident that they were not sterile. I don't know whether it was impossible for a human to fertilize a n'k or whether I am just not very fertile. I've had only one child by J, though we've never used any birth control methods. So I presume that I am at fault.

But, as J has several times remarked, thank goodness virility has nothing to do with fertility.

THE WAY IT WAS WITH O

In his second novel about me, B gives a somewhat bowdlerized and distorted account of my "affair" with O, Countess C. (Lovely woman, she is dead now. After her much older husband died, she remarried and had four children, one of whom I met while he served with the Free French in World War II.)

B says that O and I were alone in her house, though our assignation had, in the beginning, no sexual intent. But we were in each other's arms when her husband, warned by that despicable blackmailer, her brother, entered with intent to kill.

I don't know what would have happened if he had not burst in on us. I myself was not sure what my conduct should be, since I was not sure of the rules in this particular case. I suspect that I would have followed my natural inclinations unless O had said no, and she did not seem likely to do so.

I was neither engaged nor married and was on the rebound from J. As far as I knew, J and I would never see each other again. But I did want to follow the rules of society. The trouble here was that I did not know what the rules were in this particular contest.

Adultery was illegal, but I had observed that humans often did what was illegal and did not consider adultery immoral. At least, not very immoral.

I myself had none of the moral objections to sexual conduct by which humans are supposed to guide themselves. Though adultery is frowned upon by the n'k, everybody practices it. If caught, they suffer physical punishment, not the pangs of conscience or ostracism from society. Once the beating is over, the thing is done.

I was in Paris, and I knew that the rules depended upon the situation. Some French men would kill you if they caught you with their wives. Others accepted it as long as the business was conducted discreetly.

So what, I wondered, was the context of the situation with O? To which group did her husband belong?

While I was wrestling with this problem, O was preparing to disrobe. Whatever her husband's attitude, she was getting ready to mate with me.

I wasn't, as B implied, "loath" to mate. But I did intend to ask her what her husband thought about this.

Then he burst in with a loaded cane and tried to kill me with it. I lost my temper, and I reverted to my normal state of the threatened n'k. If O had not cried out so vehemently, I would have killed him as a terrier kills a rat. But I stopped; and then, cooling off, I felt that I should abide by the human rules. I had made a mistake and must suffer the consequence. Hence, the duel which B describes wherein I refused to fire back at him. Hence, my lie about the seriousness of the intentions of his wife and myself.

A number of B's critics have said that I acted as if I had been born in King Arthur's court. No real human being would have acted as self-sacrificingly as I did. What they overlooked is that I felt obligated to obey the rules because I was not thoroughly human.

Later on, after I had comprehended the extent of the hypocrisy of humans, I would not have behaved so chivalrously. I would have lied to save O, taken the blame, but I would have shot the count in the arm and rendered him hors de combat.

But then I would never have gotten into the situation in the first place.

HOW I ESCAPED PUBLICITY

If events had been exactly as B described them, the whole world would have been cognizant of me, and nobody would now think of me as a fictional character. The publicity would have turned my life into hell. My only escape would have been to plunge back into the jungle.

D* was well aware of what would happen if my story became known. He was afraid that publicity might destroy me.

My cousin had already inherited the title, and I did not wish to file my claim on it. As B says, I sacrificed my rightful inheritance because I thought that J wished to marry my cousin. I was willing to give up everything if it meant that J would be happy.

I know that this sounds like the noble act of the hero of a romantic novel. But it happened. Perhaps it happened so easily because I had read such novels and thought that I should abide by the rules expressed and implied in them. But I don't really think so. I loved J, and I loathed my cousin because he had, I thought, won out over me. But I did not hate J because she had rejected me. I could understand why she, a highly cultured person, would not want to marry a man raised by beasts. (She thought the n'k were some kind of apes, but even if I had been raised in an Amazonian Indian tribe, she would have hesitated. Or so I thought.)

B says nothing about my difficulties in getting a passport in Port-Gentil† and taking passage to France. But D knew that there would be much trouble when I entered the town unless a suitable story was prepared. Otherwise, the authorities would have thrown me into gaol while they investigated my unauthorized presence in the French territory of Gabon.

While I waited in the jungle outside Libreville, D arranged with some of the bribable authorities to get me a passport. My borrowed identity was that of a Monsieur Jeanne Charles Corday, a Norman trader. Corday's post was far up the Ogouée River, but he was at that time in Port-Gentil. For the sum D promised him, Corday was quite willing to surrender his passport. It was arranged that Corday would be smuggled out of Gabon and back to France at a later date. Corday would then pick up the

---

* D is presumably the French naval lieutenant who brought Greystoke to civilization.
† A town in Gabon, an area on the west coast of equatorial Africa.

passport in France as if he had had it all along. By then I was to have assumed a new identity, that of an Englishman.

All this cost D much, but he was quite wealthy and willing to spend much for the man who had saved his life.

As it turned out, after we got to France, D received word that Corday had died of a fever and had been secretly buried by a man in on the deal. So I remained Corday for a long time. Corday had no relatives and had been out of France for fourteen years so there were no problems in the familial area.

My imperfect French and unfamiliarity with French customs was explained to those authorities not in on the plot as the result of an accident. A blow on the head had impaired my mental functions, and I was returning to France for treatment.

Events transpired somewhat as B has described them. I lived in Paris, studied the English and French languages and the people, read books on many subjects, learning to read while I read, smoked cigarettes, drank absinthe, beat up some thugs who attacked me and then some policemen who tried to arrest me, went through the affair of O and the count, and then traveled to America. There I drove to Wisconsin, saved J from a forest fire, was rejected by J, and received the telegram that told me that the fingerprints on my father's diary were indeed mine. I was the rightful heir to the fortune and the title. Though I must add that I was neither the viscount B said I was nor the duke and earl that F* facetiously said I was.

I am titled, and I am descended from viscounts, dukes, and royalty. But I am only a b. . . .†

F constructed a highly romantic and grandiose lineage

---

* Your editor.
† The rest is deleted by Greystoke. B could stand for baron or baronet. If it is the latter, Greystoke would be addressed as Sir, not Lord. Nor would he be a noble. Baronets are a sort of hereditary knights.

for me in his "biography."* He claims to be more of a
realistic writer than B, but he is a romantic who clothes
his fantasizing with the trappings of reality. He could
have told more of the true story in his biography without
disclosing my real identity, but he couldn't resist the
temptation to gild the lily more than a little. However,
I am in Burke's *Peerage*, though not under Greystoke,
of course. I am descended from the historical Barons
Greystoke and related to the Howards. But that can be
said of hundreds of people or, for all I know, thousands.

There was only one way I could have gotten the title
and the money without publicity. Nor do I know why
B did not tell the real story in his account of how I became. . . .† Perhaps he felt the publication of the novel
was too close in time to the real events. He may have
felt that somebody might have investigated and have
been lucky enough to detect the fraud. After all, all one
had to do was to reread the English newspapers of a few
years back. However, he would not have found that a
young English . . . .† had been shipwrecked off
the coast of Africa and, after some hardships, had been
rescued. T's‡ yacht, contrary to what B said, was only
disabled, not sunk.

On the other hand, my father had been on a secret
mission for the British government, and when he and
his wife disappeared, the government gave out a totally
misleading report. So I can't be tracked down through
that account.

Even if some determined person did come across the
proper clues, he wouldn't find me. I have already faked
my death. Nor would he dare make a public accusation.
He would be laughed to scorn and undoubtedly sued by
my family. B has done me the inestimable favor of establishing once and for all in the minds of the public
that I am a purely fictional person.

Half of the events told in B's second novel had their

* Philip José Farmer, *Tarzan Alive*, (New York: Popular Library, 1973).
† Deleted by Greystoke.
‡ T is Greystoke's cousin.

parallel in reality. It is not true that J was abducted by men who would have had to trail me across half of Africa if B's account had been true. Actually, though I did find that lost city, those Cold Lairs inhabited by a few survivors of an ancient Caucasian people, that "rose-red city half as old as time," before I returned to the west coast, I was not to visit it again until some years later.

I did find my cousin* dying on the west coast, and he told me how he had been aware that I was the true heir but had concealed it from J.

After he had died, J told me what would happen if I stepped forth to make my claim. I would never know a moment's privacy while I lived in the civilized world.

"I wouldn't either," J said. "As your wife, I'd be subject to just as much publicity."

"Then I won't claim it," I said.

"No," she said. "You have a right to it."

She looked at her dead fiancé and said, "We've commented on how much you look like him. So. . . ."

My cousin was only an inch shorter than I and had an athlete's physique. His features were much like mine, which wasn't surprising considering that my grandfather and his father were brothers. And he had the same black hair and grey eyes.

"Technically, it's illegal," she said. "But it's not a criminal fraud. You wouldn't be getting anything you aren't entitled to."

So that is why we buried him there and journeyed up the coast to where the rest of the shipwrecked party was. Nobody there who knew my cousin was fooled, of course. But after J had explained what I was going to do and why, they agreed to keep silent. D was the only one from the French ship that rescued us who knew my identity, and he thought that the deception was a splendid idea.

N† remained to be dealt with. He would have been glad to keep silent, too, if I would pay him blackmail.

---

* This is not T but WC, Greystoke's nearest relative.
† O's brother, a member of the party but under an assumed name and wanted by the French police.

Of that we were all sure. But he had no idea that my cousin had died, and we did not tell him. He was put in the ship's brig and turned over to the French police at Marseilles. I returned to England as my cousin.

We were taking a long chance, though not as long as it might seem at first sight. My cousin had been out of England for a year, taking a sort of Grand Tour before he went to Oxford. He was only nineteen and hence might reasonably be expected to have grown another inch in a year's time. The scars on my forehead and body could be accounted for as a result of the accident to the ship and the jungle hardships. Since I am a gifted mimic, I had no trouble imitating his voice, the timbre of which resembled mine somewhat in any case. His parents were dead, and he had seen no close relatives for years. The servants at the ancestral hall and the villagers nearby were a sticky problem. But they were described to me, their photographs shown, if available, and I was filled in on them by my third cousin, Lord. . . .* He was, as B said, a member of the party, in fact, the owner of the yacht which had sunk. He was marrying J's best friend, and he was very sympathetic when he heard my story. He furnished me with all the information he had about the servants and the villagers.

He also told me as much as he knew about my cousin's friends and his schoolmates. He had gone to Rugby, too, though he was three years ahead of my cousin. He had kept in contact with him after school. They ran in the same circles and belonged to the same clubs.

Still, I was bound to run into friends and relatives of my cousin about whom I would know nothing. So it was thought best to pretend that I had suffered partial amnesia as a result of the shipwreck.

This story got me through a number of difficult situations.

The servants and the villagers must have thought that my African experience had made me rather odd. But if

---

* Deleted by Greystoke.

they suspected that I was not who I was supposed to be, they did not bruit it about.

About a year later, N escaped from the French prison. He looked up his old crony in crime, P, and they came to England. Why, I don't know. But somehow they found out that I had taken my cousin's place. They were in a position to blackmail me and would have done so if they had not known that I would kill them regardless of the consequences. Instead, they kidnapped my baby and J and carried them off to Africa. J was to be sold to some desert sultan, and my son was to be raised as a black savage. In this respect, B was correct. But much of the third novel is grossly exaggerated, and many things he describes never happened.

My son died of a jungle fever; N was killed much as B describes. P escaped but was never heard of again, though B used him as a character in the fourth novel. I imagine he died in the jungle shortly after escaping.

And that is how I was able to claim my inheritance with only a few people knowing that I was not my cousin.

HIS EARLY LIFE IN THE RAIN FOREST

"In the beginning was the Word."

True perhaps for the creation of the world. But not true in my case. In the beginning was a pair of large soft brown breasts with enormous pink nipples. These constitute my earliest memory, which goes back, I believe, to when I was two or three years old. I was not completely weaned until I was about six years old; and when my mother (foster mother, rather) told me I could suckle no more, I went into a screaming rage. I felt that I was no longer loved, that I had been rejected by the only person I loved. She expected this and was prepared. Instead of cuffing me, as she often did when I was misbehaving, she took me into her arms. She explained that I couldn't expect to be treated any longer as a baby, since I was not a baby. I had to become independent of her. She had suckled me for a far longer time than any infant of the tribe was suckled. My playmates were jeering at me because I was still taking her milk, and this added to my burden of being different from the others. I needed to become as much like them as possible. This was one more step toward making them forget my alienness.

Moreover, to nurse me so long, she had given up mating, and while she had no particular desire for any male of the tribe, she was suffering from lack of sexual intercourse. Also, the women and the male elders were urging her to mate again. The tribe needed every infant it could get in order to keep its numbers at a constant level.

That she refused me her breasts did not mean that she no longer loved me. She was doing this for my own good and for the good of the tribe.

None of this except the statement that she still loved me meant anything to me. I would have seen the whole tribe dead before I would have given up the delicious and warm and cozy feeling of suckling. In fact, if I had been big enough and strong enough, I would at that moment have scooped up my mother and run away with her into the forest. And I suppose that if I had been that big and strong, I would have mated with her. There was a diffuse element of sexuality in this suckling. At least, I always got an erection when I suckled. My mother took no especial notice of this, though some of my playmates commented on it. Erections were common among both adults and children of the tribe and accepted with a blaséness that human beings would have regarded as shockingly immoral. Civilized human beings, anyway. There are some preliterate peoples who regard this as natural. Among some peoples of the Sudan area, where the male is naked, if a male should happen to pass by a female and get an erection, the female looks upon it as a compliment. And if no one else is around, the two are liable to go into the bushes.

So it was with the tribe, though there was seldom a chance to commit adultery. Its members felt uneasy when out of sight of the tribe, which is why expulsion was the worst thing that could happen to a member. If he or she could not quickly find another tribe and be adopted into it, he or she just sat down and within a few days grieved themselves to death. This happened far sooner than starvation can account for. The heart was broken and simply quit beating.

I never felt this uneasiness; and if I had been exiled, I would have reacted with rage, not depression. This stemmed from my feeling of alienness, of course, but it was a healthy expression. Better to be mad than sad. Though this feeling of alienness sometimes made me unhappy, it was in the long run a survival factor. Certainly, without it, I could never have spent those days by myself in the cabin teaching myself how to read English. Nor would I have been able to leave the tribe, forever, I thought, when I finally did find people like myself.

I've read Freud and the other great interpreters of the human psyche, Jung, Adler, Sullivan, and so on. On first reading Freud, I believed that every word he said was true. The Oedipal situation seemed to me to be a universal phenomenon. But that was because Freud had certain personal attitudes that coincided with mine. My attitudes came about because of the similarity of his familial situation and mine. I had a mother who was the center of my universe. Or, at least, the only other center of which I was aware. I don't think anybody ever gets over the infant feeling that he is truly the focus of the world. Not completely, anyway. Maturity is a relative state; the most mature are those who have traveled the most distance from that infantile attitude. But nobody has ever gone over the horizon and out of sight of it.

My mother loved only me and I loved only her, outside of our own selves of course. My stepfather hated me, and I knew from an early age that if I didn't kill him first he would kill me. And I was, of course, intensely jealous of him. He was always importuning K'l to mate with him, and though she would always say no, I was afraid that someday she would weaken and say yes. That meant that I'd be sharing her with him, which would have been as traumatic for me as losing an arm or leg or going blind.

Thus we had a sort of *Oedipus Rex* in the jungle, with
P/t as King Laius, K'l as Jocasta, and myself as Oedipus.
P/t was no king and never would be. But I fantasized
from an early age that I would be king someday, which
meant that I would have to kill the king, Kck, in combat. Kck tried many times to get K'l to slip away into
the bushes with him, and since he knew that she would
do so if it were not for me, he hated me almost as much
as P/t did. So, in a sense, both P/t and Kck represented
King Laius.

I don't want to strain this analogy too far. My read-
ings of Freud and his critics, plus my own observations
of many human societies, have convinced me that Freud
often applied his own peculiar familial situation as a
general principle to all of humanity. I don't think that
the majority of male children hate their fathers because
of any sexual jealousy. Nor do I think that any but a
small minority of female children have penis envy. They
might envy the physical superiority and the economic
and political benefits that having a penis automatically
confer upon the male. There is as much evidence that
males might have a vagina envy. That is, very little evidence at all.

On the other hand, Freud did bring the concept of
the unconscious mind to its fullest fruition; and he did
discover that sexuality is much more diffuse than previously thought, that it pervades and influences most of
the elements of human behavior. Sexuality is, in short,
a field that stretches far beyond the genital; or, put differently, the genital invades every area of human behavior. The Westerners of his day were loath to accept
this, and there are still many who reject this concept.

This rejection is founded on hypocrisy. In fact, society
is founded on hypocrisy (among other things). It is my
belief that if hypocrisy were eliminated overnight as if
it were fecal matter, and people became completely hon-
est, society would fall apart. This dictum applies to all
human societies, literate or preliterate.

Hypocrisy has caused much misery and injustice, in

fact, the deaths of millions of people over a period of perhaps a million years. But hypocrisy is one of the bonds that keeps human society from collapsing like an old castle in a hurricane.

I loathe and abominate hypocrisy; yet, when I am among humans, I have to practice it myself to a certain extent. If I didn't, I wouldn't be able to operate effectively in human society. As it is, I don't operate with a high efficiency. Though I am under no compulsion to be frank when I am disgusted with hypocrites, which means that I can keep silent under most conditions, I seem to radiate disgust. I betray myself in a silent language with certain inflections of stance, gesture, and facial expression; and most humans detect this. They resent it, of course, which makes it difficult to generate any warmth, any feeling of closeness or of equality, between me and most human beings.

As for frankness, I have observed that people who boast of being frank generally are so for one reason. They want to hurt others. They say they are frank because of their love for truth. But they lie to themselves and fail to deceive others with this lie.

I spoke of equality above. There is much talk of equality in human society but very little exists. Human beings have a pecking order just as animals and the subhumans of my tribe have one. Even two individuals of assumed social equality fight on a conscious or unconscious level for a subtly superior position. However, the pecking order is much less rigid in human society than among animals or in my tribe. Among animals the order is usually established in a very short time. It does change but not very often. Death and sickness are the chief operands. In my tribe, the order is somewhat more fluid, and the structure is dual. That is, the females' status is not altogether dependent upon the status of her mate. If she is exceptionally fertile, she may be accorded a higher position than her mate. But this usually results in some male trying to acquire her so he may acquire more status. This sounds contradictory in view of what I've said about the mate of the exceptionally fertile female not gaining status also. But the society of my tribe, like human society, contains a number of contradictory attitudes. If a male can take an exceptionally fertile female away from another male, by physical or verbal means, then this acquisition confers additional status on the male. A male with two females as mates is higher in the pecking order than a male with only one. A male with three females, two of which are infertile or not very productive of infants, has less status than a male with two fertile females. At the same time, his females may have a higher standing in the female pecking order than he has in the male order.

This could result in the females of a lower male having a higher status than the mates of the king. It seldom does because the king is keenly aware that the status of his females is a reflection of his own. The younger and more vigorous of the adult males begin thinking of challenging the king when this occurs. But the king knows this, and so he takes the fertile females away from the lower male. This is not usually done by an open and brutal assault upon the lower male. The king asks the females to become his mates. They have the option of rejecting him, but they seldom do. The females of my tribe are as impressed by social position as are the females of human society.

If the females should refuse the king, the king may then harass the lower male in a hundred different ways. If, for instance, the lower male feels that his particular feeding territory has been invaded by another male, he will appeal to the king to settle the case. The king, though he knows that the claimant's case is just, may decide against him. The king may treat the lower male with an obvious contempt or with open insults which go beyond that determined by the male's position in the pecking order. The rest of the tribe quickly perceive this, and in a short time the male is relegated to an even more inferior position.

The male can then fight the males who are pushing

him on down. If he loses, he goes down to the very bottom of the hierarchy. In effect, he has to fight every male above and below him, usually in one day, and even the strongest would tire halfway through this ordeal. So he's doomed to plumb the social abyss unless he challenges the king himself.

Possibly, he might win, in which case he comes out on top. The king doesn't then go to the lowest rank; the king is dead. Most fights between males end when one male confesses that he is beaten, but the battle for kingship is to the death.

Unless the lower male is unusually powerful, or the king is getting old, the lower male usually does not challenge the king. But he is frantic at losing status, and this may cause him to challenge the king. The king knows this, and he also knows that chance or the sheer desperation of the male may result in him (the king) being defeated. So, as often happens in human society, some sort of compromise is worked out. The king takes the fertile females of the lower male but gives the lower male his own infertile or less physically desirable females. The male retains his original status, since it is felt that a male who gets the king's females, even though they were rejected, gains a certain status. This gain cancels the loss of his fertile females.

The pecking order is not as complex or as fluid as that in human society, but it is complex enough that a 50,000-word book could be written about it.

When I say that the king can take or give away females, I do not mean that the females have no say in this. A male can divorce a female, or she him, with a simple declaration within the hearing of the king and the majority of the tribe. This applies even to the females of the king, though I never saw such an instance.

On the other hand, taking a female is not as simple as among the baboons, for instance. The male cannot take a mate just because he is a physical superior of another male. The female is free to accept or reject. And this is what my mother did. After adopting me, she divorced

P/t, and she refused the king's advances. This offended both males. P/t could get no females to become his permanent mates, though I observed that he sometimes talked a female into lying with him when the two were out of sight of the others. This gave me an advantage over him. I would inform him that I'd spied on him. I would threaten to tell the mate of the female if P/t did not cease his persecution of me. P/t would rage, but he feared being beaten up by the cuckolded male and would leave me alone for a long time.

P/t was often beaten up, anyway. He had a bad temper and could not refrain from showing his resentment when the other males shoved him to the rear of the tribal assemblies or transgressed on his small feeding territory. Sometimes, he beat the other male, and it was only this that kept him from going to the very bottom of the order.

It was this bad temper, plus his ugliness, caused by a broken nose, that made the females reject him. Without at least one female as a permanent mate, he could get only so high in the order. This social inferiority thoroughly ruined a disposition that had never been sweet to begin with.

He blamed me for this, but, as B has shown, I didn't take his persecution passively. I gave more than I got; I was a constant torment to him with my tricks. Also, when I was about twelve, I thought of another way to force him to leave me in peace. I had observed that he was in fear when I threatened to tell the tribe about his adulteries. Then it occurred to me to threaten P/t with tales of wholly imaginary adulteries. In other words, I invented the lie.

P/t was so outraged at my first threat that I had to flee through the trees, take to the higher branches where he was too heavy to follow me. After he had cooled off, he realized that I had him in my control. And once more he ignored me, though, after a time, he forgot my threat and started to bedevil me. Then I had to threaten him again.

P/t was so outraged because lying was unknown to

the tribe. Its members had many human qualities, since they were subhumans or prehumans. But they weren't human enough to have thought of lying. Or intelligent enough, perhaps. He was both angered and shocked when I first proposed my lie. I believe that he never did quite understand what I was doing. Or, if he did, he thought my threat was unnatural, a perversion. It was something monstrous.

So it was, from his viewpoint.

B has recorded that my native intelligence allowed me to invent a number of things new to the tribe. Such as the running noose, the full-nelson, swimming, et al. B did not record my invention of untruth, but this was because he did not know about it.

Later on, when I taught myself to read English from the books I had found in the cabin of my true parents, I discovered that humans abhorred lying. And so, in my effort to become human, I too abhorred lying. After I became acquainted with humans, I found out that this abhorrence is only a pose, a major and indeed vital hypocrisy, of human society. But by then I had ingrained myself too deeply with this abhorrence. I never lie now except when survival demands it. I believe that most humans, excepting compulsive liars, don't lie except when their survival is threatened by the truth, but when they think of survival, they think of survival of their social image, of survival of their emotional and socioeconomic relationships, in fact, of a thousand things that will be endangered if they don't lie. Each individual has his own hierarchy of lying; some lies are permitted, others are forbidden, though if the going gets rough enough, the tabus are quickly shed.

Nor do humans seem to resent lies in the political field. There is a general feeling that all politicians are liars, that, in fact, a man can't be a politician unless he is a liar. I've never been able to understand this attitude. Politicians control the state; and so the welfare of the citizens depends upon being told the truth, both before and after the politician has been elected to office.

I've also never understood why the poor and the oppressed have endured their miserable state for so many thousands of years. They've always outnumbered the wealthy and the oppressors. So why didn't they just rise up and take over the government?

This is why I've never taken any interest in social reform, though I have in individuals who are suffering from poverty and injustice. But that is just because they happened to become personally involved with me.

This attitude has resulted in my being accused of being both an extreme rightist and an extreme leftist. Though by different people, of course. I won't try to change the system myself, since I am well off under it. But I am perfectly willing to grant that the poor and the oppressed should rise in revolution, a bloody one if need be, and take away from the rich and the oppressor.

I know from my reading of history that from time to time the masses have risen up but that usually they were slaughtered. These failures came about only because of disunity and fear among the masses. With a well-planned organization and enough willing to sacrifice themselves (after all, what did they have to lose?), the poor and the oppressed could have revolted successfully several thousand years ago and set up a new system. The male and female servants of the rich, for instance, were in a position to massacre their employers, wipe out the ruling class almost overnight.

But they did none of these things, just turned like rats and bit futilely when their state became so wretched they could no longer endure it. And they died like rats.

On the other hand, how many revolutions succeeded in their aims when they did conquer the ruling class? France got the Terror and then Napoleon I and then Napoleon III. The Russian Revolution wasn't really a revolt of the masses, and a small group got control and has retained it ever since. Are the Russians really better off than they would have been if the Czars were still in power? Are the Chinese better off under the Communists?

Some say they are; some say they aren't. For me the

question is academic, since I personally do not care. All I know is that, if the masses under the Communists (or any other ideology) are being oppressed, why don't they do something about it?

D says that I don't understand this because I don't understand human psychology, or sociopoliticoeconomics. He may be right.

K'l's love for me resulted in much suffering for her. Because she refused to mate and because she nursed an alien, she went down to the bottom of the social scale. As the saying goes, she had to suck hind tit. When there was a kill and the tribe lined up for meat, she was last in line and lucky to get anything. She had to endure verbal abuse, though she was too powerful for another female to attack her. Also, the tribe had doubts about her mental stability. No sane female would refuse to mate or insist on suckling a being like me. Thus, she must be mad. This belief in her insanity made the females afraid to push her too far. Like most primitive peoples, and they were more primitive than even the Australian aborigine or Digger Indians, they were in awe of anybody who might be "possessed."

K'l was last in line at the table, but she was intelligent and industrious and so a good food provider. Though it scared her to go far from the vicinity of the tribe, she did so. And hence she foraged ahead of the others. Grubs, worms, eggs, grasshoppers, small rodents, birds, baby antelopes, dead animals, anything that was protein and didn't move fast enough to elude her became part of our diet. Most of her diet consisted of roots, nuts, fruits, and berries, of course, since she was primarily a vegetarian. Many of the roots she ate contained too much siliceous matter for me, and I rejected this from instinct, I suppose. Even when she offered me premasticated vegetable matter, I rejected it. The coarse gritty stuff would in time have worn away my teeth. I did not realize this consciously, but I knew I didn't like the stuff. So, in addition to much mother's milk, I ate many berries, nuts (after she had cracked them open), and fruit and pieces of raw meat from the creatures she caught. In the beginning I could not masticate the raw meat, but K'l chewed these up for me, and these I accepted eagerly.

So, though K'l suffered from a semiostracism, and I suffered too after I became aware of this attitude, we were far from being always unhappy.

Also, that we were alone against the others made us draw much more closely together than the normal mother and child of the tribe.

I sometimes believe in Goethe's theory of elective affinities. Certainly this is the only thing that can account for K'l's fierceness in raising me despite all the objections of the tribe and the abuse she had to take.

I was lucky that it was she and not some other female who had lost her infant the same day my parents died. If her baby had not been killed, she would not have wanted to replace it with me. And Kck would have killed me, too, after slaying my father. But, as chance would have it, she wanted me to replace her just-dead infant, and so she snatched me from the cradle and ran off with me. Never mind that I was a queer, even repulsive looking, creature from her viewpoint. She accepted me and from the moment I began suckling, she loved me. So, at least, she told me in afteryears. Even if her love for me at first sight was really an event of retrospect and not of reality, there was no doubt that she soon did come to love me.

Since she had no one else to talk to or to love, she spent all her energies, outside of food-gathering and hunting, on me. She was, for me, a castle with a host of defenders, which is why I had a tremendous sense of security despite my early years of alienation from the other members of the tribe. Her continuous talking to me also resulted in an acceleration of my intelligence. No doubt, I would have outstripped my contemporaries anyway, since a human being is more intelligent and faster talking than the prehumans of my tribe.

It was also my good fortune to have been adopted by a

female who was possibly the brightest individual of her people.

DESCRIPTION OF THE N'K

B first heard of me when he was living in Chicago. But in the first novel he wrote about me, he pretended that he had learned of me while visiting London. His informant was supposed to have been an official of the British Foreign Service. This man was acquainted with my story because he had access to top secret documents in the Service's files. These supposedly included my father's diary, written in French, which recorded the events that led up to, and included part of, the day on which he was killed by Kck and I was taken from my cradle by K'l.

According to B, the official disclosed my story when he was drunk. When B scoffed at this, the official then showed him documents, though he had no right to reveal these and would have been discharged and possibly gaoled if the Service had known of his act.

The truth is that B was not in London at that time. As far as I know, he has never been in England. His informant was an American who had heard some of my story from an Englishman. Thus B got his facts third-hand. Nor had his immediate informant seen any documents. If these had been in the Foreign Service files, the Service would have known about my fraud. And it would have felt obligated to expose me.

After B's first novel came out, I realized that someone had talked about me. I knew that the original source of information had to be somebody close to me. It did not take me long to eliminate all but one. I confronted T,* and he confessed that he might have talked about me to an American during one of his alcoholic sprees. T was a splendid man. I liked and respected him very much, except for one facet of his character. Now and then he succumbed to his compulsion and would disappear for days

---

* Probably Greystoke's third cousin, a baron.

or even weeks. Poor H* would track him down and bring him home and dry him out. He had enough character, however, not to make a promise he might not be able to keep. He would only say that he would fight against his demon with all the strength he could muster.

As the Americans say, I chewed him out. He was very contrite and shaken up, so much so that he did not drink alcohol for three years. Nor, as far as I know, did he ever say anything of me again while drunk.

Well, he has been dead for many years now, killed while fighting Jerry. He died a hero's death, as they say, and was posthumously awarded Britain's highest medal for valor. I miss him.

B, realizing that his informant had given him the germ of a unique story, wrote a novel. Since he had few facts to begin with, most of the novel is incorrect in its details. It is also considerably romanticized. But he captured the spirit, the essence, of what really happened, and all honor to him for that.

One of the criticisms of B's story was that there were no such creatures as his language-using "great apes." Thus, his novel had to be sheer fantasy, as much modern mythology as Kipling's *The Jungle Book*.

The "great apes" had not been discovered by reputable scientists and hence could not exist.

This criticism came only twelve years after the discovery of the okapi, the existence of which had been scoffed at for years by scientists.

The pygmy elephant and hippopotamus were also supposed to be a mere fable of the natives. But more than one zoo now exhibits them.

There have also been rumors for years of a small maneless spotted lion existing in the forests of Kenya and Uganda. The existence of these is denied, but I have seen them. Whether or not any specimens will ever come to the attention of the scientists is another matter. They were never very numerous, and they may now be extinct.

---

* T's wife, an American, and J's best woman friend.

The point I'm making is that scientists have been wrong. They are perfectly correct in refusing to acknowledge the existence of such creatures until proof is presented of their existence. But too many scientists, and educated laymen, have denied that they could, in fact, exist. And that is an unscientific attitude.

B's critics denied that any unknown species of ape could exist in Africa. They also scoffed at B because his apes ate meat. Chimpanzees and gorillas don't eat meat, they said. Therefore, no apes (even of the mythological variety) are carnivores. It seems to be true that gorillas are pure herbivores in their natural state. But Goodall has shown that chimpanzees in the wild state do eat meat whenever they get a chance; and it is known that baboons, which are monkeys, also eat meat.

The truth is that both B and his critics were half-right and half-wrong.

There is a species of primate which has not been discovered by the scientific community. Or there was, at least. I saw them several times during my childhood and youth, but they may be extinct now. It is this species which has given rise to tales of the Kenyan *agogwe* and the "wild men" observed in the eastern, central, and western areas of Africa. They are about four feet high and very hairy, but they walk upright. Hence, they are not apes, not in a scientific sense. Their pelvic girdles and feet are so similar to men that they would have to be classified as some species of australopithecoid, creatures halfway between ape and man. I doubt that they are the "missing link." It is more probable that they are a cousin of the creature that was in the direct line of man's ancestry.

In any event, I have seen them, though I never had any direct contact with them. They fled my tribe as quickly as they did humans.

My own people are, I believe, another species of hominid or perhaps a giant variety of the *agogwe*. They are not missing links, either, but cousins of man. They are not the great apes described by B, but they do, or did, exist; and it was among them that I was raised.

B was not given any clear description of them and so he visualized them as gorilloids. He had them using a language, which was correct. But in his novels he also attributed language use to the gorillas and monkeys. While it is true that the higher primates can communicate more effectively than the zoologists believe, they do not have a language in the human sense. They use signals, not verbal symbols.

It was lucky for me that the n'k were language users. If I'd been raised by true apes, I would have passed the mental stage beyond which language learning becomes possible. And I would have been not much better than an idiot. Authentic cases of feral humans bear me out in this. If the child has not experienced a human language before the age of five to eight (or perhaps earlier) he becomes incapable of learning language.

So, in a sense, I am not a true feral man. Those who raised me were quite capable linguistically. And their capabilities for learning other things were higher than those of any animals.

B didn't know this. After learning the truth, he was forced to continue the original description in order to be consistent. Not that he cared. He was a storyteller, not an anthropologist.

I have said that my people were possibly a giant variety of paranthropus. Giant is a relative term here, since the tallest was actually only about six feet. When I'd attained my full growth, I had three inches on the tallest, old Kck. He didn't like my looking down on him, and this was one more thing to make him hate and fear me.

But he was much stronger; and if it hadn't been for my father's knife, I would have been killed when he finally challenged me.

The n'k looked hairy, though this was because their body hair grew to a four or five-inch length and was as coarse as a chimpanzee's. The numbers of hairs were actually less than that of humans. The breasts of both male and female were innocent of hair; both had short bushy beards and stiff head hairs not more than two inches long.

The n'k head was long and low, bread-loaf-shaped. They had very little forehead, and the supraorbital ridges of the adult male were almost as massive as a gorilla's. A bony crest, like a gorilla's though smaller, ran from the front to the back of the skull of the males. These were necessary to support the massive chewing muscles. The nose was not quite as flat and as wide-nostrilled as a gorilla's. The ears were close to the head and shaped exactly like a human's but about one-fourth larger. The jaws were prognathous, about halfway in protrusion between man's and the gorilla's. The lips were not the thin lips of the chimpanzee and the gorilla; they were as fully everted as the average Caucasian's. The teeth were large, fitted for grinding the tough siliceous roots or cracking the nuts which formed a large part of their diet. Contrary to B's description, they did not have the long canines of the gorilla. The teeth were quite hominid, the molars having five cusps in a Y pattern. A primatologist would see at a glance that they belonged to a creature nearer to man than the apes. The palate was not quite as arched as that of the human. The jaws, seen from above, formed a bow shape, unlike the U shape of ape jaws.

The head was carried further forward than that of the human. The pelvis was not as efficiently shaped for walking as the human's. The legs were shorter in proportion to the torso than the human's, and they were less straight. The feet were flat, and there was a wide separation between the big toe and the other toes. The arms were somewhat longer in proportion to the torso than those of a man. The hands were larger and thicker than a man's. The thumb was shorter and thicker in proportion. None of the tribe could come near my manual dexterity.

Their muscles are not only more massive than a human's but superior in quality. Even the smallest female is much stronger than the greatest human weightlifter. The muscles are attached to thick and dense bones. My own skeleton is denser than that of any modern man's. I attribute this to my feral life, to unceasing activity and hard exertion. As I understand it, the bones of the early caveman were also denser due to his exceedingly active life.

Their hair color varies from a dull black to a russet brown. The eyebrows are very bushy and black. Their eyes are russet brown; their skin, coffee with three spoonfuls of cream. Like most rain forest dwellers, they don't have or need many sweat glands. Their body odor differs from that of man. The English language does not contain the vocabulary items needed to decribe it accurately. I can only say that to a keen nose it has elements both of the odor of Homo sapiens and of the gorilla with an indescribable element that is unique to them. Their anal excrement is softer but more adhesive than that of Homo sapiens and not nearly as offensive. This, I presume, is because their diet is largely vegetarian. Their urine, curiously enough, reminds me of civet cat urine, yet I would not mistake one for the other.

Unlike the gorilla, they do not foul their own nest. When one has to defecate, he retreats to some distance from the feeding ground. This seems to have nothing to do with modesty. A number of adult males and females and children will retreat at the same time to the same place and there relieve themselves side by side while chatting away unembarrassedly. Nor do they leave the feeding area to urinate.

In going some distance from their feeding or sleeping places to defecate, however, they exhibit a fastidiousness superior to that of the Australian aborigine. The latter will defecate while among a group squatting around a fire and eating.

Their sense of smell is keener than that of Homo sapiens but not nearly as keen as a dog's, whose sense of smell is estimated to be a million times sharper than man's.

B has exaggerated my own olfactory powers. They are not as strong as a n'k's, though they are superior to any human I've ever met. But this is a matter of training. And after I've been in a city for a while, it becomes comparatively deadened. A good thing, too. During my first few days in a city, I become nauseated with the many offensive odors that exude from man and his artifacts.

WIND AND SEX AMONG THE N'K

While I was learning to read, I was startled and sometimes shocked. I discovered things that were completely contrary to what the n'k believed and, hence, what I believed.

One of these was that it was the wind that caused trees and their leaves to move. The n'k always believed just the opposite. Trees and grass were living things; and so, when they moved, they caused motion of the air.

Once I had read that the wind was the responsible agent, I saw why. I reproached myself for my stupidity. I should have noticed that if the tree caused the wind, the wind should have flowed out from the tree in all directions. That discovery made me determined that from then on I would be more observant. Nor would I believe anything that had been told me until it was proved.

I was upset again when I learned that there was a direct connection between copulation and reproduction. The n'k did not know this. They believed that rain and lightning fertilized women. The latter caused the birth of exceptionally strong or intelligent individuals.

When I made the discovery about the true origin of the wind, I hastened to tell the n'k. They would not believe me, even after I had offered them proof. In fact, I was scorned and laughed at, and several commented that I was not as bright as I was supposed to be. Indeed, I must be suffering a mental breakdown.

So, when I discovered the link between copulation and fertilization, I kept silent. The n'k did not want to be enlightened. They resented the truth as if it threatened them. In this respect, they are like most humans.

Every human society has adopted rules for sexual conduct by which its members are supposed to guide themselves. Conduct which breaks these rules is regarded as unlawful but not perverted, or unlawful and perverted. The former conduct can be broken down into two subclasses. One, that which is regarded with a certain limited tolerance. Two, that which is simply not tolerated, if the conduct becomes known to laymen and police.

My reading of the novels did not help me much in determining exactly what modes of sexual behavior were in what classifications. The *Encyclopaedia Britannica* was of some help, but it had been published in 1885 and was thus far from frank. The most I could find out from my reading was that certain undescribed sexual acts and attitudes were regarded by most people as disgusting and illegal and deserving of long sentences in gaol or even death.

My own sexual attitudes were determined by n'k society. Theirs were at the same time much more rigid and far more liberal than those of any civilized human society.

Much of what was permitted would be regarded as unnatural by Western societies of that day, but any deviation from the rules was regarded as perverted by the n'k. Or I should say would have been regarded so. I never saw or heard of any deviations while I was with the n'k.

Open masturbation among the children was permitted. In fact, if a child did not masturbate, he/she was an object of concern. There must be something wrong with him/her. This included both self- and mutual masturbation.

The males who were unable to get females as mates because of their low position in the pecking order performed self- or mutual masturbation. In their cases, however, they did so out of sight of the tribe. Not from any modesty but because they would be objects of derision from the upper class males.

Lawful copulation took place in view of the tribe. The sexual activities of the king were watched closely because any lack of vitality was regarded as a sign of weakening. When this took place, the males considered challenging the king.

Unlawful copulation, that is, adultery, occurred in the

bushes, of course. The males were very jealous of their mates. If another male copulated with his mate(s), he was challenging his order in the social scale.

The females could be put into three classes. One included the majority of females, those who took advantage of every opportunity to commit adultery. The second consisted of females who would commit adultery only with males on a higher social plane than their mates. The third, a small minority, were always faithful.

On consideration, there was a fourth class which was a minority of one. This was K'l, my foster mother. During my infancy and childhood and early youth, she refused to take a mate. This was her right, but it caused her to be regarded as perverted. At the same time, it made her more desirable. The males thought that if they could talk her into mating, they would automatically rise in the order.

Of course, this mating would have to be done publicly. And I am not certain that K'l did not now and then succumb to her sexual drive while in the bushes. She must have been very discreet, however, since I had no suspicions that this was occurring. If I had, I would have been very jealous.

Now that I look back on it, I would not blame her if she had taken the opportunity to relieve her sexual tensions.

The favorite position of the n'k during copulation was with the female on her back and the male on top. Entry from the rear with the female standing but bent over, braced against a tree, was often performed. The king, Kck, preferred this.

Kissing as sexual foreplay was as common among the n'k as among humans. But kissing involved not only the lips and the breasts. The n'k kissed each other all over. Fellatio and cunnilingus and soixante-neuf were often indulged in, though these were not conducted to the point of climax. Though the n'k knew nothing of the connection between copulation and reproduction, as I have said, they thought that the male must ejaculate within the vagina.

Of course, accidents happened; but when they did, the couple were derided.

Though the lower scale males mutually masturbated or performed fellatio, they were not compulsive homosexuals. If a single male managed to get a permanent mate, he at once ceased any homosexual activities.

Anal intercourse was never performed, at least, not to my knowledge, and if anyone should know, I should. I was often in the trees or behind the bushes, observing the hidden activities of the tribe.

Incidence of sexual activity was much higher than the average in Western human society. The king was thought to be approaching senility if he did not copulate with his three or four females at least three times a day. In addition, he was on his good days liable to copulate with three or four other females in the bushes.

I believe that the males of Western human society would be capable of this frequency, too, if the social attitudes were different. In Polynesian societies, for instance, when the whites first encountered them, a male was thought senile if he did not copulate with his wife three or four times daily and, in addition, copulated with several of his sisters-in-law. This high sexual activity results, I believe, not from the physical superiority of the Polynesian male to the Western male but from the social attitude toward sex.

The only cases of impotency I saw among the n'k were very old males (forty-five years of age was the equivalent of the human eighty) and one young male, Lmp.* And his condition probably resulted from some physical deficiency, though I cannot prove this.

This brief sketch should indicate why I found the human attitudes toward sex ludicrous, incredible, and comicotragical. And it shows why J was so horrified about my attitudes.

But she got over it.

---

* This is so close to "limp" that Greystoke may be making a little joke.

THE LANGUAGE OF THE N'K

The anthropologist Grover Krantz has studied the fossil skulls of early man (*Homo erectus*) and of his predecessors *Paranthropus* and *Australopithecus*. He speculates that the brain volume which divides man from his forerunners and cousins is 750 cc. The brain volume of modern man averages 1,400 cc. The gorilla's and *Australopithecus*' is 500 cc. *Homo erectus*' was between 750 and 1,400 cc.

In the late '30s I returned to my native area and looked for n'k skulls. I found three female and five male skulls and measured their capacity. The average for the females was 900 cc and that of the males was 1,200. I also studied the brain of an old male who had died from pneumonia shortly after I rejoined the tribe. I was especially interested in the development of the frontal lobes and of the three primary speech control areas: Broca's, Wernicke's, and the angular gyrus. I also dissected the oral cavity, the larynx, and the pharynx. I did this to compare them to man's and to analyze the anatomical and neural limitations of the n'k in regard to speech.

Krantz says that, at the end of his first year, the human baby's brain is approximately 750 cc. Within six months, the baby begins to talk. Based on this, Krantz suggests that the 750-cc volume is the threshold of the ability to use language. Krantz reconstructed the oral cavities, pharynx, and larynx of *Homo erectus*. Based on these, he concluded that the vocal apparatus of *Homo erectus* was closer to that of a newborn baby's than to an adult of *Homo sapiens*. Consequently, *Homo erectus* had a larynx that was situated higher in the throat than modern man's. This limited the size of the pharynx above it. *Homo erectus*' tongue, consequently, was almost entirely in the mouth; relatively little of it was in the throat. This meant that the tongue of *Homo erectus* could not act on the pharynx but was limited to varying the size of the mouth in producing speech sounds.

Homo erectus thus did not have a pharynx capable of producing the vowel sounds *a* (as in father), *i* (as in ma-

chine) and u (as in tool). He also suggested that the
three brain areas I mentioned above were less developed
than in modern man.

All these limitations, plus the low-slung and heavy
jaws, meant that *Homo erectus* had a very limited speech
repertoire and probably spoke very slowly.

It would follow from this that the less evolved *Paranthropus* and *Australopithecus* had even more limitations,
that his linguistic capabilities were even less than very
early man's.

The facts are that the n'k could produce one vowel
sound, similar to that found in the English *the* when it
precedes a consonant or that of the vowel in *cut*. This
occurred in about one out of ten n'k words. It was, however, unvoiced; that is, it was produced without any vibra-
tions taking place in the vocal bands of the larynx. Nor
were the consonants which English speakers voice, *n*, *l*,
and *w*, voiced by the n'k. These were accompanied by a
heavy aspiration. But the n'k could control the vocal
bands enough to produce a glottal stop. By closing them,
they produced a consonant which is found in many
human tongues, Danish, Scots English, Nahuatl, et al.
This stop also occurs in standard English, but it has no
significance, and most English speakers are not even
aware that they produce it.

In addition, the n'k speech contains four click consonants. One of these is similar to that produced by a carriage driver when he is urging his horse to a faster speed
or to that which is often spelled *tsk! tsk!*

N'k speech sounds perfectly natural to me, but J and
D say that it is weird. The long strings of whispered consonants with no intervening vowels, the clicks, and the
glottal stops seem unhuman to J and D. But there is at
least one human group, a California Indian tribe, which
uses words with whispered consonants and only an oc-
casional vowel, also unvoiced. And the click consonants
are common in the Bushman and Hottentot languages
found in some Nahuatl dialects.

The brain size of the n'k child doesn't attain 750 cc

until he is six years old. This is when he starts to babble, though the babbling is much slower than that of a human baby's and more restricted in the variety of sounds.

I started babbling shortly after K'l adopted me and was speaking as fluently as any adult n'k by the time I was four. This amazed the n'k and compensated in K'l's eyes for my lack of speed in physical development and my lengthy dependence on her. I was also able to talk, literally, five times as fast as the n'k.

If any linguists read this, they may wonder how I was able to voice sounds after I came into contact with humans. Theoretically, since I had had no experience in voicing speech sounds in my formative years, I should, as an adult, have been unable to reproduce them.

But I am a natural mimic. When I eavesdropped on the blacks of the river village, I would try to imitate the sounds of their language. At first, I had little success in vibrating my vocal bands. But I persevered. After a while I was able to imitate perfectly both the unvoiced and voiced sounds of the blacks.

The n'k sounds are:

Vowel: the unvoiced vowel of English *the* or *done*, represented here by e.
Consonants: p, t, k, ', h, s, c, m, n, l, w, /, //, ///, †.
   p is the same as in English but is always heavily aspirated, that is, followed by a puff of air.
   t is like the English t but made with the tip of the tongue higher up.
   k is that in *keen* and is always aspirated.
   ' stands for the glottal stop, the catch in the throat called by the Spanish linguists the *saltillo*, the little jump.

F misinterpreted something I said about the glottal stop in n'k and so made an error in the biography he wrote about me. F stated that the n'k regarded the ' as a vowel. He should have known better, since he has some knowledge of linguistics. What I said was that B often used a vowel in place of the glottal stop when he spelled out n'k words. In any case, the n'k had never heard of a vowel or, indeed, of anything connected with phonetics or grammar.

> h stands for the fricative *ch* sound in the German *ach* or Scots *loch*.
> s is the same as in English.
> c stands for the *ch* in *church*.
> m is the English *m* but unvoiced.
> n equals an English *n* unvoiced.
> l is an unvoiced sound halfway between the English *l* and *r*. B used either *l* or *r* in his system of spelling n'k words, I suppose for the sake of variety.
> w is like the English but totally unvoiced.
> / stands for a click consonant made by flattening the tip of the tongue against the front teeth and then quickly withdrawing it.
> // stands for a click made against the gums above the teeth.
> /// stands for a palatal click.
> † stands for a click made with the side of the tongue close to the right side of the cheek.
> B used b, d, g, and z respectively to represent these clicks. He also used z to represent s sometimes.

Each syllable of n'k consists of two or three consonants or combinations of consonants plus e, e plus consonant, consonant plus e plus consonant, or two consonants plus e.

Each word is a monosyllable, disyllable, or trisyllable, excluding the monosyllabic gender prefix.

The stress or accent is lighter than in English but relatively stronger on the second syllable within a word.

Tone, or pitch, is mid-level in a declarative phrase and abruptly chopped off at the end of the phrase.

Exclamatory, hortatory, interrogative, and conditional phrases use a rising pitch similar to that in English. This rising pitch is an important grammatical feature. B indicates this in his description of the difference between the phrase, "Do you surrender?" and "I surrender." The former is distinguished by the rising pitch; the latter is a flat "/// //."

Though the n'k speech is about five times as slow as human speech, it has juncture. That is, it has a difference in the speed of transition between the sounds in a word, between words, and between complete phrases. The second is twice as long as the first, and the third is twice as long as the second.

The n'k vocabulary items are few, possibly no more than five hundred. Its grammar is truly primitive and can be quickly described.

The parts of speech are:

Personal names.
Entity indicator: tnt = elephant; w'l = nest; "// = rock; c/// = sky; k' = I; 'sh = wind; mp// = mother.
Attribute indicator: ///e = red; klk = dangerous; s'l = skin; pkt = dead; wn// = beneficial, tasty, healthy; cs† = angry; pks = motionless; 'et = state of possession; tk' = many.
Negator: tn// = no, not.
Action indicator: ///'m = run; /n// = kill; sps = snarl; h'h = laugh; ///tn = looking gloomy.
Temporal indicator: tw' = soon; //p// = sometime in the past; nw/// = dawn; nwk = between dawn and high noon; nl/ = high noon; ns† = between high noon and dusk; nw// = dusk; smk = night.
Locative indicator: wc = there; s's = out of sight; ksw = right; //e' = left; c// = above.
Gender indicator: b' = male; m' = female.

The entity indicator refers to anything that is considered in n'k as an object which is completely separate from other objects. It includes what we would classify as personal pronouns. The n'k is not as conscious of ego differentiation as the human is. At least, that is my impression.

Though he behaves as an individual with self-consciousness, he is not as sharply aware of his aloneness as a human is. *K'* means not only *I* but *we*. Where a human would say *we*, a n'k gestures to indicate that others are part of his *I*. Or he is part of them.

There is no word in n'k corresponding to the human *you* or *they*. The personal name is used instead when addressing an individual; and if *they* is indicated, a gesture indicates this.

Indeed, the *I* is not often used in a phrase, though its existence is implicit.

Why do I include the word for *skin* as an attribute indicator, something that humans would call a noun? This is because the skin is classified as an inherent undiscrete part that makes up the whole. It is no more separable than the color of the skin. Thus, my personal name, s'n-t'l, is made up of two attribute indicators.

The word for *mother*, mp//, is not used in the generic sense. A mother is an entity, either my mother or your mother. A n'k could not speak of many mothers. There is no word for father. A *father* is the mate of your mother, and the word used for him is b'-cpm, meaning *he-mate*.

The n'k have no general word to indicate emotion or feeling. The emotions or feelings have to be specific and refer to states invisible to the beholder. If a n'k feels sick, he says, "tn// wn//." That is, "Not healthy," or if he wishes to emphasize it, "k' tn// wn//," or "I am not healthy."

It seems strange to an English speaker to classify a verb, 'et, meaning *to possess*, as an attribute. But this word indicates a nonphysical relationship, an invisible connection between the speaker and the object referred to. No physical action is implied. The relationship referred to is as unchanging as the color of one's eyes. For example, take a sentence translated as, "She is my mother." In the first place, no n'k would say *she*. He would use her personal name. If I said this in n'k, I would say "k'l wc. mp// wc. k' 'et k'l."

Literally, "K'l there. Mother there. I state-of-possession-K'l."

The indefinite plural indicators and the numerical indicators, *many, few* (more than two), and the numbers one through ten are thought of as attributes. Ten is as high as the n'k can count. Anything more is *many*.

An action indicator describes or prescribes movement. Movement includes facial expressions of internal states. To a n'k, rain is not drops falling but an entity that appears from time to time. He would not say, "It is raining." He would say, "Rain here." Or "Rain there." Or "Rain soon."

N'k is uninflected except for the gender prefix, which is always attached to the entity indicator, but to that only.

There is no tense. To indicate the past or future, a temporal indicator is used.

There are no words to indicate aspect, that is, whether the action occurred some time ago and then stopped, occurred in the past and is still operating, is now occurring but will soon stop, is now occurring but will run for a long time.

A n'k phrase seldom consists of more than three words and often only of one. Where gesticulation will suffice, a n'k prefers not to verbalize.

There are no connectives such as *and, but,* or *or.*

N'k has no passive voice, and tone indicates the difference of indicative, subjunctive, imperative, potential, conditional, and obligative modes. Actually, the same tone is used for all but the indicative. The others can be lumped together in the mood of dubiety.

The word order of the most complex phrase is locative indicator-temporal indicator-personal name or entity indicator-attribute indicator-action indicator. The negator is used just before the indicator to which it is most relevant. The attribute indicator is the only one which cannot be used as a complete phrase, though, since personal names often consist of attribute indicators, this is an exception. One n'k can utter another's name to attract his attention.

B has described me in the first novel and in a short story as teaching myself to read English. This is correct. I started off with children's picture books, which my mother (my human mother, of course) had intended to use to teach me to read. I associated the letters of the alphabet with the pictures just as B depicted me. I started with the simplest word-picture books and progressed to the less elementary books. But this was fortuitous. If I had not just happened to pick up the most basic book first, the one that my mother would have used when she started teaching me, I may not have made any progress at all.

One of the things B neglected mentioning when he described my self education in literacy is punctuation. I had no idea, of course, that these were aids, auxiliaries, for bridging the wide gap between the spoken and the written. I thought they were words too. It took me almost two years to grasp their nature. And I pronounced them, too, giving each a syllabic value.

One of the many features of English that I had trouble with was grasping the distinction between the definite and indefinite article, between "a" or "an" and "the." N'k has neither, but then this lack is nothing special in human languages. Many neither use nor need these articles.

Inflection and conjugation, prepositions and adverbs, and the verb *to be*, caused me much trouble also. These features are totally lacking in n'k; and if I had not been both so curious and intelligent, I might never have understood their use. But I persevered, and I began to comprehend, though, truth to tell, it was not until later after I had been living among English speakers that I fully understood them.

Or I should say, among English and French speakers. After all, French was my first spoken human language.

If anybody other than myself ever reads these words, he or she will probably smile at my egotism when he reads that I call myself intelligent. But this is not egotism. I lack false humility, since I was not raised in a human society. I tell facts as I know them, and the truth is that I have an I.Q. of 197 on the Terman scale. I don't know that this means much; the various I.Q. tests are much subject to criticism. Nor would I have ever succeeded in my self-education if I had not had a tremendous drive to learn. I might not have had this if it had not been for my feeling of alienation from the tribe. I identified only partially with them, and the discovery that there were others like me in the world made me lust to know everything about them. I intended to find human beings some day and to live with them. I expected to be accepted by them, to dwell with them completely happy. Of course, this was in the early days of my self-education. When I began to read with some fluency the novels and the history books and the *Encyclopaedia Britannica* in my parents' library, I also began to understand that things would not be so simple. It would take more than just being born in a society to be accepted and to be happy.

RELIGION

When I got deep enough into the books, I despaired. Apparently, a man had to have much money (a concept I never understood from just reading about it). A man had to be on guard all the time to keep others from taking his money away. A man had to watch other men to make sure that they did not take his mate away from him. A man might not even want his mate after a while because, inevitably, he and she would be struggling for dominance in familial affairs. Or the mate would be possessed by drives over which she had no control; she might have enough money but not a high enough position in the pecking order. She might be rejected or think she was being rejected by her parents, and she could not rest until she had fulfilled their image of what a daughter should be. And so on. Of course, men were in the same unhappy situation.

Then there were religious conflicts in history and in the novels. I did not understand this at all, perhaps because the religious sense in the n'k was so rudimentary. But I did understand that the religious sense in human beings was highly developed, yet they had no idea of what was true and what wasn't true in their religions. The

Christians claimed fiercely that only their religion was true, that they alone had access to divine revelation. Yet the Christians were divided among themselves, calling each other liars and wicked; and while preaching charity and love and peacefulness, they were killing and torturing each other.

It all seemed simple and clear-cut to me. If you had a creation, then you had a Creator. At least, it seemed obvious to me at first. Later I went through the stage that every person of any intelligence goes through. Who created the Creator? How could the world have come out of nothingness? What existed before time began? Why were suffering, illness, and death inevitable?

If I had been presented with only one explanation of these, if, say, I had only the Bible available, I might have believed a monolithic explanation. But the books told me that there had been many differing explanations; and quite possibly, all were false.

I didn't think religious or philosophical issues were worth fighting over or even getting excited about.

I could understand why men schemed and fought for control of land and money and position in the pecking order. Survival is dependent upon these.

But, I asked myself, if man is so intelligent, why hasn't he developed a system where hypocrisy and greed and ruthlessness and oppression are not necessary?

I still ask myself this question, though I know that there isn't any answer. I also know that if there were an answer, it would be rejected by most people. Most humans are not much advanced beyond the n'k when it comes to freeing themselves from their social conditioning. Those who do so generally only seem to do so. They extricate themselves from one set of conditioning only to switch to another. And they do this because of their genetic dispositions. I am convinced that individuals are born Catholics or Methodists or Moslems or Jews, born Tories or Whigs or anarchists. Their genes predetermine them to a certain form of religion or ideology or economics. Some are never able to free themselves from their parents' religion or ideology, and this results in unhappiness for them. Others are able to do so, though their struggles make them unhappy.

As for me, my being an alien, an outsider to both the n'k and the humans, resulted in an unhappiness and confusion in my childhood and youth. But no longer. I am insular. The troubled waters of others affect me only in a physical sense. I am sometimes swept into the difficulties of others, and I have often sided with one group against the other. But the question of which side is morally right or wrong doesn't concern me.

I happen to be a British citizen because circumstances made me so. I was born of British parents, but in my early contacts with civilization I could easily have become a French citizen. Only the fact that my British parentage was established and that this meant I could gain a high position in British society without much effort determined me to be British. If I had been, say, Russian, I might have become Russian and fought for the Russians.

On the other hand, being much more rational and objective than most humans, because I was an outsider, I would have observed that the British society was relatively freer and contained more justice. The conditions of British society were appalling; but compared to those in Russian society, they were less objectionable.

At first sight, American society might seem relatively freer. But it didn't take me long after I'd been in the United States to see that it was a slave society. The whites denied this, of course, but the blacks knew it was a fact. And though the whites thought they were free men and democratic, the fact that they were living in a slave society colored their every thought and action and institution and made them, in a sense, slaves to their slaves. They might not know it, but it did. There can be no truly free men where some citizens are slaves.

This applies not only to ethnic, but to economic, attitudes. The poor are, in fact, slaves, though a white person can get out of that slavery if he is vigorous and intelligent enough. Or ruthless enough.

All human societies are slave societies, some more than others.

To return to my reading.

At first, I could not distinguish between fact and fiction. I thought the novels were true stories. Then I found out that they were only exercises of the imagination. I shouldn't say *only*, since the concept of fiction was new to me. It was, in fact, staggering. The n'k had no fictional stories with which to entertain themselves; any tales they told were of events that had happened in reality.

After I was able to ingest this concept, I still believed that the histories and the sacred books were true. But when I came across references to the Koran and the Book of Mormon and the Christian Science books and the religions of ancient peoples, I saw at once that they couldn't all be true. Somebody was lying. In the end, I concluded that they all were. Or, if one was right, there was no way of finding out which one.

All contained some truths, though even these were distorted.

Then there were the scientists. They denied the claims of the religionists. But scientists had often been wrong and probably still were wrong in many of their conclusions. The scientists were just as prone to dogma and prejudice as the religionists.

The difference between them and the religionists was their method of searching for the truth. Actually, the religionists were no longer searching. They had found the truth, and their searches were only for rationalizations to bolster their claims. The true scientist doubted anything unless it could be proven to be fact. And he still had a mental reservation, because he knew that what seemed established today might be unseated tomorrow.

But though scientists could uncover physical truths, they were as helpless as the religionists in the supernatural or in the cosmogony and cosmology of things and spirits. Nobody could answer my youthful questions nor was anyone ever going to answer them.

Neither deliberately blind faith or highly rationalized

faith was for me. I told myself that all religions were, to be blunt, nonsense skillfully arranged to look like sense.

Human economic and political systems were not nonsense. They were machines for the operation of society. But they were all, capitalist, socialist, communist, highly inefficient, and the rationalizations for justifying them were often as transparently false as those used in religion.

That's the way it was and is and probably will be.

The admission of this does not mean that I am cynical or bitter or despairing or depressed. I am not like that "ape-man" in that story by the Czech author,* who killed himself because he could not endure the hypocrisy, greed, and injustice of civilization.

I accept this as the way things are, and I adjust accordingly. I had a very difficult time in my early contacts with humans because I didn't know the rules. People learn the thousand and more subtle laws of social behavior easily because they are brought up from infancy surrounded by adults who know them intimately. The children only have to imitate their examples. Even so, if they are thrust into a segment of society where the rules differ, they make mistakes. And quite often they are incapable of adjusting themselves.

I wasn't entirely innocent when I ventured into civilization, since I had read the novels and histories. But these more often confused than helped me. They gave a partially false picture and, also, the rules had changed somewhat between the time the books were written and the time I experienced society. But I learn quickly. If need be, I can pass as easily for a London dock laborer or a Yorkshire farmer as an English aristocrat. Or, for that matter, skin color and hair aside, for a Masai cattle herder or a Texas rancher.

My ear for sounds and rhythm of a language and my ability at mimicry enable me to do this. Inside of course I am still the "ape-man."

---

* Josef Nesvadba, *The Death of an Apeman*, in *The Lost Face; Best Science Fiction From Czechoslovakia*, Taplinger Publishing Co., 1971.

TIME HAS NO SHADOWS

In the beginning was greenness and timelessness.

The rain-forest trees with their thick canopy of vegetation binding them cast few shadows. And time cast no shadow at all.

Those who've read Hudson's *Green Mansions* know that the rain forest is not the same as the bush jungle. Large areas of the latter are often comparatively clear beneath the trees and their connecting many-leveled awnings of branch, vine, and creeper. A twilight and a hush spread through the rain forest; the trunks of the trees soar upward branchless for a hundred feet, looking like the columns of a huge badly lit temple. Most of the forest life, the birds, monkeys, civets, rodents, etc., is in the upper levels; and it is only seldom that a ground-dweller glides through the semidusk.

The n'k's territory was mainly in the rain forest, though part of it was in the bush jungle of the lower ground near the ocean or that along a nearby river.

The silence was often broken by the speech or cries of the n'k but even their language was whispering and quite appropriate for the living temple in which they dwelt.

This can be easily visualized by people who have never been to the rain forest.

But I have never met a person who could truly comprehend my sense of timelessness. On the other hand, I do not truly understand the sense of time which humans have.

I suppose that I have more of it than the n'k, since I am genetically a Homo sapiens. But I don't have much more.

How can I describe something for which no human languages seem to have words?

The preliterate and less technologically advanced peoples perhaps have a somewhat similar attitude. But they, too, are bound to their economics, which is considerably more complicated than that of the n'k. The latter are not even much guided by the sun, which they may not see

for days or sometimes weeks except for fleeting appear-
ances through a break in the canopy. The night pales
into the semitwilight, and they may or may not rise with
dawn. They eat when hungry, which is, however, most
of the day. Being primarily root-grubbers, they spend
much time digging up roots and stuffing their paunches,
which are as big and rounded as those of the gorilla.

They have almost no ritual or ceremony except the
feast under the full moon, when the entire tribe dances.
If a large animal has been killed, or a member of an
enemy tribe of n'k (which doesn't happen often), they
eat the body as a climax to the dance. B, by the way, was
correct when he said that an earthen drum is pounded by
three old females while the tribe dances. I know that
some critics have maintained that B got the idea for this
from descriptions of chimpanzees pounding on earth or
logs with sticks. But they are wrong.

I've asked the n'k why it was always three females who
drum, but they didn't know. It is just the custom, they
said.

If the tribe happens to be in a completely covered area
where the full moon is not visible, the tribe doesn't
dance. Nor does it seem to know that it's missing its
monthly event.

The point is that the n'k have no sense of time except
when arranging meetings, and that seldom happens. Nor
does their sense of tense extend beyond today, the day
after today, and a vague past. They don't even have a
distinction between the rainy and dry seasons. Gabon
gets abundant rain through most of the year, and there is
little variation of temperatures.

The essential difference in the attitude toward time
between the n'k (and hence mine) and humans is this:
Humans think of time as a steady flow which can be
sectioned by natural or artificial means. The natural is
comprised of the sun, the moon, the stars, and the seasons. The artificial is comprised of clocks and calendars.

The n'k think of the sun, moon, and stars as living
beings and wouldn't be surprised, though they would be

dismayed, if the sun did not appear when it should. They just exist in the now, and the past and the near future are nearby limits to now.

That is the best I can do in trying to explain my original sense of time or lack of it. I'm sure that if some human could look through my mind and eyes, he would be lost and perhaps even scared. He would not know what he was experiencing. The closest he could come to describing it would be to compare it to a nightmare. Dreams are lost in timelessness; things are out of sequence; there is often no causality.

Of course, I became somewhat aware of the concept of time through reading the books in my parents' cabin. But I didn't truly comprehend it until I was in civilization. Even so, I never came to accept time-markers as natural. I went along with clocks because humans lived by them, and I was trying to live by their rules. But I never felt the sense of urgency that accompanies clocks and calendars.

And when I am back in the jungle, it is with relief that I sink back into my natural timelessness. I become one with the beasts and the trees, and I can laze away weeks or months with no thought beyond the now. If I were a true n'k, I would be unable to imagine beyond now.

This was the essential difference between the n'k and me. They had very little imagination, just enough to distinguish them from the beasts. This little difference is, of course, enormous, since it does make them partly human. But I had much imagination. And so I was all human.

Despite this, I am much closer to the n'k than to humans in my sense of time. Perhaps imagination is the ability to comprehend time. The greater the comprehension, the greater the imagination.

FOREWORD to

Tarzan of the Grapes

Gene Wolfe is one of the finest writers in the science
fiction field. But this story is not science fiction. It is
modern myth, generated by one of the three greatest
literary characters of the twentieth century. Myth begets
myth; and Tarzan, Sherlock Holmes, and Leopold Bloom
have begot many others.

Tarzan of the Grapes

BY GENE WOLFE

SHIMMERING in the heat, the long rows of vines stretched row on row uphill, so that the hill seemed to be a great, swelling wave in an ocean of grey-green. Prescott, the deputy, said, "You think he's really in there? We'll get him if he is."

Brown shook his head. "I don't think he exists. Here or anywhere else. I think he's a phantom of the public mind."

"You bastards write enough about him. We'll clear out some of them anyway." Without waiting for Brown to reply, Prescott picked up the riot gun leaning against the sheriff's car and ducked into the aisle between two rows of trellises.

To his back Brown said, "I interviewed the witnesses and reported what they told me." He checked his camera before following.

The trellises were seven feet high, five wired, strung on redwood posts. A five-foot space between rows was adequate for spraying and fertilization, and for the pickers who would soon harvest the crop. Brown picked some as he walked, purple-ripe and bursting with juice, and popped them into his mouth. To the sheriff, a big-bellied man who had lived all his life within twenty miles of this vineyard, he had said, "Once the harvest begins they'll leave."

"Sure they will." The sheriff's leather belt was four inches wide, and he thrust his thumbs into it when he pontificated. Brown thought: No one should be so damn pompous and right too.

"Sure they will. They'll go back and brag their heads off about what a great time they had here, and next year we'll have ten times more. Either we stop this now, the first season, or we'll be fighting it the rest of our lives." The sheriff had looked up at the thrashing helicopter as he spoke, as though just by looking he could tell if the pilot saw anything. Actually the pilot had been talking with Prescott on the radio in the car. Brown could hear their voices without being able to make out words. More plainly the sheriff's thoughts had said: "They lay down in the shadows when they hear him coming, damn them. The only time he can see them is high noon."

Prescott was walking fast and Brown hurried to catch up, spitting seeds and resisting the temptation to pick more grapes. What was it Prescott had told him? "You've written enough about him."

He had done more than that. He had invented the figure; he and Culough and the teletype girl.

Culough was his editor, and thinking back, Brown decided it was the publicity the town had gotten when the pickers were being unionized that had set him off. There had been organizers, professionals and volunteers, from the AFL-CIO and the Teamsters, and sound trucks, picnics, and whoop-de-doo. Coverage by AP, UPI, CBS, ABC, NBC, *Time*, and *Life*, as well as the Los Angeles papers. The circulation of their own had shot up, only to drop again when the thing was over—leaving Culough, perhaps, to dream of those days of glory. The idea of a hip contemplating his toes in the vineyards had been his, and as he had explained it, it had seemed easy and hardly criminal.

"All you have to do," (leveling a big finger at Brown), "is go into Haight-Ashbury or one of those places and hire some kid for a couple of days. These nuts are top news now. They grow pot on their own farms, and they're practically sun worshipers. Why shouldn't one decide to start camping out in the grapes?"

"Wouldn't it be better," Brown had objected, "to have four or five? You know, kind of a love-in."

"Too much chance of somebody talking, and it would cost too much." It was typical of Culough that before calling Brown in he had ripped covers from his collection of magazines and taped them to the walls of his office. There were an impressive number of them, with some of the most important represented two or even three times. Culough's finger stabbed toward one featuring a handsome young man with wavy lines painted on his face. "Get me one who looks like that."

And Brown had, as nearly as he could. A UCLA student on vacation who possessed dirty bare feet, longish hair, sun-glasses with perfectly circular lenses, and a cotton poncho dotted with three-fingers-together leopard spots. It had been the poncho, Brown thought, that had done it. That poncho had given everyone something to hang a story on.

The student had made no trouble at all. He had accepted the deal as offered, had come for two days, and had appeared at the edges of the vineyards whenever it had seemed likely that he could startle someone by so doing. At the end of the two days Brown had three good interviews with local people who had "sighted" him, and the student had gone quietly back to San Diego. The story Brown wrote was headlined GRAPE MAN APPEARS HERE.

The teletype operator, however, must have been influenced by the leopard-skin poncho. She had sent Brown's piece out under a slightly different heading, and it had been picked up elsewhere under such titles as APE MAN APPEARS IN VINEYARDS.

That had accomplished everything Culough wanted. And more.

Ahead, Prescott stopped and raised his riot gun. Over his shoulder Brown could see an unkempt figure disappearing through some hole in the vines, but it was too late to get a picture. The riot gun roared, and a little puff of dust rose in the hot, clear air. It looked like a tiny cloud against the pitiless sky.

Prescott spread the vines with his hands until he had a big enough hole to thrust his head through, and looked into the next aisle to see if the boy he had shot at was there. Apparently he was not, since he drew back in a moment with a grunt of disgust and began trying to raise the helicopter on his walkie-talkie. "I had one here, did you see him? Hello? Mike?"

The odd thing about the "ape man" was that people continued to see him even after he had gone. At first Brown had been surprised at this, but the mysterious figure in leopard skin had become a handy catchall for any hitch-hiker or half-seen vine dresser. The publicity generated more reports, and Culough gave each a prominent spot.

Still trying to contact the helicopter, now on the far side of the hill, Prescott jerked back the slide of his gun to jack a new shell into the chamber. The empty, red as a firecracker, plopped onto the sandy ground. It had a brass that caught the sun in hard points of light. "You might have killed him," Brown said. He had tried to suppress the protest.

Prescott was surly at having missed his shot. "Fleeing from a peace officer while committing an act of malicious trespass," he said. "I got a right to fire."

"Why don't you just arrest these people in town? My God, they panhandle on the street; they even buy yogurt and that kind of garbage at the A&P." Brown had not been in church since he was a child, but he found a quotation, ghost-like, in his mind: *As against a robber have you come out, with swords and clubs. When I was daily with you in the temple, you did not stretch forth your hands against me.* He could not have known what that meant when he had last heard it.

"The worse ones don't," Prescott said, voicing an argument Brown had heard before. "They stay out here in the grapes. You don't see that Tarzan guy in town, do you?"

"He's a myth, damn it," Brown insisted wearily. The

young people (in his own mind he did not know what to call them; very few were really hips, but then he was coming to realize that there were very few real hips) who had begun drifting into the area almost as soon as his first stories had been picked up spoke of the "ape man" as their leader, or at least their ideal; and unfortunately they spoke to the police and the press at times. Only a few claimed to have seen him, but they called him "Tarzan" or "Simba" (there was a fad for Swahili). By nonhips he was still reported often, and in one case was under accusation of statutory rape.

"People around here ain't going to take it," Prescott was saying. He was no longer looking at Brown, but prowling ahead down the endless corridor between the trellises. One hand held the radio to his ear while his free arm cradled the riot gun, its butt on his hip. "They used to take all these sit-ins and all that crap, but not any more. People are mad. You think you're going to crucify me in that sheet of yours if I blast one of these guys? You read your letters column. Read your own editorials."

"They don't do any harm. They sleep on the sand in here and talk and eat a few grapes. Less than the birds. What harm does that do?"

"You try telling that to one of these growers. They—" Prescott stiffened in midsentence, his head up, listening to the walkie-talkie. "Hey! The copter's got one spotted. Come on!"

He was off at a clumsy run before Brown could collect his wits enough to follow, then ducked sideways through a hole in the vines much as the boy he had shot at earlier had. Afraid that he would miss the action entirely, Brown was forced to sprint to keep him in sight. There were distant shouts from other deputies moving unseen down other aisles. Apparently in response to his radio Prescott bulled his way through the trellises again, Brown closer behind him now.

Ahead of them a figure with flying hair dashed away. Prescott halted and raised his gun, then lowered it again and set off in pursuit. The helicopter close overhead made a sound like a washing machine and, whipping the leaves like a hurricane, blew choking dust.

Looking past Prescott, Brown saw their quarry, a girl in a gaudy op-art smock, trying to break through the wall of green into another aisle. Beyond her he glimpsed the blue-clad deputy who had cut off her escape. Prescott shouted something and fired into the air.

The girl stopped and turned to face them, her arms dangling loose at her sides. Tears were cutting bright channels through the dirt the helicopter had blown onto her face. "Up! Get them up!" The girl raised her hands slowly.

Brown thought: I brought her. She read what I wrote and thought the vineyards would be a new kick, a new game. It was as though the girl were his daughter, and he was powerless to help her. She had blue eyes and long legs like a colt's, heavily tanned. Brown legs, he thought. Brown face. Brown hair.

The other deputy came up behind her, puffing and red faced. "All right," Prescott demanded, "what's your name?"

"Jane," the girl said. She held her head proudly, but the tears were streaming down her cheeks.

"Where are you from, Jane?"

"Oz."

"Don't give me any of that." Prescott advanced a step toward her. "Where are you from?" He had hooked the radio on his belt, and with the riot gun resting in the crook of his elbow, he held pencil poised over note pad.

"Tarzana."

"That's part of L.A., ain't it?" He looked at her suspiciously. "I thought that place changed its name."

"If you say so."

A third deputy arrived, thrusting his way through the vines, and looked curiously at the girl. "Better bring her out, Prescott. Sheriff says he wants to see her." Brown took a picture of the three of them with her, the flash almost invisible in the brilliant sunshine. With him bringing up the rear they began the walk back to the road, feet crunching softly in the dry sand, the girl erect as a young palm between Prescott and the second deputy.

When they had gone perhaps a hundred feet Brown halted, changing plates in the camera and exchanging the spent flash bulb for a fresh one. Culough would want a picture of the sheriff with the girl.

Fingers drove his nose and lips back, crushing them against the bony parts of his face, and held them there. He thrust out his arms, flinging away the camera as he was jerked backward into the tangle of vines; then he jolted against the ground and was staring up into a broad, sun-darkened face framed in straggling hair.

"If you yell, I'll break your back."

"I won't yell." Blood from his lips ran salty in his mouth, but Brown forced himself to relax, lying back against the sand. In leopard-patterned shorts the other towered over him, his shoulders wide as a bulldozer blade and his arms as thick as Brown's thighs. Unexpectedly he bent down again, slipping his hands inside Brown's coat to touch his chest and armpits. "I don't have a gun," Brown said. "I'm a newspaper reporter. Honestly."

The young giant twitched his head almost imperceptibly in the direction the deputies had taken. "I'm going to fight them. You going to fight for them?"

"To help them?" Brown shook his head. "No. I only want to watch so I can write about it later, Tarzan."

The broad face remained immobile, but Brown sensed that he had scored, if only ever so slightly. A muscle-beach boy? Wrestler? Someone who wandered in here looking for a leader and found himself cast in the part.

As Brown spat away blood, the giant turned and loped off down the corridor between the trellis rows, pausing only occasionally to peer through the leaves into the aisle the deputies had taken. At last he stopped, and Brown, who had sprung up to follow, was able to catch up. Through the living barrier, he could hear the deep mutter of the deputies' voices.

Then the giant plunged through.

By the time Brown could follow, the group had ex-

ploded like a herd of prize steers ambushed by a tiger.
One burly officer actually flew, both feet in the air from
the force of the blow he had taken, and the ground shook
when he fell.

Then Prescott's riot gun flashed back, and forward, the
stock slamming against the giant's head. A second time,
and the wooden butt splintered. The giant pitched on his
face. Brown ran to get his camera.

When he returned, Prescott was putting handcuffs on
the unconscious man's huge wrists. The deputy he had
seen sailing through the air a few moments before was
sitting up, moaning with pain as the third officer tried to
straighten the suddenly warped line of his chin. "I
wouldn't touch that if I were you," Brown said. "His
jaw's broken. Where's the girl?"

"She got away." Prescott stood up as the cuffs clicked
shut. "What the hell do you think? But we got the big
guy here, and he's worth more than all the rest put together." For a moment he looked down at the injured
deputy, then nodded in agreement with Brown's diagno-
sis. "That's busted all right." To the uninjured one he
said, "Help him up and take him to the car so they can
get him to the hospital. I'll stay here with the prisoner
until he can walk or you can send somebody out."

Brown helped lift the deputy with the fractured jaw to
his feet, and Prescott asked, "You want to go with them?"

Brown shook his head, gesturing at the unconscious
giant. "This is where the story is. I'll stay here." The two
deputies left.

After a moment Prescott asked, "Say, where were you
when the fight started?"

"Back a way," Brown said vaguely. Now that the excitement was over he was beginning to feel the heat again.
Even in the dry air his shirt was soaked with sweat. He
fanned himself with his hat, and for a few minutes neither
of them spoke. The thrashing of the helicopter was no
longer audible.

Prescott picked up his riot gun, dusted sand from it,
then dropped it again. Besides the damage to the stock,

the barrel was at least fifteen degrees out of true. "Well, you can put it in your story that this kook busted a hell of a good Winchester gun for me."

Brown did not answer. He was watching the prisoner, whose eyes now showed a tiny crevice of awareness at the base of the lids. His arms had not moved, but they were knotted now with effort. Brown looked away, pretending to search the sky for the helicopter, hoping that Prescott would be deceived by the misdirection. The steel link that held the manacles snapped.

FOREWORD to

Relic

Most feral human stories are unrelieved by humor. This is a funny yet grim tale of an aging "Lord Greystoke" in a meatless mechanized future. When this time has come, and it soon may, it won't seem funny.

Relic

BY MACK REYNOLDS

H E was an inoffensive old man, or should have
been. In his day he had probably gone six and
a half feet tall, and his thinning, white hair
had undoubtedly been black, jet black. In his
day the now grayish skin would have taken a tan as none
other. In his day he would have put a Hawaiian beach
boy to shame.

But this was no longer his day. There was a bit of the
shamble in his walk, and his once wide shoulders drooped
in the inevitable slouch of age. Still, there was some arrogance remaining.

Muttering the vexations of his years, he found himself
a table and chair in the auto-cafeteria and peered unhappily at the menu set into the table top. He grumbled at
the small type, peered about at his few neighbors, muttered again and brought forth a pair of steel-bound spectacles, one lens of which was cracked. He fumbled them
onto his nose and went back to his perusal.

He said waveringly into the ordermike, "Steak tartare.
Steak tartare without capers."

A mechanically tinny voice said, "We are sorreeeee, we
do not include that dish on our menyouuu."

His tone was peevish now. "You take a pound of fresh
ground raw sirloin, a half cup of finely chopped onions,
an egg yolk, salt and pepper. Form the meat into a patty
and make a small indentation into which you drop the
egg yolk, then garnish with the onions."

"We are sorreeeee, we do not include that dish on our menyouuu."

He glared at the mike for a long moment in frustration, but then sent his eyes back to the menu, his mouth working.

Finally he said, "A double tenderloin steak, very rare. Very rare, understand? Barely seared on each side. Nothing else, just the steak."

"Thank-kew."

He went back to his unconscious, faint mutterings while he waited.

Within five minutes, the delivery area of the table sank, to return with a large platter upon which rested an enormous steak.

Growling low in his throat, he reached forth and brought it to him. Almost as though it was an afterthought, he reached for knife and fork and jabbed the prongs of the latter utensil into the meat.

His quivering lips went back over yellowing teeth and he banged the fork back on the table.

He said querulously into the ordermike, "I said rare. I distinctly said very rare. This steak is burned to a cinder."

"We are sorreeeee. We cannot accept returns of orders. If you have ennnny complaints, please speak to the manager."

"Blitherit! I want another steak. A rare steak, understand?"

"We are sorreeeee. If you have ennny complaints, please speak to the manager."

An ordinarily faint scar across his forehead began to go reddish. His wavering voice found strength and he snapped, "By George, I'll do just that!"

Trembling his irritation, he shuffled to his feet, took up the platter complete with the debated steak and glared around the enormous dining room. Nobody bothered to look up from their automated feeding.

There was a sign at the far end of the restaurant indicating the preserve of the manager of this assembly-line eatery. He stomped in that direction, growling incoherently in his throat.

He pushed through the door without knocking, glared about through watery eyes. There was a desk, but no one at it. Beyond were rows of gleaming mechanized restaurant equipment, each device boasting impressive banks of dials, meters, switches and screens. A middle-aged man in shirt sleeves and with a harassed expression on his face prowled up and down. He would stare into a screen, automatically reach out and throw a switch; he would scowl at a dial, hover a finger over a button, but then shake his head and hurry on to the next device which, perhaps, was throwing a red light.

At the entrance of the newcomer, he looked around, his face as querulous as that of his indignant visitor.

He came up, after banging a release which turned off the red light. "Now what!" he snapped. He put his hands on his hips.

"This steak. . . ."

"What's the matter with the bloody steak? It looks all right to me."

"That's what's the matter with it!" the other snarled, with surprising fervor in view of his advanced years. "It is not bloody! I asked for a rare steak, do you understand!"

The restaurateur cast his eyes ceilingward, in search of divine guidance. "Fifty thousand meals a day. Fifty thousand, get it, and on top of all my other duties I've got to put up with cranky old duffers who don't know a good steak when they see one."

"Cranky old duffer, eh?" The older man growled low in his throat. "Listen, you young bounder, I was eating steaks better than this hydroponic farm-raised, over-fat mush you call meat, before your grandfather knew what it was all about!"

He took the steak, platter and all and dashed it to the floor.

The harassed manager had had it today. He reached

out to grasp the oldster's jacket front. "Now you clean that up! If you don't like our food, you needn't pay, but you're going to clean that . . ."

However, he had made his mistake.

At the touch of the hand, the low growling which had sounded no more than an old man's complaint, suddenly deepened, unbelievingly, to a warning rumble. And suddenly he who had been doddering crouched slightly and leapt backward, breaking the other's hold.

The growl became a snarl and thin hands shot out for the restaurant man's throat. Thin and veined, but they were hands of steel. Even as the younger man's eyes bulged terror, they tightened.

"Thus," the other was growling, "did I deal with Bolgani when but a boy. Thus did I deal with Terkoz. And thus do I deal with you, whom I respect no more than Dango the hyena."

The pressure of the hands on the throat tightened, and the victim's eyes bugged in stress. There was a sharp crack, the body lost its stiffness, the fists ceased their drumming on the horrible old man's chest.

The body dropped to the floor, and the oldster, glaring still, put one foot on it, beat his fists against his chest, opened his mouth as though to roar, but then caught himself. He looked down at his victim, obviously dead, went back into a semi-crouch and darted his eyes about the restaurant's office, *cum* kitchen control center. There were no others present.

He hurried his way to what was obviously a back door, probably leading onto an alley from which restaurant supplies could be unloaded by the robos.

Lieutenant Webster entered after a grumbled response to his knock and looked at his chief.

Cosgrove looked back as though in weary resignation.

"Sorry to bother you, Inspector. You said anything at all, anything that might be a lead."

"What've you got now?"

"Probably nothing. You know this kid from Trans-World?"

"Stimbol? That young cloddy they sent over to haunt us. What in Zen do they need a reporter for in this day and age?"

"Well, he's got a bug in his bonnet."

"About the Monster? What is it?"

"He wouldn't tell me."

"Send him in," Inspector Cosgrove sighed. "He's probably been watching some of those old TriD tapes where the intrepid reporter solves the crime."

Webster left and shortly after Jerry Stimbol entered. He couldn't have been more than twenty-five and actually looked a good five years younger. He was too thin, too intense, and made the Inspector tired just to look at him. He carried a couple of books and some folders in his hands.

Cosgrove said, "Well? Webster said this idea was so hot you wouldn't tell him about it. You got some angle for a story?"

The cub reporter said, "Now look, Inspector, let me build up to this. Don't say no until you've thought about it. I think I've got it all figured out." He scowled unhappily. "Except why he came to America, and how he's maintaining himself."

Cosgrove sighed again. "Let's hear your fling, son."

The reporter approached, laid his books and folders down on the other's desk and pulled up a chair. He scratched between his nose and upper lip, as though he had a mustache, which he didn't.

"Well, now look at this first." He handed over the heavier of the books, opened and with a section marked with a penciled box.

Cosgrove kept the place with one finger, looked at the cover.

"*Burke's Peerage?*"

"Yes, sir, I got it from the library."

The Inspector shrugged and began to read, muttering

a word or two from time to time. "Greystoke . . . viscount
. . . West Africa . . . married . . . Porter, an American
. . . one son. . . ."

He finished finally and looked up. "All right, so what?"

"Look at the date of his birth."

The Inspector looked. "All right, late 19th Century.
So?"

"Look at the date of his death."

"It doesn't give a date of death."

"I know," Stimbol said.

The Inspector looked at him.

Stimbol said nervously, "Sir, have you ever considered
how many fictional characters are actually based on real
people?"

The Inspector held his peace.

The reporter squirmed in his chair. "Take Huck Finn
and Tom Sawyer; both were boys Mark Twain had known
in Missouri. In fact, Tom Sawyer was Mark Twain; he
was autobiographical. Take that other classic character of
early American literature, Mike Hammer. Did you know
he was based on a real private detective Spillane knew?"

He hurried on, as though afraid the other would inter-
rupt him. "Jack London's characters were often based on
real people, and certainly Scott Fitzgerald's were. Take
Hemingway's colonel in 'Across the River and Into the
Trees'; he was based on a real person."

"All right," the Inspector said. "I get your drift."

"Well, what I'm driving at, isn't it probable that a lot
of other supposedly fictional characters were actually
strongly based on actual people?"

"Greystoke," the Inspector muttered. "West Africa.
Wait a minute. Some story tapes I used to scan when I
was a kid."

Stimbol leaned forward. "Yes," he said excitedly.
"Based on a real person. Brought up by animals as a boy.
Other cases have been known. Saw some fantastic adventures in early Africa. Somehow, the author of the stories
got in touch with him and fictionalized his experiences."

The Inspector snorted. "Fictionalized is right. They're

some of the most far out yarns of all time." He snorted
again. "My old man used to wallop me for reading them.
What're you leading up to?"

The young reporter opened one of his folders. "Now,
I don't know how many of the books you read when you
were a kid, but I could almost recite them. Here's a list in
correct order, that is, chronological."

"I remember vaguely," the Inspector said. He grinned
suddenly. "Remember that one where all the men had
tails?"

"And the one where he got reduced to the height of
about one foot?"

"And the time he found the city of gold?"

They were both laughing.

The Inspector stopped suddenly. "What in Zen's this
got to do with our drivel-happy killer?"

Stimbol, seemingly ignoring the question, took up another folder. "Well now, what you said just now ties in.
This mysterious Monster doing all these meaningless killings obviously needs psychiatric care. Now, you notice in
those books that whoever was doing the story telling continued to go further and further out. The first one was
admittedly a hard to believe adventure yarn, but it was
downright conservative compared to what came later.
Toward the end, he was even doing such things as going
to the center of the earth, not to speak of finding lost
colonies of Crusaders and lost Roman Legions in the
middle of Africa."

"What's all this jetsam got to do with . . ." the Inspector ground to a halt. His eyes narrowed. Now he rasped,
"Oh, no."

"Now wait a minute, sir. Now, look. My theory is that
as the years went by, he was slipping further and further
into paranoia. All you have to do is read the books. He
was getting delusions of grandeur. Patrolling the jungles
and deserts, righting everything *he* thought was wrong.
A regular one man lynch law to himself. Killing off everybody who hindered him in no matter how small. . . ."

The Inspector was on his feet. He said, his tone very

low and even, "Get . . . out . . . of . . . here. You silly clod, get out of my office. In fact, get out of the building!" His voice was rising now, just short of the shrill point. "I'm issuing immediate orders to Roberts that if you ever show your stupid face around here again. . . ."

The keeper said, "Hey there, old boy, don't pester the anmuls!"

The other looked around. He had obviously ducked under the steel rail in order to get nearer to the cages.

He said testily, after noting the keeper's blue uniform, "I am not pestering the animals, as you put it. I am talking to my friend here, Manu, the monkey."

"Oh," the custodian said with sour cynicism. "And what did he say?"

"Manu says he is unhappy penned up in this hut of steel. He says it is not fit for a Gomangani, and well is it known throughout the jungle that the Gomangani will live in filth."

The keeper hadn't bothered to follow. The monkey was upset, all right. The old yoke must have scared him. The little fellow was chattering and jittering and running around the back of his cage as though something was after him.

"Okay, okay," the keeper said. "But suppose you go on about your business. If the monk has any complaints he can tell them to the curator."

The old timer looked at him levelly. "You seek to jest with me? Even the balus will tell you it is not wise to jest with the Lord of the Jungle."

Oh, great. Another screwball. Last week they had some kid of supposedly Spanish descent who'd hopped into a grazing pen with a bull, armed with a red colored blanket. He was, he explained later, in the curator's office, an es-pontáneo, getting in a bit of practice in case the fiesta brava ever made a comeback.

"Listen, all I'm telling you, old man, is if you bother any more of the anmuls I'll run you in. Can't you read those signs? Don't feed or tease the anmuls."

"But I had planned to exchange greetings with Tantor."

"Who in Zen's Tantor?"

A thin red line, obviously an old scar, was beginning to manifest itself across the other's forehead. "Tantor! Tantor the elephant!"

The other shook his head in sour despair. He reached out to grasp the old man's arm with the intention of escorting him to the gate.

A few minutes later on the other side of the zoo, one of the visitors came to a sudden halt, his face scowling puzzlement.

"What's the matter, dear?" his wife said. She hated these weekly expeditions to look at the animals. For that matter, she hated the half dozen years her husband had spent stationed in Africa; it was all the old bore ever talked about.

He said, "I didn't know they had a gorilla here."

"They haven't," she said. "We've seen every moth eaten beast in the place twenty times over. No gorillas."

The sound came again.

"There. Did you hear it? The roar of a bull gorilla, proclaiming its victory. Or, at least, something awfully like a gorilla."

His wife made a contemptuous moué. "If that was a gorilla roaring victory, it must have been a conquest of some flea that had been giving it a hard time. You've got a glass ear, darling. Didn't you hear that squeaky break when he hit high? If that's a gorilla, it's a mighty decrepit one."

"I still say it sounded like a gorilla," her husband said argumentatively.

The body of the keeper wasn't found until several hours later. It had been hidden in the rushes in the duck pool.

The editor-in-chief had closed his eyes in acute pain long minutes before. Under his breath he murmured something that involved somebody's uncle owning a controlling share or otherwise he would . . . .

Finally he said, "Now look, Jerry. Let's be astute about this. I read those books when I was a kid, just the way you did. In fact, I was the neighborhood authority. It wasn't until I was in my middle-teens that I found out such little discrepancies as the fact that there isn't any jungle in Africa in which you could swing through the trees. Maybe in South America, but not Africa. It's mostly bush, or plains, or desert. Even the Ituri rain forest doesn't have the kind of trees you could swing through. You would have done better here in North America back when the live oak covered the country."

"Now I can explain that," Stimbol interrupted.

"Hold it, blast it, let me add a few more little items. Those great apes that supposedly raised him. What were they, chimpanzees? Because that's the largest ape in Africa, other than the gorilla, and his foster parents supposedly weren't gorillas. And don't tell me they might have been orangutans, because they come from Borneo, and while the author we're talking about probably did more lousing up of geography than any other in history, I don't think he'd mistake West Africa for Sarawak."

"That's what I mean," Jerry Stimbol said plaintively, urgently. "I'll admit the author had never been out of the States until he'd written several of the books. The stories must have been told to him. Admittedly the teller probably magnified. Then, on top of the magnification, the author, in fictionalizing the accounts, magnified still more. And that's what eventually led to the trouble."

"What trouble?" the other grunted. He looked desperately at the sheaf of reports on his desk. On top was the latest Monster victim story, and here he was, like a yoke, spending his time on this kid's jetsam.

"It's like any kind of lie. To keep it going, it's got to grow bigger and bigger. In the first book and the second, he was a fairly easygoing type, trying to get along against an hostile environment. But to keep the reader's attention and to continue to receive the egoboo he was getting on a worldwide basis, he had to make the adventures further and further out, the lies bigger and bigger."

He scratched his upper lip nervously even as he scowled, trying to put his fling over against what he knew were impossible odds. He raised his voice to keep the other from interrupting.

"And it evidently got to be a worm in his brain. He really began believing it all. I wish I could figure out what he's doing in America, and how in the world he's maintaining himself."

His chief sighed deeply. "Look Jerry, let's let everything else go by. Let's admit everything you say is right. But there's just one other thing that's wrong."

"What?" the reporter demanded.

"He's dead."

"Burke's Peerage doesn't say so."

The editor's voice was going impatient. "Now look. Remember, I read the damn books too. In the first one he's raised by the overgrown monks, okay. In the second one, he gets married to this mopsy, Jane. The third one is about his son. Mind you, all this takes place before the First World War. Both he and his son participate in that fighting against the Germans in Africa. Now, mind you, he's already a grandfather at that time. How in the name of Holy Jumping Zen can you suggest he's still alive?"

Stimbol had been nodding, as though only awaiting his own chance to talk. Now he said doggedly, "It points out in one of the stories that he regularly got rejuvenations from a witchdoctor, or witchwoman, or something."

The editor's eyes closed in acute pain again.

Jerry Stimbol pressed it earnestly. "Would you deny that medical science makes it possible today to prolong life for at least a couple of hundred years?"

The eyes opened. "With organ transplants and all our modern developments, yes. But back before the first World War? And a Bantu witchwoman? No!"

Stimbol leaned forward. "You're being prejudiced. How about the primitives using foxglove as a heart stimulant before the laboratories ever dreamed of digitalis? How about the natives using the bark of the cinchona against malaria long before the supposedly scientific doctors dreamed of the real nature of the disease and of quinine?"

His superior glared at him, hopelessly.

The reporter thought he was making his point, at long last. He pushed his advantage. "Maybe whatever rites he went through were what finally sent him off his rocker. Possibly, to keep his youth, he took some native narcotic that wound him up with his screws loose."

The ire was rising fast. "Listen, Stimbol, whatever got you going on this?"

"Yes, sir," Jerry nodded, still thinking he was beginning to get through. "I traced the killings back. They didn't start here in Greater Washington. There was a similar outbreak in London, a few months before, same sort of thing. And when they started in Greater Washington, they stopped in England. But it was the London killings that gave me my first clue."

"So what happened in London?"

"He strung up one of his victims with a grass rope."

"A grass rope?"

"Yes, sir. Don't you remember? Even when he wore Western type clothing, he used to wind his grass rope around his stomach, underneath. That and his hunting knife were his last resort weapons. You remember how often he resorted to the hunting knife."

"As I recall from my childhood studies of our hero, he killed half the population of Africa with it, Negro, Arab and animal."

"Yes, sir," Stimbol beamed. "And note how many of these Monster killings are knife jobs. Oh, he's still got that old hunting knife all right."

"And I've got two more ulcers since you came in here and started this," the other told him nastily. "Now listen here, Stimbol, I've stopped caring who your uncle is and how much TransWorld stock he owns. You're off crime as of this minute, understand?"

The other was flabbergasted. "Off crime? You mean . . . you mean you're not going to let me follow through on the Monster story?"

"My boy, I wouldn't put you on a crime story that involved ten-year-old kids pilfering from the pneumatic delivery chutes from the ultra-markets. How are you on covering marriages? Or, better still, obituaries?"

"But that's all automated," Jerry Stimbol wailed.

"We'll un-automate obits," his chief snarled. "As of now, it's the good old days in the obituary department."

The aged ape-man stretched out on his back, his hands behind his head, and stared up at the ceiling, his mind going back, as so often it did these days, to his memories of yesteryear.

It wasn't so easy to separate the real memories from the written accounts of his adventures. He should have been more firm with that blithering scribbling Yankee who had wormed out of him so many of his deeds of daring. Lot of confounded nonsense, mixed up with the reality. Those jewels he had, uhh, liberated in Opar, for instance. There hadn't been nearly as many as reported. In fact, they weren't exactly jewels at all, but sort of costume jewelry some itinerant Arab had unloaded on the local natives, largely made in Japan.

And that hand to hand battle he'd had with Bolgani, the gorilla. That was highly exaggerated. He hadn't been nearly as badly hurt as reported. The ape-man snorted. Of course, it was kind of a baby gorilla, but he'd forgotten to tell the American that. At any rate, he hadn't been nearly as hurt as came out in the published story. This scar he'd got across his forehead—he traced it now with a thin, freckled but still wiry finger. From the book accounts, you'd think the blow he had taken to his head had all but incapacitated him. Actually, his head still throbbed from time to time and seemed to get worse, now that he was older, but it wasn't as though Bolgani had all but finished him.

He scowled, his memory blurring then clearing again as he tried to send it back over the long years. Come to think of it, that Bolgani probably wasn't a gorilla at all.

It had been kind of dim there in the forest. Possibly it had been a baboon. A moderately large baboon.

He shook his head. But no, he distinctly recalled that it was a full grown, bull gorilla. And he, the Lord of the Jungle, had killed it. He, the adopted son of Kala, who had nursed him. He of the tribe of the Mangani great apes, headed by Kerchak the king. He who had loved Teeka, the beautiful she ape. Yes, yes, he could remember quite clearly now, he had killed the giant Bolgani with his knife.

That was the trouble with his memories, these days, he told himself in continuing irritation. It was hard to recall where the reality ended and his memories of the books began. Those long years in the institution. He had passed the time reading the books over and over again.

He brushed that from his mind and shifted his position on the bed where he sprawled, fully dressed. Watery eyes went about the room, in disgust. Ha! This was not as it had been in the old days, when he had lived out in the great jungles and scorned a roof over his head.

How even the cities of the Tarmangani had changed. He'd had to search full many a day to find this cellar room with a window so that he could at least have fresh air, rather than conditioned, machinery polluted air, for his jungle-bred lungs. Yes, how all had changed.

He closed his eyes to shut out the here and now and sent his mind to dwell on Jad-bal-ja, the Golden Lion, and to Tantor the elephant and Sheeta the leopard. He pictured himself swinging through the trees clad in naught but a loin cloth. His spear and sometimes a shield slung on his back, along with his great bow and quiver of arrows, his rope slung over his shoulders, his long knife at his side.

He brought himself up at the memory. How in the name of heaven did that blithering scribbler expect him to be able to carry all that muck with him through the trees? Especially when he was also burdened down with a female Tarmangani who was often unconscious and couldn't even hang on.

But suddenly through the open window there came an odor which he could hardly believe. Surely, it couldn't be true. His once keen nostrils twitched.

He sat up quickly, bringing his feet around to the floor. Yes. Yes, it could only be.

His arch enemy, Ibn Jad, the Bedouin sheik who came to steal his Waziri youths to be sold as slaves to the Arabs of Saudi Arabia. Ibn Jad, the forgotten of Allah!

His nose twitched again even as he tottered over to the small bureau, opened the bottom drawer and dug out from behind the soiled clothing where he had hidden it, the long hunting knife once the property of his shipwrecked father.

This was an Arab smell if he had ever smelled one, and even his aged nose could not mistake an Arab. And he would wager all the jewels of the lost mines of Sheba that it was Ibn Jad—in spite of the fact that he'd managed to contract a slight cold in this impossible climate and had the sniffles.

In a half crouch, the failing ape-man left the building by his private entrance. Night had fallen and, as so often in the past, he was following a spoor.

Jerry Stimbol said unhappily, "Let's make it as brief as possible, I'm personally paying for this call."

"Very good, sir," the man in the screen said. "I have checked the records thoroughly. It would seem that his Lordship was never quite the same after Lady Jane ran off with the beatnik poet."

"Beatnik poet?" Jerry said blankly.

"Yes, sir. It seems that she left a note," the other continued stiffly. "She was an American, you know, and evidently not used to the ways of a British spouse."

"What did the note say?"

"She was evidently spiffed at his continually running off on what she called drunken expeditions. At least, she assumed they were drunken what with the stories with which he returned."

"Well, what happened then?"

The British private investigator cleared his throat. "Well, it would seem that his Lordship's son was somewhat distressed over the manner in which the African estates were being managed. Among other things, it would seem his Lordship was subsidizing a whole tribe of natives, continuing them in the primitive state they had originally known. Ornate head-dresses, spears, shields, war dances, that sort of thing, don't you know? Didn't allow them even bicycles, not to speak of Jeeps or station wagons."

"The Waziri," Jerry Stimbol breathed.

"Yes, sir, that would appear to be their tribal name, sir. Suffice to say, when his Lordship's son took the matter to the courts, the conduct of what remained of the once extensive estates was turned over to his management."

Jerry looked at his watch unhappily. A photo-phone call to London was no small item. "But the important thing," he said. "What happened to, uh, the Viscount?"

The Englishman looked down at his notes. "He was committed to a rest home in Leopoldville, the nearest suitable for a distinguished gentleman who insisted upon remaining in Africa."

"Committed to a rest home!" Jerry blurted.

"Yes, sir. It would seem that his Lordship put up quite a show before they were able to get him into a straitjacket. Several of the establishment's employees were reported indisposed for some time."

"Institutionalized in Leopoldville," Jerry breathed. "And then what happened?"

"Why, sir, it is to be assumed he died there. His son acceded to the title."

"Now wait a minute. What do you mean *it is assumed* . . . ?"

"Why, sir, as you know there were considerable civil disturbances in the Congo, during which most records were destroyed. That period was the very latest to which I could trace his Lordship."

"Well, are there any surviving members of the family now? Somebody I could get in touch with?"

"Theoretically, sir, the great-great-grandson of his Lordship now bears the title. However, it would prove rather difficult to contact him." The British investigator cleared his throat still once again. "It would seem he operates a, ah, honky-tonk, I believe is the American expression, in Singapore."

"Honky-tonk! I thought the family was rolling in dough? How about the jewels of Opar, the City of Gold, all the rest of it?"

The other said stiffly, "I wouldn't know anything about how the family acquired its original wealth, sir. I do know, however, that by the time his Lordship was committed to the, ah, rest home, he had spent considerable amounts for such, ah, rather unrewarding investments as space research."

"Space research!" Jerry shot an agonized glance at his watch.

"Yes, sir, however, it would seem that his Lordship failed even to get into orbit."

Jerry said, "Look, get all this on paper and rocket it to me."

"Certainly, sir, and I'll send my bill at the same time."

Jerry winced, even as the other's image failed.

For a long moment he stared at the empty screen. "I wish," he muttered, "I knew what he was doing in America, and how he's maintaining himself. Even if he had money, he couldn't get it out of England, what with the currency controls."

Jerry Stimbol was on the carpet.

"So you did it, eh!" his editor bellowed.

"Well, yes, sir, I guess I did. I wanted to warn people, bring home to them the nature of their danger."

His superior hit the paper spread out before him. "Half the sheets on our chain ran it. All of them treating it like a silly-season story. What does that make us look like? Right on top of that poor Arab Union consulate official getting his throat slit on the streets of Greater Washington. Right on top of that, to run a Monster story with a gag slant."

"It wasn't a gag, sir. I keep telling you. I have all the evidence. Remember all those terrible killings that took place in the Congo, way back when they were still fighting their civil wars?"

"What in confounded Holy Jumping Zen has that got to do with the Monster, and smuggling through a silly-season story?"

"Well, sir, my theory is that all that killing that took place wasn't committed by the Simbas."

"Listen," his superior said ominously. "Forget the Congo. How did you get this story on the wire?"

Jerry blinked his apprehension. "It seems that last night McPherson became indisposed."

"Indisposed! He was drenched! You filled him full of guzzle and then talked him into letting you take his place."

"Well, yes sir, in a way." Jerry Stimbol scratched his nonexistent mustache.

"I thought I told you you were off crime and on obituaries."

"Well, yes, sir. I just sort of used my own time to continue my theories on the Monster."

The editor beamed at him. "Oh, you did. And I suppose that in spite of all, you figure on continuing on your own time?"

Jerry felt emboldened. "Well, yes I do. After all, it's my time."

"And sooner or later, you'll figure out some way to get another story onto the wires, making TransWorld look like an idiot."

Jerry swallowed and kept his peace.

The beam in the other's eye had a growing ominous quality. "Well, Jerry my lad, guess what? We're taking you off obits here in Greater Washington. Yes, sir, you've been promoted."

"Promoted?"

"Jerry, old man, old demon reporter of the old school,

obviously we couldn't come right out and fire you. Not with your uncle feeling the way he does about you starting at the bottom and working your way up in this business. On the other hand, you wouldn't quit under any circumstances. It might antagonize that same uncle. So we'll solve everything by just naming you . . ." his voice was rising to a crescendo now ". . . to be our sole representative in Byrd City, Antarctica!"

"Oh, *no*," Jerry whimpered.

"Oh yes, and we'll see just how many apes you run into there!"

The President of the United States of the Americas enjoyed a good press. Not since F.D.R. had the fourth estate found a chief executive so quick with the quip, so humorous of sally. They liked him. There was never a press conference but that you could count on a few laughs to lighten the load.

Today he sat in the news conference hall, flanked by Senator Fillite and Congressman Higgins and backed, as usual, by his press aides. The subject had been the dumping of Chinese surplus wheat on the world markets, and it had been a touchy one.

The president at long last grinned and said, "Well, gentlemen, we've all been on the grim side today. Any last question?"

Someone called, "Mr. President, did you read the TransWorld dispatch on the identity of the Monster, this morning?"

The president grinned his famous grin, worth at least twenty million votes at the polls. "Yes, Bob, I did. And all I can say is that the Lord of the Jungle is going to have all the resources of the F.B.I. and the C.I.A. combined thrown against him."

Senator Fillite got into the act. "In fact, gentlemen, I plan to present to the Senate a declaration of war on this enemy."

Higgins was not one to let a bit of personal publicity go by. He puffed out his cheeks and announced, "I must

remind the President and my honorable colleague of the
Senate, that a declaration of war must pass *both* houses.
However, the full support of the House of Representa-
tives will be thrown into the matter, I can guarantee."

A laugh went through the room.

"Thank you, Mr. President," the senior newsman
called.

In his dismal cellar room, the senile ape-man squinted
the moist eyes that had once been the sharpest in the
jungle. He was finding it difficult to read, these days, even
with his spectacles.

But the story got through to him.

Though not the humor intended.

The government of the United States of the Americas
had the audacity to seek him out as a common felon. It
had, if he understood this blithering American newspaper correctly, declared war upon him. All, evidently, as
a result of their objecting to his righteous wrath expressed
against his foes.

What in the world was he doing in America, anyway?
He scowled. Oh, yes. The last great expedition, the last
great project. He was going to go to the rescue of John
Carter, who seemed to be having a rough go of it, up
there. He had finally given up trying to make enough
money in such places as the carnival, to resume his own
researches. He had read that the Americans were about
to send a small colony to Mars. Very well, it would not
be the first time the Lord of the Jungle, utilizing his jungle stealth, had stowed aboard some ship, or other trans-
port.

He looked at the paper again. But this, obviously, must
be attended to first.

It was not the first time he had been confronted by the
combined force of a whole government. And he'd toppled whole governments before, and with very little assistance, as a rule. That Roman government of the lost
Legion, or was he thinking of the two Crusader colonies,
or still again, the degenerate government of Opar?

It was hard to recall these things clearly, these days. It was lucky he periodically reread the books, to keep matters fresh.

At any rate, yes, it was obvious that this challenge must be met, if he was to keep his own respect and that of the world. The gauntlet had been thrown down, and never had one been so quick to take challenge as the ape-man. He had half a mind to go out onto the street and bellow the battle cry of the Mangani into the sky.

But no, the odds were great. The stealth of the jungle must be relied upon. He growled low in his throat and began to make plans. Finally, he came to his feet, went over to the bureau drawer in which he kept the long hunting knife and slipped that weapon into his belt, beneath his coat.

First he would go down to the relief offices and collect his unemployment insurance benefit check which these blithering Yankees seemed to hand out to anyone who applied.

Then he would start stalking these Senators and Representatives who evidently were the governing body of this mad country. What were the names of these two who had initiated the movement against him? Higgins and Fillite. They'd be first. He flexed his once mighty thews.

FOREWORD to
One Against a Wilderness

The author of this story is one of the great mysteries of
twentieth-century literature. No one knows anything
about him except that he wrote four novels, all of which
were first printed in Blue Book magazine, about a
character called Kioga. His agent knew William L.
Chester only through receipt of the manuscripts and
correspondence. No one knows if Chester was his true or
pen name, though the former seems likely, since he
dedicated his first book to Irene Lang Chester. She may
have been his wife, mother, sister, or aunt.

Hawk of the Wilderness, the first novel, was serialized
in Blue Book in 1935. Harper published it as a
hardcover in 1936; Grosset and Dunlap reprinted it a
short time later; Ace Books issued it in softcover in
the 1960s. In 1936 it was made into a motion picture
starring Herman Brix (Bruce Bennett).

The first book was so popular that readers demanded
sequels. Chester obliged with Kioga of the Wilderness,
One Against a Wilderness, and Kioga of the Unknown
Land. These were his only works, or, at least, the only
ones published under the Chester byline.

Sometime before the 1960s, he, along with Irene,
disappeared. Several publishing firms and private
individuals tried to locate him, but the search needed
a Sherlock Holmes, and even he may have failed.

Ace Books wished to reprint Hawk of the Wilderness.
Since they could not find Chester or anything about

him, Ace made arrangements with the original publishers. Royalties on the book went into a trust account for Chester. So far, neither he nor his heirs have appeared to claim it. The Chesters, along with Judge Crater and Ambrose Bierce, seem to have been swallowed by the earth.

Your editor, on the advice of his agent, has set aside a sum to be paid Chester or his estate for the printing of Part I of One Against a Wilderness. This is a complete story in itself and is the first of the detailed adventures of Kioga (Snow Hawk) as a juvenile.

The setting for Kioga's exploits is a land above the Arctic circle. This was once connected to both Asia and North America and has fauna and flora of both continents. Volcanoes and geysers warm it, giving it a climate like mid-Canada's. It is a land of vast forests, many rivers and cataracts, and rugged mountains. In it roam tribes of Amerinds, descendants of people who settled down in this hidden place during the millenia-long migrations of Indians from Asia to the Americas. It is also populated by Siberian tigers, snow leopards, Kodiak bears, and some beasts extinct elsewhere, including mammoths and mastodons.

Kioga's parents and their friend Mokuyi, an Iroquois Indian, were cast away on this savage land. Lincoln Rand, Jr., or Kioga, was born in Nato'wa (Sun Land) and raised among the tribe that had taken in the castaways. After his parents were murdered, Kioga was adopted by Mokuyi, who taught him to speak, read, and write English. Kioga was a lonely boy because the other children of the village mocked and persecuted him. Mokuyi gave Kioga a captured bear cub, Aki, as a pet, and the two became inseparable. Later, the cub's mother breached the village's stockade and took her cub back into the wilderness. The following year, the unhappy Kioga joined Aki and her mother and lived for a year and a half with the bears. Though he returned to dwell with the Indians, Kioga often visited the bears and several times took refuge with them. Like Tarzan, he became a master at traveling through the trees and at establishing symbiotic relationships with various animals. Eventually, he became chief of a group of tribes, met a white girl, Beth LaSalle, and went with her to the States.

Kioga is not a truly feral man in that he was not adopted as an infant and raised for a long period by animals. He is a sort of reverse feral man. Instead of being adopted by the beasts, he adopted them. But he did acquire a feral man's physique and psyche. Like them, he was beast-strong and an Outsider; he was rejected for a long time by humans and found his happiness in communing with animals. Also, like Tarzan, he became a trickster.

The hidden land in the Far North with its lost races has been a theme used by a number of writers. It is, alas, in this day of extensive air exploration and satellite observation, no longer possible to postulate such a romantic place. The door has been locked on this genre. But the millions of readers of Burroughs, Haggard, Chester, and Merritt don't care. To them, Opar and Cathne-Athne, Kôr and Zu-Vendis, Nato'wa, and the Shadowed-Land are as real as, and more interesting than, Chicago, Paris, and Moscow.

Just so, the maps of these countries are more fascinating than of those that do exist.

Man is an amphibian. When he starts to dry out on the shore of reality, he takes to the waters of imagination.

One Against a Wilderness

BY WILLIAM L. CHESTER

I<small>N</small> far Nato'wa—that new-found land within the Arctic Circle—deep in the still, primeval forest called by the red-skinned natives Indegara, there stands a great rock called Chieftain's Head, supposed to be the image of Mialoka, legendary First-Chief of all the Shoni tribes. When the eyes of Chieftain's Head light up, Two-Star, the little son of Mialoka, will return to take his place among mortal men, so goes the legend, implicitly believed among the Shoni.

Below this rock, towering sentry-like a hundred feet above the neighboring forest, three rushing rivers meet. Their meeting-place is known as the Caldrons of the Yei, a name which well describes the foamy chaos into which the mingling rivers churn each other. Two of these rivers are glacier-born; the third springs from its sources boiling, heated by volcanic fires; and where hot and frigid waters meet, there hangs above the Caldrons a pillar of dense gray mist.

Little is known of this lone, unearthly place, reverberant with the hollow roar of waters through the scoured-out caves which honeycomb its rim. But of one thing the Shoni witch-doctors long were certain: Human bodies, of enemy or village-sacrifice, consigned to the Caldrons, were never seen again. The hungry Yei—mythical spirits of the rivers—ate them, so the Indians believed.

What the Caldrons finally discard at their southern edges is sucked into the vortex of a mighty cataract be-

111

yond, then smashed and swept into eternity . . . For centuries no human foot had ever pressed this place of peril, nor human eye looked on its inner mysteries and returned to tell of what it saw. . . .

One day, not many years ago, somewhere between Hopeka and the Caldrons of the Yei, a forest denizen stood belly-deep, fishing in the Hiwasi River. More clown than fisherman, the great brown bear leaped among the shining salmon arrowing upstream to their spawning-beds.

Not once in fifty times did his swinging claw-armed paw hook out a shimmering fish. More often the clumsy bruin missed, and fairly stood upon his head amid the silvery horde.

From somewhere near the brush-grown bank a peal of care-free laughter echoed forth. The bruin's small red eyes turned toward the sound, beholding in the shadows a familiar human figure, of a youth of perhaps fifteen. In one strong hand he grasped a pointed chipping-stone, and in the other a half-finished arrow-head, one edge cunningly sharpened, the other still quite dull. Pausing in his primitive task, he laughed again.

Discomfited, perhaps, the bear regained his poise, reared up, and with a sudden lucky pass scooped a big salmon high in air, batting it fiercely toward the bank before it fell.

By sheerest chance the salmon hurtled toward the standing figure. Quick as the flick of sparrow's wing the supple youth dodged, twisting to one side. But for all his haste the writhing fish got in one flat resounding blow, delivered stingingly. The outline of a salmon's tail glowed redly on a brown bare hip.

Much hurt and out of dignity—of which the middle teens may have great store—the figure leaped down upon the flopping fish, which got away. Then belated self-command ensued. He turned back to the bank. Standing—by painful preference—he meditated on the perils of his wilderness.

The feathers of the Snow Hawk—or Kioga, to call him by his Shoni name—were ruffled. Aki, his wild companion, was laughing at him silently, if expression meant anything at all. High on the bank, with lolling tongue, a fox grinned down on him. Kioga flung a stick—and missed the mark. All things went wrong this day! Again he stood straight and silent as the trees beyond him.

Tall for his fifteen years, already Kioga gave promise of the man he was to be. Lithe and graceful, with long leopard-muscles, he almost matched a full-grown warrior in strength. In quickness and agility, he far excelled the practiced wrestlers and runners of the Shoni tribes—a nation of athletes.

Eager to forget his earlier embarrassment, Kioga plunged forthwith into the river. For a while he wrestled and gamboled with his friendly partner the bear. As if born and existing only to guard him from harm, time and again the huge brute dragged him bodily upon the bank. And soon Kioga forgot his earlier uncomfortable experience in the excitement of diving to elude his burly companion. In the liquid element the lad Kioga was as adept, and elusive, almost, as the salmon. Aki was no match for such tactics.

So for an hour amusement crowded all other thoughts from his mind. Suddenly Kioga felt the bruin stiffen, nostrils twitching toward upstream. Kioga too, chin-deep in water, grew still, clutching Aki's shaggy coat. Presently his own nostrils, little less sharp than his wild companion's, caught the scent of smoke-tanned garments, worn on the backs of men.

"Come, Aki!" whispered Kioga urgently, pressing the rough shoulder. If not in true obedience, then solely to be with him, the bear swam quietly ashore. The Snow Hawk, still hanging on, went with him, without an effort.

Then from below the bank two pairs of watchful eyes observed a tall canoe move into their line of vision. On the forward seat a withered dried-up figure sat—Inkato the shaman, famed and feared for the power of his magic. Hideous with self-mutilation, he sat with scarce a movement, only his glittering eyes denying him to be a mummy.

Behind Inkato a slim boy about ten years old sat pale-faced, with eyes of fear, thongs binding arms behind him immovably.

Astern a lesser shaman propelled the craft downriver and, when the captive struggled, struck him callously with the flat of the paddle.

Watching through slitted lids, behind which the greenish eyes blazed like melting emeralds, the Snow Hawk growled back in his throat. And on a deeper, gruffer note the brute beside him did the same—Kioga's foes were Aki's too.

Well Kioga knew where and to what fate the youthful victim went. For one black mark stands against the Seven Tribes. Whereas their music and arts are things to marvel at, the age-old custom of human sacrifice still survives.

But a wrinkle of perplexity deepened between Kioga's eyes. On some pretext or other, the shamans had decreed death for this unlucky captive. But why such unaccustomed secrecy? Why no chants, no beat of drums, no myriad witnesses to the high ceremony of human sacrifice? Ofttimes before his keen young eyes had seen the hapless victim knifed and hurled headlong into the churning waters—but never in such furtive fashion. Always the village witch-doctors had been on hand in full grotesque regalia.

Clearly something was afoot, something too dark and dread, almost, to think about, if all the other village shamans were not supposed to know of it.

The canoe passed near the recent playspot. The victim's eyes turned momentarily shoreward, as if seeking a way of escape in that direction. The quickness of his indrawn breath sent the eyes of Inkato also shoreward. With a start he hissed back to his assistant: "Kansa! Saw you some one disappearing in the bush?"

"I glimpsed a bear," said the other.

"No human leg with fish-tail mark upon it?" persisted Inkato.

"Not so. Perhaps I looked too late."

"My lying eyes betrayed me," muttered the old shaman

uneasily. "But there is no time to lose. The Yei are hungry. Push on!"

Behind him the luckless little captive slumped lower, stoicism crushed by fear of death.

Push on the second shaman did, until the mighty mill-race just above the Caldrons came into view. On either side black basalt walls reared up, cracked and broken. Ahead, the pall of mist above the Caldrons eddied densely, shrouds-to-be of the Shoni boy.

"Now!" came Inkato's voice, instinct with cruelty. With a quick swing, Kansa flung the victim overside, holding the prey afloat while the older shaman crept back with keen knife drawn.

Up went the corded old hand, the bone blade gleaming.

Then suddenly something pale, oval and speckled—the great egg of an emperor goose—hurtled from above. The wielder of the knife shrank back—too late! The half-pound egg, too long unhatched, burst hard against his temple, its evil-smelling contents spattering, and streaming down Inkato's grimacing face.

To the hurler of that egg, the boyish victim's face was not unknown. He was a lad from Hopeka—the name escaped Kioga—recently stricken dumb when lightning struck near where he stood.

Startled, the younger shaman released his grip. Caught in the currents, the bound body was drawn beyond his reach. With eyes of fury Inkato watched it go.

"No matter," he muttered finally. "The Yei take them dead or alive. And they return no sacrifice. Back, careless fool! The current pulls us!"

And Inkato, himself fearful of the death he meted out so casually to others, seized a paddle, forgetful even of the stench which hung about his head. A moment later, mouthing malediction on the mother of that pungent egg, the two were gone upstream, their ends achieved, so far as they could know.

But Inkato was wrong: Whereas the river-Yei had swallowed up the victim, they did not quite digest the mouthful.

Near where the mists were swirling, a second body struck the surface like a flying lance, glancing deeply. Beside the unconscious sacrifice a head appeared. Its owner might have been a river-Yei in person, up from the depths to claim the slender body; for around one strong fist the younger lad's braid was twisted.

A moment, his supple strength against the coiling sinews of three mighty rivers, Kioga fought the currents. Alone he might have had a chance, as does the reed that bends before a hurricane. But encumbered thus, the waters had their way with him.

Tenacity, however, was in his fiber. The will to survive blazed with a fierce white flame—else he had never lived this long. His grip upon that braid tightened in a hold that only death would slacken. And in his dire extremity, one single name escaped him, loud as healthy lungs could shout it out:

"Aki! *Aki!* Aкı!"

A momentary hush ensued, broken only by the sound of rushing waters. Then came a roar like rolling thunder, a splash close by as if a ton of rock had fallen, and a great wave covered Kioga and his burden. When shaggy fur came beneath his hand, the Snow Hawk clutched it, clinging like a limpet.

Now vast primordial strength was laboring for him— five hundred pounds of solid buoyant brawn, delivering power through four thrusting paws. Gasping stertorously, the bear obliquely stemmed the hungry eddies, slowly neared the carved-out caves.

Dragged coughing to the surface, Kioga caught a breath of air. He had but one thought, to keep his hold on that dark braid and on Aki; only one command to utter fiercely through clenched teeth: "Swim, Aki—*swim!*"

The loyal, selfless heart, already pumping near to bursting, responded, drawing on unknown reserves of power. Seeming hours were but minutes. The thrashing claws scraped bottom, gripped, hooked onto stone, and held. Then surging mightily, Aki dragged himself ashore.

Kioga felt his grip loosening, and again the currents struggled to possess him. Then the patient bruin did him violence, taking one forearm in gin-trap jaws and dragging him for the hundredth time to solid ground—and with Kioga came that other limp, shackled body.

Kioga came to, consciousness rising from a sea of pain. A warm moist roughness licked soothingly across his naked chest. A hot breath thawed his tense and rigid muscles. He saw a vast dark shape bulking huge beside him, and rose up spent and trembling, his first thought for the one he had rescued.

Beside Kioga, at full stretch, the body lay without a movement. The Snow Hawk wore no knife, nor aught else either; but with a chip of stone he sawed through the leather cords, loosened the boy's apparel, and began to chafe the victim back to life.

Swift moments passed; the rescued one showed signs of life. A ray of pale auroral light came through the opening of the cave and fell upon a thin wan face, colored slightly with returning blood—a face of innocence, marked by an ugly bruise on one temple.

More gently now Kioga chafed anew, luring the boy back to consciousness. And as he worked, his eyes narrowed; amazement, resentment, anger grew within him—then black and bitter hatred of those who had worked this crime against a helpless child.

The common bond of youth made that offense seem greater. Until this hour Kioga had loathed the brethren who devised such acts of horror—but with a detached and general kind of loathing. Face to face with dread reality, his hatred crystallized and sought some one on whom to fasten. He thought of the two who had brought the sacrifice down-river—old Inkato and Kansa, his confederate.

"They fed the Yei in secret," he muttered hotly, devising a thousand mental tortures for the guilty pair. "I wonder why? But they'll pay! Blood for thy blood, little brother!"

What the rousing sacrifice thought, waking in that reverberant cave to see a bloody figure crouched above him and a dripping bear near by, cannot be known. If fear, Kioga sought to calm it.

"Be not afraid," he shouted in Shoni, above the roar of waters. "None may do you hurt while I am near. I am Kioga—the outcast of Hopeka!"

Then wasting no time on further useless talk, Kioga armed himself with a rock and explored about him, seeking means of egress from this cave-pierced shore of the Caldrons. Aki shuffled after him.

One ledge ended at a whirlpool. Above, sheer rock, slippery with condensing mist, offered no encouragement. The foam-capped waters—he had no wish to challenge them again! Returning, he found another route, along connecting caves, and passed from one to another in an upstream direction. Somewhere, soon, he thought, the area of the Caldrons must abut upon the neighboring forest. But the underground path he followed ended in a wall.

In disappointment he hurled his stone against it. Some slabs of rock, weakened by erosion, slid from the wall. He hurled the stone again; a threat of air, cool and dry, blew through from somewhere, bringing with it scent of pine and hemlock. Encouraged, Kioga hammered afresh, desisting only when his stone fell apart in his hands. With naked hands he tugged and strained. But for all his efforts, he had only made an opening large enough to get one hand through. One huge slab moved slightly. If that could only be moved a little more—

Behind him Aki sneezed with the sound as of a parting compressed-air coupling. Kioga jumped in surprise—but with a great idea dawning. Directing the bear's attention to the opening, "Smell, Aki!" he commanded. The brute sniffed eagerly, caught the scent of outer liberty and understood. Exerting all his strength, he pulled upon that slab. Kioga also pulled. With a rumble the slab fell inward. The way was clear.

A few minutes later Kioga carried the Shoni boy out, carefully concealing the new-made entrance to the Caldrons; for here was another retreat in time of peril.

Guarded on his way by one no other wilderness brute dared face, Kioga moved north and westward through the forest labyrinths, never hesitating, though changing direction a hundred times.

From thicket, cave and deep ravine, eyes saw the little trio pass—eyes that were bright as heated coins, eyes like mirrors reflecting flame, many only curious, many more hot with hungry menace. The Shoni boy shivered in fear.

Kioga soothed him, bantering a little. "Fear not, little brother. Who dares molest Kioga and his friends? What is thy name?" he asked; then as he spoke he remembered that the boy was dumb. But to his surprise, the other answered:

"I am Ohali. My father is a chief. My brothers all are warriors."

"But you were dumb! I heard the shamans say it."

"When the river took me, I cried out. My voice came back."

"Why did the shamans give thee to the Yei?"

Ohali shivered. "I do not know. They seized me in the night. I struggled, but could not cry out."

A gust of fury swept Kioga afresh, tearing out this vow: "They'll pay! Before the sun and moon and all the stars, I swear it!"

"Where are we going? Back—where Inkato and Kansa are?"

Kioga heard the boy's teeth chatter. "Not so, little brother. While Inkato and Kansa live, you'll not be safe in all Hopeka. Yet since they did not kill thee, why should I kill them? There must be a better way. First we will rest and eat."

"Where do you live?" Ohali asked.

"Where once a tiger couched. That is Kioga's home."

In awe Ohali heard these words. "Who are you?"

Thoughtfully Kioga answered, putting into words dim thoughts, maturing ideals of youth at shining manhood's threshold: "I am a friend to all like thee, Ohali. I place small birds back in the nest. I kill no doe with young. I aid the weak, destroy the wicked strong and make them fear me. Hast ever heard of Robin Hood?"

"Ra-bin-hud?" echoed Ohali, repeating the English words with unaccustomed lips. Smiling, Kioga bade him forget the question.

"A friend of mine you would not know, Ohali."

Perplexed, the thin young arms, dark with the marks of cutting thongs, tightened around Kioga's neck. "I do not fear Kioga."

"Nor I the shamans," muttered Kioga. But Ohali heard him not. He was asleep.

Presently Kioga turned off the trail, climbed a steep narrow path to a point halfway up a frowning cliff. Pausing before a mat of growing vines, he pushed them aside, exposing a huge log door chinked with mud and mosses. Manipulating a latch, Kioga pushed in the door and entered, placing his burden gently on a pile of thick soft furs.

With curving stick and leather thong, he kindled sparks and blew them into flame and made a fire. A veritable pirate's den, that cave, hung all about with bows and arrows, coils of leather rope, long whips that were the dread of every brute that prowled the forest, and many kinds of Indian garments, and hideous devil-masks.

One of the garments Kioga fastened round his waist with cord of buckskin. The slight demands of modesty thus satisfied, he went forth through the night again, returning in an hour, laden with nuts and berries and wild birds' eggs.

Upon the coals he set an earthen pot, filled with water from a rock-spring bubbling in the recesses of his cave: and into this flung quantities of dried meat and vegetables from his basket stores.

Then, beholding Ohali's tattered garments, from a leather case he pulled out fringed buckskin shirt and leggings of hide, cured soft and white, with moccasins to match—his own gala boy's attire, long since outgrown but treasured none the less, because a loved one's fingers had sewn upon them. These, with other ornaments he placed where Ohali must see them when he first awoke.

His body stretched to rest before the bubbling stew, Kioga pondered: How return Ohali to Hopeka without delivering him back into the hands of Inkato—who, one way failing, would find other means of persecuting the boy?

Still wrestling with that problem, Kioga slept—in utter weariness.

Meanwhile, pulling for Hopeka town upon the Hiwasi River, Inkato had rested uneasily upon his paddle.

"A leg with fish-tail mark upon it—I cannot put that out of mind," he told his companion. "Let us go back and look along the shore. If it were known we did this thing—"

Then came Kansa's voice, guttural and deep: "What have we gained by this great risk? Because his father cursed you when his son was stricken dumb—was that cause enough to take Ohali's life?"

"We did not take a life," corrected Inkato, drawing a fine distinction. "We gave it—unto the Yei. You see things crookedly, O Kansa. I fear you will never be a famous shaman."

"What would our fellow-shamans say, learning that we did this secretly, without their knowledge?"

"How will they ever know—unless you babble, Kansa? Cease sniveling!"

Uneasily Kansa shook his head, pushing downstream toward the point where movement had earlier caught the older shaman's eye. When they had arrived, Inkato spoke.

"Go you ashore and look about. I will watch, with bow in hand, to see that no harm befalls you."

Kansa took up his spear and disembarked, scanning the bank on every hand. Then suddenly he straightened with a hiss. "The footprints of a bear, I see—and others, man-like but smaller than a warrior's."

"I knew it!" cried the old villain fiercely. "We were seen—and know you who made those tracks?"

Kansa shook his head, wondering at the other's agitation.

"Kioga!" snarled Inkato, the weapons quivering in his hand. "He who runs with the bears of Indegara!"

"*Agh!*" choked Kansa, his face losing color. "What if he saw us throw Ohali into the river!"

"That egg—I should have known!" remembered In kato. "Back to the Caldrons, Kansa! Make haste! Methinks there is no good in this!"

The startled shamans returned to the scene of their outrage. And after searching long, they came upon fresher tracks, again of youth and bear together. One look at the human spoor, and Inkato stiffened. "He carried a burden. And look you, Kansa—all were wet. There's mud within the prints. And here—two smaller prints!"

"Ohali lives," muttered Kansa. "We are betrayed!"

Inkato shook his head defiantly. "Not yet, you shivering fool. Back to Hopeka—bend your paddle, Kansa, or it may be you will never bend it again!"

Awaking in the cave, the first object Kioga's eyes fell upon was Ohali, standing straight and slender, clad all in new white buckskin, capped with crown of hawk-wing plumes, on either wrist a ruddy copper bracelet; and glittering and flashing in the firelight, fine beadwork upon his breast and back.

A spark of inspiration touched Kioga off.

"*Ahai!* I see the way!"

"What way?" demanded Ohali, puzzled by the words.

"The way to put Ohali beyond the reach of such as Inkato. Hast heard the legend, that when the eyes of Mialoka, the First Chief, are seen to burn, the son of Mialoka will return to dwell with living men?"

"*Ahi,*" answered Ohali, not understanding.

"You shall be Mialoka's son. The eyes of Mialoka will burn tomorrow night!"

Ohali had shivered at mention of the shaman Inkato. His poise was swiftly gone, and fear looked from his eyes.

Kioga's mind worked swiftly. Were it known what now he contemplated, all Shoni shaman-hood would work against him. Those less fanatic medicine-men who worked with roots and herbs and sought no power in primitive politics, would frown on his scheme. Even the common populace would restrain him.

But there was the measure of Kioga's peculiar daring. Half of his short young life had been an epic struggle—one against a wilderness. A lone hand held no terrors. His wits versus theirs—one brain against a hundred—would be no new experience.

He reprimanded Ohali swiftly. "Shrink not, little brother. Stand proud and straight. From this day forth, the greatest chiefs will do thee honor. Far and near thy fame will spread." And with the words, Kioga laughed aloud and said again: "The eyes of Mialoka will burn tomorrow night. And henceforward men will know Ohali as Two Star, son of the First Chief!"

Bewildered by this rapid flow of words, Ohali straightened once again. "How can this be?"

Pursing his lips and drawing in his cheeks grotesquely, Kioga spoke as Inkato was wont to boast: "I am Kioga, greatest of all magicians!" Then again he laughed outright, and Ohali laughed with him, scarcely knowing why, save that with Kioga near he could not long be fearful or unhappy.

When their meal was done, Kioga showed Ohali tricks of sleight-of-hand; and while Ohali sat entranced, squatted there before the little lad, telling funny tales to make him laugh, and drawing pictures on a buffalo-hide for Ohali's amusement—and for his own delight as well; for when Ohali's laughter bubbled up, Kioga listened raptly, as a long-deaf person might who heard a sudden note of flutelike music. Not often had Kioga human friend to share his solitude. . . .

Sometimes, though, a shadow crossed Ohali's face—a face too young to bear such marks of haunting fear. Then pity filled the Snow Hawk's heart; and to erase the shadow, he called in Aki from his guard-post outside the door, and to the trill of Pan-pipes made Aki rear and dance, and bear Ohali on his shaggy shoulders.

All in all, it was a merry evening, ending far too soon in weariness. Ohali slept as never in his life before.

Banking the fire, Kioga again quit the cave, then to the broad Hiwasi went, sought out his hidden bark canoe and on the central stronger current came swiftly toward Hopeka town. Hiding his canoe, Kioga neared the palisaded village afoot, gained secret ingress, and prowling the shadows of the long-houses came to the lodge of Inkato the shaman.

Listening, he heard no sound within. Entering stealthily—no lodge is ever barred among the Shoni—Kioga found a fire glowing, by whose light his darting gaze saw many things. Above the coals a cooking-vessel simmered, of which Kioga smelled, turning up his nose. To one side hung a bunch of shriveled berries—a violent medicine, whose attributes Kioga well remembered.

On a wicked impulse he flung these into the cooking-pot, adding also to the broth some other near-by ingredients, which the shamans never prescribed for themselves. Then stirring slowly, he sniffed again, adding more of this and that until the odor satisfied him by its vileness.

Hearing footsteps, he hastily retreated through a side entrance to the lodge and hid himself outside, ear glued to the barken wall. Soon some one entered. He heard the lisp of Inkato's voice, speaking to a companion through toothless jaws.

"*Ehi-ehi!* A lucky thing we found their footprints. To-morrow we will track them down with warriors from the village. All will think Kioga stole Ohali from the village. And when we come upon them, we will kill the Snow Hawk. And if," added the shaman meaningly, "Ohali is also killed, it will be by accident—will it not, Kansa—eh?"

"It will need doing quickly," answered Kansa darkly, "lest Ohali himself betray us."

"Then see you carry springy bow and sharp arrows. Leave Kioga to my spear."

Outside the lodge Kioga listened, missing not a word. Beyond doubt the shamans knew Ohali was still alive.

If they had their way, he would bear the blame for the boy's kidnaping, and all his plans would go awry. To return and efface the trail to the cave could yet be done, but that required time. What other way? What better, quicker way?

Much that had been not clear before was now explained. The outrage they had perpetrated on the river had not even the slight redeeming color of religious sacrifice. It had been attempted child-murder, brutal, vicious, and hidden even from the other medicine-men.

Among the Shoni there is no penalty for the taking of a life. By custom, as among the old-time Iroquois, the killer waits beside the body of his victim, until discovered. Life may call for life; or a gift to the nearest of the dead man's kin to satisfy the spirit of the departed. Thus the elements of primitive honor prevail.

Not so with Inkato and Kansa. Their crime was so far without the pale that not even their own fraternity must know, much less the family of Ohali. Upon this fact the quick wits of the Snow Hawk seized at once. His problem was resolving rapidly.

But once more Inkato was speaking, as if he had not recently returned from doing foulest deed: "Come, Kansa! Fill the bowls. My belly is an empty gourd."

Through a crack Kioga saw Kansa approach the cooking-pot, fill one bowl, then sniff the contents doubtfully.

"This soup—how strange it smells! I think—" began Kansa, but Inkato cut him short indignantly.

"Rich and full of strength! Fresh this very morning. Drink heartily, O Kansa, and mayhap it will make you great—like Inkato!" And snatching the brimming bowl the old shaman emptied it in greedy gulps.

Not daring to offend his host afresh, Kansa held his nose and also drank. The two put down their bowls and sat in silence.

Then Inkato to Kansa spoke: "Why is your face so pale?"

Kansa made a sickly grimace, answering in a stranger's voice, "I would have asked the same—of you."

Inkato gave a sudden mighty start, clutching at his middle.

And presently, grinning with satisfaction, Kioga went away. One hour, at least, would pass before these two could go about again . . . .

This time Kioga visited the longest tongue in all Hopeka town. He found her crouched before her lodge and stood above her quietly.

"Some one is near," said the old crone harshly. "Who is it?"

"Who brought thee sweets and cakes and wood to burn and water from the spring, when others all forsook thee, Mother Iska?"

A moment she was silent, her blind mask softening. Then: "Kioga, lightener of my sightless misery! How dare you enter Hopeka, where so many wish you ill? What would you have of eyeless Iska? But ask, and it is yours."

He pressed her gnarled old claws tenderly. "I ask no gift. I bring you one. The gift you love the best," Kioga answered.

"Something to whisper in my ear!" she exclaimed in excitement, bending nearer avidly. For news, the spoken word, twenty kinds of gossip—all these made Iska's darkened world endurable.

"A juicy something," Kioga agreed, and sitting close beside old Iska, spoke long and earnestly—just as in years gone by he had brought her other choice gems of information.

In rapt attention she heard him. "Eh-eh-eh? Go on— go on!" And as he spoke, she stiffened. "O hearts more black than midnight! What do you say to me, Kioga?"

" 'Tis true," he assured her. "With these two eyes I saw them throw Ohali in. In these ears he told me all that I tell thee. *The eyes of Mialoka will burn tomorrow night!*"

"O wonder!" Old Iska fairly trembled with the weight of this disclosure. "It will shake all Hopeka. And I"—her face lit up with joy—"sightless, aged, crippled old Iska, I alone know it is to happen. . . . Ask any boon for this great gift, Kioga!"

"Some other time, Mother," he said. "But tell this to no living soul," Kioga admonished mysteriously, the more certainly to ensure a wide broadcast of all he had confided.

Then leaving excited Iska, Kioga returned without misadventure to his canoe and hurried downstream toward the Caldrons, approaching Chieftain's Head on foot from its one accessible side.

Along the broad ledge that simulates a human brow, and in the hollows so like eyes, he heaped a pile of brush and firewood, ready to be kindled with a spark. That done, he returned again to his forest cave, found all there well, and had four hours of sleep before the morning dawned.

Rising with the sun, Kioga woke Ohali, broke fast on fruit and some acorn-cakes smuggled from Hopeka, and told him of his activities. "Iska knows that you are alive. Iska will tell the whole village. The people will await the coming of Two-Star back to this earth. And then it will be the turn of Kansa and Inkato to shiver in their blankets!"

But poor Ohali did not seem to feel enthusiastic, and to lighten his fears Kioga took down a book from a covered shelf. This and many other volumes he had salvaged from the cabin of a sinking hulk off the seashore; and from it he read to Ohali a tale of Sherwood Forest, translating the English as best he could for Ohali. Thus also had Mokuyi done when teaching Kioga to read and speak English, the mother tongue. And hearing the strange stories of an unknown civilized world, Ohali calmed again.

Then Kioga put the book aside, and after a moment of silence asked: "Hast ever seen a river-Yei, Ohali?"

"No," answered the Shoni boy. "But they look like men, with devils' heads. So my father told me."

"And hands webbed like a duck's, and great brown spots upon their bodies," added Kioga reflectively.

"Have *you* seen one?" asked Ohali curiously.

"No," said Kioga, "though I have poked long poles in every river-hole seeking to bring one forth."

Ohali's eyes grew great. "You dared—do that?"

"Aki was with me," explained Kioga. "Together we fear nothing. And tomorrow," continued Kioga, "the Shoni will see a river-Yei. Now listen well, Ohali."

Rounder still grew Ohali's great dark eyes, as the Snow Hawk spoke. And when Kioga had done: "I dare not—I dare not!" whispered Ohali, pale with fear again.

"If I am close behind, Ohali—then will you dare?"

Ohali's fears grew less. Return to home and family in prospect, and with the Snow Hawk his ally? "Yes—yes!" he said at last.

"Good, little warrior," commended Kioga. "Now watch."

On a buckskin he drew the outlines of his hands, and with a whetted knife cut out four pieces; and sewed the four together with needle of bone and sinew thread, into the shape of overlarge gloves, save that he left the fingers joined together like the toes of Paddle-foot, the wild duck.

Next from the wall he took down his most hideous medicine-mask, fringed about the open neck with human hair and made to be worn upon the head like a helmet. Then taking deer-grease in a small stone cup, he added to it reddish earthy pigment, mixing the two together.

These several adjuncts to his ambitious schemes he wrapped up in a deer-skin, fastening the bundle to the shoulders of faithful Aki. Then he set leisurely forth, whip in belt, and Ohali by his side, toward his canoe.

Along the way Aki, guardian of their every previous step, roamed off the trail, lured by some vagrant scent or other. Where the forest paths were open, Ohali walked beside Kioga. In tangled places the Snow Hawk lifted him easily in his arms, moving by leaps and bounds as if he were no weight at all. Now and then he dropped from cliff to bough, while Ohali hung tightly on, certain that they must plummet far to earth.

But nothing like that happened. Impossible places

passed easily beneath his knowing feet; and once indeed, they took six long drops in quick succession. But by now Ohali knew no further fear and enjoyed the swift exhilarating descent.

Almost to the river grave hazard growled fiercely at them from a trail-side cave. With back-laid ears and lashing tail, a great snow-leopard appeared.

Were Aki here, he had not dared venture forth. Now, unmenaced, in another instant he would spring, and rend.

Ohali, standing mesmerized by the golden cat's fire circled stare, was struck rigid with terror. Not so Kioga.

Before the brute was halfway out, he flicked his length of leather whip behind him. Then, with a move too quick for eye to follow, the long lash slithered forward. Beneath the leopard's hanging jaw the hissing whang-strip barked like an exploded pistol. Then twice again—crack! crack! —the long lash made the fur fly up.

Checked in full intent to spring, the stung leopard arched up its spine and hissing like any common alley cat, broke ground before the baffling thong. Once more resounding whack and the brute turned. And when the lash flicked forth again, the beast was gone.

Gone, too, in another moment, were Kioga and Ohali, who reached the canoe without further incident. Aki found them there, delivered up his shoulder pack, and when the little craft turned downriver, swam powerfully, close behind.

When they had gone a little way, Kioga let the craft drift of its own volition, and reaching into the bundle, took forth the deer-fat paint he had mixed in the cave, handing it to Ohali.

"Now paint me," he said, "so that if any Yei should see me, he would come and call me brother."

In Hopeka events transpired as Kioga had hoped. As always, the Hopeka women paused, to visit a while with the poor blind Iska, human clearing-house of village information.

Unable to contain her wondrous secret, the aged crone let slip—a word here, a word there—the burning rumor Kioga had confided to her.

The village women, filled with wonder, told other women, in strictest confidence. *"The eyes of Mialoka will burn tonight!"* To those who doubted, "Iska told me," they said, by way of proof. The gossip-pot boiled up; the lid blew off. Like swift wildfire, then, the news flew round. Ohali was in truth, said Iska, the son of First-Chief, come humbly back to earth in the guise of a minor chieftain's child. Ohali's mother, hearing, grew faint.

Corn-cakes burned; meals grew cold; clothing went unmended.

And in his lodge cruel Inkato and Kansa his confederate, ill as men could ever be, lay groaning on the floor. An hour passed before they recovered from the effects of Kioga's potpourri.

Kansa, going to the door, returned with tidings that made Inkato's own blood flow swiftly once again. "The village folk are rising! There is a wondrous stir. Strange rumors are afloat: Iska spreads them even now. 'Tis said Ohali is not mortal child but the son of the First-Chief, Mialoka!"

Up to his feet sprang Inkato. Quivering to vague apprehensions, they looked at one another. "Quick! Knives and tomahawks. Mayhap even now we have waited too long."

Inkato quivered, recalling Ohali's warrior-brothers, his chieftain father, and all those eager knives that waited.

But he was quick to recover a measure of his composure. "Come!" he said to Kansa. "Let us look and listen, and learn what is going on."

To accomplish that, the shamans had but to follow the crowd in their own canoe, downriver.

Along the broad Hiwasi, the village canoes had gathered thickly, filled with Indians from Hopeka. No torch yet blazed above the curving prows. All was dusk within shadow. There came the click and buzz of whispered conversation. Hundreds of dark eyes fastened upon a distant lofty point—the crown of Chieftain's Head, above the Caldrons, coming slowly into view.

"The legend is come true! The eyes of Mialoka burn!"

Suddenly a cry of awe—the eyes far overhead were lighting uncannily: a halo glowed about the rocky mist-draped crown; smoke poured from the stony lips. It was the sign, the portent of some great happening, which blind old Iska had foretold!

Bemused, enthralled by wonder, the Shoni saw the burning eyes grow dim, the fiery chaplet fade against the sky.

The prow and helmsmen breathed upon their punk-wood tinder, preparing. As the last glow dimmed on Chieftain's Head, they fanned their sparks to flame and lit the smoking torchlights stem and stern. For thus had blind old Iska earlier counseled them to do.

Quivering shadows wriggled on the coaly waters. The river, dark before, became a sea of yellowish light, save where a rocky point threw ebon shade from shore to shore.

Then something pale and ghostly seemed to float from nowhere. The outlines of a small canoe were seen. Within, a dimly gleaming figure knelt. As the craft came slowly forward, this was seen to be a youth in full regalia. Forth from the gloomy shades his craft of beauty came —canoe of birch-bark white as snow. Forward knelt the figure, robed in frosty cloud. And as the torchlights illumined him, his gala raiment seemed on fire.

Wide-eyed and open-mouthed, the watchers stared, bedazzled.

Then some one sharp of eye saw and recognized: "Ohali—Ohali! 'Tis he, indeed! Ohali is the son of Mialoka!"

From behind Ohali, hitherto almost unseen, a crouching thing of horror reared its goblin head—not head of man but more like devil. Its hands seemed not as common hands, but webbed as if for swimming. Its human body, lithe and muscular, was mottled with great liver-colored spots. No thing like this had ever walked the earth before—yet children among the assemblage well knew it for the ogre with whose name women frighten small offenders.

"A Yei—a river-Yei," they whispered. "Go not too near!"

While they watched, the Yei with webbed hands propelled the snow-white craft along, pausing now and then to jabber weirdly. Thus, with its cargo of comely youth and unearthly terror, the white canoe moved among the village craft. Its white-clad youth half-smiled. Its hideous ogre made furious clutching passes ever and anon, whereat the nearest women screamed and shrank away.

But seeing that no harm befell, a few canoes drew nearer, among them one containing Inkato and Kansa.

As the shamans neared, the foremost figure in the white canoe whispered, "I am afraid."

From behind him came an answer, "Fear not! Behold, they look at us in awe."

In the foremost canoe a stately figure spoke, with trembling hand outstretched. "Ohali, my son, we know not if you live or are a spirit."

Astern the goblin river-Yei muttered something. The youth then spoke in low tones—yet not one was there but heard the words distinctly: "Are you not my father Tenasi?"

A cry of awe rose up. "Miracle! Miracle! Ohali the dumb has answered! Ohali's tongue is loosened!"

Answering uncertainly, Tenasi said: "Once I called Ohali my son. But now he returns from the Caldrons, whence never human body returned before. He comes as the legend says the son of Mialoka will return. He comes back to life as Two-Star. None knew of this until blind old Iska foretold it."

Astern the river-Yei shook and choked, as in convulsion.

"The Yei cannot breathe well when out of water," a Shoni mother whispered to her son near by. "Like fish they are, with gills."

Then rose a warrior seated behind Tenasi, and said, as spokesman for his brothers: "We are your earthly brothers. What happened to Ohali?"

"He was given to the Yei," came the answer, and gesturing toward the stern: "One of their number brings me back to you."

A great indrawn breath sounded among the people. The canoe containing Inkato and Kansa moved slightly nearer. Both shamans' eyes were glued in fascination upon the white-clothed figure, whose face grew deathly pale beneath that scrutiny.

Ominous as distant thunder, the voice of the chief spoke again: "Who gave Ohali to the river-Yei?"

Still closer moved the shamans' craft. Rigid as an image sat the river-Yei, watching their every move. Muttering something, he heard Ohali repeat—swaying where he sat—

"Two men of wicked hearts."

"Name them," came the fierce appeal from Tenasi. The silent multitude strained their ears to hear. No sound was audible save the distant cough of prowling tiger.

The shaman's craft was only spear-length distant from the white canoe. The eyes of those within it bored into Ohali. Some there were who later said they heard a voice then mutter, "Courage!" Right or wrong, Ohali seemed to stiffen, though his voice fell to a whisper. He answered slowly, "The name of one was—"

Suddenly one in the craft so close beside him sprang up, with frightful yell, and in his back-drawn hand a war-ax gleamed. Ohali did not stir, but gripped the gunwales as if by some command.

In a voice like ice some one unknown finished Ohali's sentence, pronouncing the name he feared to utter: "Kansa!"

Kioga had sought only the disgrace of Kansa, not the penalty of death. But now there was no choice. He acted to save Ohali's life.

Before the younger shaman could strike, Kansa seemed to choke and wither where he stood. Those close by could hear a high-pitched *twang* and see an arrow sticking through his neck. Then Kansa toppled limply 'nto the river. And as he sank the river-Yei watched fixedlv.

Again the voice of Tenasi: "Who was the other?"

Again Ohali whispered, "The other's name–was Inkato!"

"*Yala-i!*" Shrill and terrible rose that cry from behind the chief, out of the mouths of Ohali's brothers. "Quick, after him!"

But Inkato had acted swiftly, already swung his craft out into the current, and crouching somewhat forward, presented little target to the spears that glanced the water all around.

Though they might have caught up with him, it was seen to be unnecessary—and dangerous. The shaman raised a startled yell. Slowly but inexorably, the currents were bearing him toward the fate to which he had sent so many others—straight to the Caldrons of the Yei.

In the white canoe Ohali swayed. Up rose the river-Yei to bolster him. Ohali heard swift muffled words close at his ear: "Well done, little brother! They'll trouble thee no more. Good-by, O son of Mialoka."

"Good-by," answered Ohali brokenly, and to the horror of the onlookers, threw impulsive arms about the Yei. "Ohali will never forget."

"Hang on," came Kioga's final word. Ohali gripped the gunwales tightly.

One spring, a knifelike entry with little splash—that quickly the Yei was gone beneath the surface, the same surface which carried Inkato away.

With beating heart Ohali watched for sign of him upon the water. A minute passed—another. Clutching the gunwales, the boy went paler than before. Then from somewhere in the shadows near the bank, there came a loud and imperious call:

"*Ahai! Aki! Aki!*"—followed by a whistle.

Downstream, like rat in sinking trap, Inkato heard that call, and glancing shoreward saw a naked figure vanish from the moon's new light. Seeing, Inkato stared, drop-jawed. On one bare hip he dimly saw the mark of salmon's tail. Then glancing upward he caught a last view of Chieftain's Head and stared anew. For where the fire had burned, the stony face had cracked; the Chieftain seemed to smile. Then mists enwrapped bewildered Inkato, and he was seen no more.

Ohali also heard that imperative summons and a bear's answering call. Hearing, he smiled with happy recollection of a strange exciting adventure.

But Kioga, the Snow Hawk, climbing the rims and ledges above the Caldrons, his face to the forest and the future, did not look back.

FOREWORD to
Shasta of the Wolves

Shasta is a Canadian Mowgli, though original in many ways and far from just a pale imitation.

His mother was a woman of an unspecified Indian tribe who had been killed during an Assiniboine raid. His own father, Red Fox, abandoned the papoose in the snow. A nursing she-wolf found him and carried him off to her den, where she brought him up with her own young. And so Shasta ran with the wolves in the northern forests; made friends with Gomposh (Shasta's Baloo); fought Kennebec, the eagle (Shasta's Shere Khan); and, like Mowgli, lived with his own kind, for a while, at least.

Though Shasta of the Wolves seems to be based on The Jungle Books, it stands on its own. It is fluidly written; its style is not imitative of Kipling's; and it evokes the remoteness and mystery of the Canadian forests, the magic of a human child who talks with the beasts, and the struggle between a human heritage and a lupine environment.

It ought to be reprinted more often. Children will love it (my eight-year-old granddaughter does), and adults who love Mowgli and Mowgli-like characters should thoroughly enjoy it. I know I did.

These selections, the original chapters II, III, V, and XVIII, carry Shasta through his early days to the end of the book, where his conflict is not yet solved. Will

he stay in the tribe of man or return to dwell with
the tribe of wolves?

Either way, he won't be entirely happy, which is a
realistic note. But then this story, like that of Mowgli,
is actually a realistic one with the trappings of fantasy.
All the best children's books, Alice in Wonderland,
Gulliver's Travels, the Narnia books of C. S. Lewis,
are such.

I hope these selections will stimulate the reader to
look for the complete book in the libraries or to ask the
publisher, Dodd, Mcad and Company, to rcprint it.
If it is republished, I hope that the original illustrations
by Charles Livingston Bull will be included. They add
a magic of their own to the text.

Shasta of the Wolves

THE COMING OF SHOOMOO

Now the first great day in little Shasta's wolf life was the day when he left the cave for the first time and came out into the open world. He didn't know why he was to go out, nor what going out really meant. All he knew was that, suddenly, there was a movement of all the cubs towards the place where the light came from, and that it seemed natural for him to follow the movement.

When he crawled outside, the sunlight hit him smack in the face like a hot white hand, and then, when he got over that, the world swam in upon his little brain in the way of a coloured dream. It was a very splendid dream, in which everything was new and strange and beautiful beyond all words to describe. The baby wolf-brothers sat in a row and blinked out at the dream, sniffing at it with their puppy noses because of the instinct within them that even dreams must be smelt if you would find out what they are. And it seemed to them to be a very good dream, smelling of grass and flowers, and of hot rocks, and of the sharp scent which the pine trees loose on the summer air. And there, on a rising piece of ground, sat the old wolf-mother, also smelling the good world, only that, besides the smell of the trees and rocks, she could distinguish those other odours of living creatures which drift idly down the wind.

138

Shasta, a little way behind his wolf-brothers, sat down too. When a large curious dream comes it is better to sit and watch what it will do; otherwise, if you begin to walk about in it, you may fall over something, and come to a bad end! So Shasta sat and blinked at the thing, and waggled his fingers and his toes. He smelt at the thing also, and to him, as to the others, it seemed a good and pleasant smell, and he gurgled with delight. The sound he made was so funny that the cubs turned round to see what was happening. But when they saw that it was only the foster-brother being odd as usual, they turned away again and went on smelling at the world.

High up above his head, Shasta saw something very white and hot. It was so dazzling that he couldn't look up at it for more than a moment at a time, and because the thing hurt his eyes, and set queer round plates dancing in front of them when he looked away, he gave up looking at it. Yet always he was conscious that it was there—the hot white centre to this curious dream. And once he lifted a little hairy hand to give it a cuff for being so hot and silly; only, somehow the hand didn't quite reach, and when he tried a little higher, he overbalanced and fell over on his back.

This was a signal for the cubs to rush at him and have a game. So for a long time, Shasta cuffed at them and wrestled with them, and sometimes got the better of them, and sometimes was badly beaten and worried like a rat. Of course neither he nor they had any idea that this delightful scuffling and cuffing was really the beginning of their education, and that their muscles were being trained and their limbs strengthened for their battle with the world when they should be grown up, and babies no longer.

Suddenly, as if by magic, the play stopped dead, with Shasta and the cubs locked in a fierce embrace. Old Nitka never made a sound, nor any outward sign, which ordered the play to cease. Yet in a twinkling the cubs were back into the den, while Nitka had risen from her point of observation, with her eyes set hard to the north. Shasta

sat up and stared. The last wolf-brother was wobbling his
fat body into the cave's mouth. Shasta felt, in some odd
unexplained way, that he ought to follow, and that it was
because Nitka had willed it, that the cubs had gone in.
Yet because he was a man-baby, and not a wolf-cub, he
stayed where he was and stared at his foster-mother with
large and wondering eyes. But Nitka did not look at him.
Her eyes were far away over the tops of the spruces and
pines—far away to a certain spot where a level rock jutted
out from the great "barren" that stretched like a roof
along the windy top of the world. If Shasta had followed
the direction of Nitka's eyes, he would have seen what
looked like the form of a large timber-wolf lying crouched
upon the rock, with his nose well into the wind. Only
Shasta had no eyes for anything but Nitka. He had never
seen her look so fierce before. All her great body was
stiffened as if with steel springs. Just above her tail her
hair was raised, as is the way when a wolf or dog is roused
for fight; and in her gleaming eyes, burning like dull
coals, there was a green, unpleasant light. Shasta could
not tell what ailed his foster-mother. Only, in a dim way,
he felt that something was amiss. And the feeling made
him uncomfortable, as when a grown-up person says
nothing to you, but has a slap ready in the hands.

Presently Nitka saw the other wolf slip off the rock
and disappear in the spruce scrub at its base. And then,
as before, she let herself down, and the bristles flattened
above her tail. She seemed to rest in her body, and to
give up all her bones to the warmth of the summer afternoon. Near by, the stream fell down the hill-side with a
sleepy murmur, and the grasshoppers chirruped in the
grass. There was nothing to be seen except, high up in the
air, a sweep of slow wings that bore Kennebec, the great
eagle, in his solemn circles above the canyon at the foot
of the mountain. Kennebec was a mighty person in his
own world, as many a wolf and mountain sheep knew to
their cost. Many and many a lamb and wolf-cub had gone
to the feeding of Kennebec's children in their dizzy eyrie

built among the steeples of the rocks. But as long as
Kennebec kept to his own canyon, and did not cast a
wicked eye upon her babies, Nitka did not worry about
him, and had all her senses on the watch for danger
nearer at hand. For in spite of all her look of outward
laziness, every nerve that she had, every muscle of her
strong body, was ready at a moment's notice to send her
flying at any creature which dared to venture within
striking distance of the den.

For a long time nothing happened. Then Nitka
growled softly, looking at Shasta as she did so. Now
Shasta knew perfectly well that the growl was meant for
him. Up to the present he had been disobedient, though
he didn't quite know how. Nitka wished him to return
to the cave with the cubs, and Shasta, though he felt
some instinct telling him to go, could not understand
what it meant, and so remained exactly where he was.
And so far Nitka had been very patient. She had simply
gone on wanting him to get back into safety, but she had
not looked or spoken. The soft growl, rumbling down
there in her deep throat, was not a pleasant thing to hear.
It sent a thrill down Shasta's little spine. He began to feel
dreadfully uncomfortable, and to wish that he was safe
inside the cave. Yet still he did not move, because the
man-cub inside his heart was not inclined to bow down
before the wolves.

Again Nitka growled, this time louder than before.
And to make it more pointed, she looked at Shasta as
she growled. He had never seen her look at him like that
before. The light in her eyes was not at all agreeable.
There was a threat in it, as to what she might do if Shasta
did not obey. He began to edge away towards the cave.
After he had gone two or three yards he stopped. This
behaviour of Nitka was so curious that he wanted to find
out what it meant. Something was going to happen.
Without in the least knowing what it might be, Shasta
felt that something was in the air. But there was no resisting that look in Nitka's eyes. With a whimpering cry,

Shasta scrambled to the entrance of the cave. Once inside
the den's mouth, however, his courage came to him
again, and he turned to look back.

As he peeped, he saw the form of a huge grey wolf
glide into the open space. Nitka herself was large, but
this other wolf was nearly half as big again and much
more formidable. His great limbs and deep chest were
wonderful to see. Between his shoulders was a dark patch
of hair which was thicker than the rest of his coat, and,
when the winter came, would become a sort of mane. He
stood nearly three feet high at the shoulders—a giant of
his breed.

As to Nitka herself, she was plainly in a rage. The
hackles on her back were raised; her body was crouched
low as if to leap, her limbs were bent under her like
powerful springs to send the whole weight of her great
body hurling through the air; while, if her eyes had shone
threateningly before when she looked at the disobedient
Shasta, now they gleamed with a green light that seemed
like living flame.

So the two wolves stood facing each other, the huge
stranger not seeming to like the look of things, with
Nitka snarling defiance at him, and prepared to give her
very life in the defence of her cubs.

Shasta, peeping timidly out from the mouth of the
cave, felt certain that some terrible thing was about to
happen. He was terrified by two things: first, by the mysterious coming of the stranger wolf, then by the awful
anger of Nitka, which,. if once let loose, must surely tear
the new world to pieces, hot white centre and all! Behind
him, in the cave, the cubs were motionless and made no
sound. They huddled closely together as if they knew,
though they could not see it, that, out there in the sunlight, a strange thing was happening with which it would
be fatal to interfere. So there they huddled, and pressed
their fat furry bodies against each other, and tried to be
comforted by each other's fat and fur.

Then Shasta, looking out boldly, saw a very odd thing.
He saw the he-wolf make a step towards Nitka with a

sort of friendly whine in his throat, and Nitka, instead of springing at him, remained crouched where she was. And although she kept on growling, and saying the most dreadful things as before, somehow or other she seemed less vicious, and the green glare was softening in her eyes. Seeing this, the other wolf grew bolder, and drew closer step by step.

It was a very slow approach, as if the giant he-wolf was fully aware that any sudden action of his would bring Nitka on him like a fury, with those long fangs of hers bared to strike. And then at last the two wolves were so close together that their noses touched. And in this touch of their noses, and the silent conversation which followed, everything was explained and understood, and made clear for the future.

So that was how Shasta saw the return of Shoomoo, the father of his foster-brothers, and Nitka's lawful mate. After that Shoomoo became a recognized person in the world who came and went mysteriously, never saying when he was going, nor telling you where when he had come back. Only that did not matter in the least. The really big thing was that when father Shoomoo did come back, he seldom returned empty-handed, or I should say empty-mouthed, since a wolf uses his mouth as a carry-all, instead of his paws.

SHASTA COMES VERY NEAR BEING EATEN BY A BEAR

The weeks and the months went by. Only Shasta did not know anything about time, and if the months ticked themselves off into years, he took no account of them. Each month he became more and more wolf-like, and less and less like a human child. And because he wore no clothes, hair began to grow over his naked body, so that soon there was a soft brown silky covering all over him, and the hair of his head fell upon his shoulders like a mane. And as he grew older much knowledge came to him, which is hidden from human folk, or which perhaps they have forgotten in their building of the world. He learnt not only how to see things very far off, and clearly,

as if they were near, but he learnt also to bring them close
by smelling, to know what manner of meat they were.
And if his nose or his eyes brought him no message, then
his ears gave him warning, and he caught the footsteps
that creep stealthily along the edges of the night. And he
learnt the difference between the three hunting calls of
the wolf: the howl that is long and deep, and which dies
among the spruces, or is echoed dismally among the
lonely crags; the high and ringing voice of the united
pack, on a burning scent; and that last terrible bark that
is half a howl, when the killing is at hand.

Yet it was not only of the wolves that Shasta learnt the
speech of the Wild. He knew the things the bears rumbled to each other as they went pad-padding on enormous
feet. Of the black bears he had no fear, but for the
grizzlies he had a feeling that warned him it was wiser to
keep out of their way. The feeling was not there in the
beginning, but it grew after a thing that happened one
never-to-be-forgotten day.

He had been sleeping in the cave during the hot hours,
and woke up as the light began to yellow in the waning
of the afternoon. He stretched his little hairy arms and
legs with a great feeling of rest and of happiness. He felt
so well and strong in every part of him that the joyful
life inside him seemed bubbling up and spilling over. He
was alone in the cave, for his wolf-brothers were now
grown up and were gone out into the world. Sometimes,
at sundown or dawn, he heard them sing the strange
wolf-song—the song that is as old as the world itself—or
a familiar scent would drift to him, as he sat in the entrance of the cave, and he would know it for the sweet
good smell of some wolf-brother as he passed across the
world. And sometimes Shasta would lift his child's voice
into that wild, unearthly wolf-song that is so very old.

This afternoon, something seemed to call Shasta to go
out into the sun. Nitka had made him understand that it
was not safe for him to go far from the cave when she was
away. Now she was out hunting, and Shoomoo was off
on one of his mysterious journeys, nobody knew where,

so there was all the more need for Shasta to stay close at home. Shasta did not see why he should remain in the dull den all the time that his foster-parents were away. Besides, were not his wolf-brothers all far out in the world? Perhaps he might fall in with one of them, and sniff noses together for the sake of old times. He determined to go out and try.

As he passed out, he heard the Blue Jays scolding in the trees.

Now there is a rule which all wise forest folk observe. It is this: When the Blue Jay scolds, look out!

Sometimes, of course, the Blue Jays simply scold at each other, because somebody has taken somebody else's grub, or just because they have a falling-out for fun; but the wise wild folk pay no attention to this, knowing it to be what it is. And when the Blue Jays scold in a peculiar manner, then the wise ones know that there is danger afoot, and that you must keep a sharp look out.

Now, although Shasta was so young, he was quite old enough to understand the difference in the sounds. Unfortunately, this afternoon he was in a mad mood, and he just didn't care! He saw the autumn sun bright on the rocks at the den's mouth; he saw the glimmer of the blue over the tall tops of the pines. High above the canyon, a dark blob circled slowly against the sky. Far off though it was, Shasta saw that it was Kennebec, the great eagle, who was lord of all the eagles between the mountains and the sea. Shasta watched him for a little while making wide circles on his mighty sweep of wing. Then he ran up the mountainside, and, as he ran, the Blue Jays scolded more and more.

If Shasta had not been in so mad a mood, he would have known by the chatter of the Jays that the danger was coming up-hill. Also, if he himself had not been running down-wind, he would have smelt what the danger was creeping up behind. But the something that had seemed to call him in the cave was calling to him now from the high rocks. So on he climbed, careless of what might be going on below. He climbed higher and higher.

Close by one of the big rocks a birch-tree hung itself out into the air. When he reached it he stopped to look back.

Down at the edge of the forest he saw a thing that made him shiver. From between the shadowy trunks of the pine-trees, the shape of a huge Grizzly swung out into the sun. It came on steadily up the mountain, its nose well into the wind. Shasta knew that he himself was doing the fatal thing; he was spilling himself into the wind, and even now the Grizzly was eating him through his nose!

By this time Shasta was very frightened. He looked this way and that, to see how to escape. He knew that he could not get back to the cave in time, for it lay close to the Grizzly's upward path, and already the bear was half-way there. The moving of his great limbs sent all his fur robe into ripples that were silver in the sun. He was coming at a steady pace. And, if he wanted to quicken it, Shasta knew with what a terrible quickness those furry limbs could move. As for himself, his wolf-training had taught him to run very swiftly, but he ran in a stooping way, using his hands as well as his feet. Only he doubted whether his swiftness could save him from the Grizzly over the broken ground. And far away over the canyon Kennebec swept his vast circles as calmly as though nothing was happening, because all went so very well in the blue lagoons of the air. Nothing was happening up there; but here upon the Bargloosh everything was happening, and poor little Shasta felt that everything was happening wrong.

In his terrible fear Shasta started to run up the mountain. As he ran, he looked back. He saw to his horror that the Grizzly had seen him and had also started to run. Up the rocky slopes came the terrible pad-pad of those cruel paws. And Shasta knew well that the paws had teeth in them; many cruel teeth to each paw. And still Shasta went darting upward, running swiftly like a mountain-fox.

As he ran, a thought came into his head. If he could circle down the mountain, he might hide behind the rocks till the Grizzly had passed, and so reach the cave

in time. For he had the sense to know that although a
Grizzly is more than a match for wolves in the open, it
thinks many times before it will attack them in their den.

Again Shasta looked back. He saw that the Grizzly was
gaining upon him. He turned swiftly among the boulders
to the left, dodging as he went so as to be out of sight of
his enemy. The longer he could keep up the flight the
more chance there was that either Nitka or Shoomoo
might return. He ran on wildly, the terror in him, like
the Grizzly behind, gaining ground.

He saw the long mountainside stretching out far and
far before him to the northwest. He looked eagerly to see
if any grey shadows should be moving eastwards along it
—the long, gliding shadows that would be his wolf-
parents coming home. But nothing broke the lines of
grey boulders that lay so still along the slopes. All the
great mountains seemed dead or asleep. Nothing living
moved. Shasta ran on and on, looking fearfully backwards
now and then, and expecting every moment to see the
form of the great Grizzly come bounding over the rocks.
Far below him in the timber he heard the screaming of
the Jays. There was a fresh tone in the cry. Before, it had
been a scolding of the bear: now it was a cry to Shasta:

"Run, little brother, run!"

It did not need the crying of the Blue Jays to make
Shasta run. He was covering the ground almost with the
speed of the wolves themselves.

Now he began to slant down towards the timber, darting down the mountain, leaping from boulder to boulder
in the manner of the mountain-sheep. Yet behind him,
faster and faster, as the rush of his great body gathered
force, the Grizzly launched himself downwards, an avalanche of fur!

Shasta knew only too well that, unless something happened, the chase could not go on much longer. It might
be a little sooner or a little later, but the Grizzly must
have him at the last unless he could reach the trees in
time. The trees were his only hope. If he could reach
them, he could escape. For among the many things he

had learnt of the ways of the forest folk, he had learnt this also: a Grizzly does not climb. And it was in this one thing only that he could outdo his wolf-brothers: he could climb into the trees!

He looked back. The thing was hurling itself nearer— the fearful avalanche of fur! Now he began to fear that he could not reach the timber in time. The Grizzly was gaining at a terrible pace. And then a thing happened.

Down aslant the mountain-side there came leaping in tremendous bounds the form of a big she-wolf. On it came at a furious speed, every spring of the powerful haunches sending the long grey body forward like an arrow loosed from a bow. And as she came, there rose from deep in her throat a long-drawn howl—the mustering cry of the wolves when the prey is too heavy for one to pull down alone.

The Grizzly saw her coming but could not stop. He was going too fast to turn so as to avoid the first onslaught. With a snarl of fury Nitka sprang.

Her long fangs snatched horribly. There was a gash behind the bear's left ear. He snorted with rage, and tried to pull up. Before he could do so, Nitka had snapped at his flank and leaped away. Then at last, by a supreme effort, the Grizzly pulled himself up, and turned upon his unexpected foe.

By this time Shasta was well within reach of the trees. But some instinct made him suddenly alter his course and turn towards the cave. The Grizzly, seeing this, started again in pursuit of his prey. Once more Nitka leaped, and the long fangs did their deadly work; but this time the bear, turning with remarkable quickness, hurled her off, and did so with such force that Nitka almost lost her balance. A wolf, however, is not easily thrown off its legs, and again Nitka attacked. Each time she sprang, the bear stopped to meet her. Nitka knew full well what she would have to expect if she came within striking distance of those terrible paws and not once did she allow the Grizzly to get his chance to strike. And every time the bear turned, Shasta was making good his escape, farther and farther up the slope. Yet still the bear continued the chase, as if determined, in spite of all Nitka's fierce defence, to have his kill at last.

But he did not reckon upon two enemies at once, and he did not know that a second one, even more to be dreaded than Nitka, would have to be faced before he could seize his prey.

Shasta had almost reached the cave now. He saw the shadowy mouth of it just beyond the clump of bushes where the great cliff broke down.

Yet if the Grizzly should follow him into the cave! At close quarters Nitka would be no match for the Grizzly. Those terrible paws would have the wolf within striking distance, and then, no matter how bravely Nitka fought, she must sooner or later be killed. Yet, just at the moment, the instinct for home was the strongest thing in Shasta's little mind, and so he made blindly for the cave.

As he darted into it, something shot past it in the opposite direction—something that leaped in the air with a noise that would have sounded more like the snarl of a mad dog—if Shasta had ever heard a mad dog—than any voice of wolf!

Far away in the lonely places of the great barren, Shoomoo had caught the long-drawn hunting cry of Nitka, and had answered it on feet that swept the distance like the wind. With every hair on end, with eyes that shone like green fires, with his chops wrinkled to show the gleaming fangs, Shoomoo hurled himself downwards full in the path of the advancing bear.

The Grizzly saw his coming just in time, and raised himself suddenly to give the wolf the blow which would have been his certain death. Swift as a streak of light, Shoomoo swerved as if he actually turned himself in the air. The Grizzly missed his stroke by a hair's breadth. Before he could strike again, both wolves were upon him. They sprang as with one accord, slashing mercilessly; then, in the wolf fashion, leaping away before the enemy could close.

The fight now became a sort of game. As far as mere strength went the Grizzly was far more than a match for the wolves; but their marvellous quickness put him at a disadvantage. Directly he turned to meet the onset of one, the other sprang at him from the opposite direction. They kept circling round him in a ring. It was a ring that flew and snarled and gleamed and bristled; a ring of wild wolf-bodies that seemed never to pause for a single second. Sometimes it widened, sometimes it narrowed, hemming the great bear in; but always it was a live, quivering, flying ring of shadowy bodies and gleaming teeth.

More and more the bear felt that he was no match for his opponents. Hitherto he had had no fear of wolves: he had held them almost in contempt. But these things that leaped and snapped and leaped again seemed scarcely wolves. They were wolfish Furies to which you could not give a name.

Slowly, step by step, he retreated down the slope. He had given up all thought of the strange wolf-cub now. His one idea was to defend himself from these terrible foes, the like of which he had never encountered before. Deep in his grizzly heart he knew that he was being beaten. It was a new feeling, and he did not relish it. Till now he had been monarch of his range, and other animals had respected his undisputed right. Now the tables were being turned, and a couple of wolves larger than he had ever seen were driving him steadily back. Yet he would not turn and run. Something in his little pig-like eyes told the wolves that, whatever happened, he would never take safety in flight. That is one of the ideas belonging to a king. When his back is up against a wall, he must fight to the last. And that is exactly what the bear was looking for —something against which he could place his back. To the left, about fifty yards away, a great spur of rock broke from the mountain-side. If he could once reach that, he knew that he could keep his foes at bay. He knew also, that in order to reach it, he would have to fight every yard of the way.

And up above on the slope, a little wild face peered

out from the shelter of the rocks, and watched and watched with shining eyes.

GOMPOSH, THE WISE ONE

The moons went by and the moons went by. The slow moons slipped into each other and were tied into bundles, a summer and a winter to each bundle, and so made up the years.

Shasta did not know anything about that measuring of time, nor that people talked of growing older out there in the world. All he knew was that there were day and night, and that the great lights came and went in the heavens, stepping very slowly upon gold and silver feet. But he knew when the loon, the great northern diver, cried forlornly in the night, that the long cold was at hand, and that he would have to stay in the cave to keep himself from freezing to death. And then it was that Nitka and Shoomoo exerted all their arts to keep the man-cub alive; and when the small game grew scarce, and the caribou hunting began, many and many a chunk of venison the little Shasta devoured, and throve marvellously upon the uncooked meat. The meat made him warm, and kept the rich blood at full beat in his veins; and that he might be the warmer when he slept, he scooped a hole in the side of the cave, filling it with dry grass and leaves and a lining of fur and feathers torn from the outside of his meat. He learnt this nest-making from the homes of the wild creatures he discovered in his ramblings in the early spring and summer; for everything you learnt then seemed somehow to be in preparation for the grim time of the winter, when the blizzard howled from the north, and even the wolves, and the caribou they hunted, had to flee before the blast.

It was after many summers and winters had been tied together in bundles that one bright September morning Shasta left the cave and made for a tall rock, overlooking the gorge of the stream. When he reached it, he squatted down and watched what might happen below. No one saw him there—the little brown thing on the rock; and no one minded him, which was even more important, because he perched above the level of the run-ways, and of the creatures whose noses are always asking questions of the lower air.

But some one whom Shasta did not know, and who was wiser than all the other wise folk of the forest, was also out for a walk that wonderful autumn morning, and on soft and padded feet came softly down the mountain slopes above Shasta's airy perch. And this was Gomposh, the old black bear.

Gomposh was very old and of a wonderful blackness. When he walked out in the sun the light upon his fur rippled in silver waves. As for his years, not even Goohooperay, the white owl, could tell you how many they were, much less Gomposh himself.

It was not any sound Gomposh made that told Shasta of his presence, but suddenly, without any warning to his eyes, or ears, or nose, Shasta knew. And this was owing to that unexplained sixth sense which the wild animals possess, and which Shasta, after his long dwelling among them, shared to a remarkable degree. He turned round all of a sudden, and there, not fifty feet away, stood Gomposh the Old in all the wonder of his black, black fur.

For the first moment Shasta felt afraid. Here was another bear—smaller, indeed, than the grizzly, but none the less a bear! And now, if the black bear meant mischief, escape was impossible because the rock was too steep for any foothold on the outer face of it, and between its inner side and the open mountain stood the bear. Then, in some odd way which he did not understand, the fear passed, and he knew that this time he was in no danger at all, and that the newcomer with the black robe would do him no harm.

Gomposh waited for a while, observing Shasta with his little wise eyes and making notes of him inside his big wise head. Then, very deliberately and slowly, he came down the slope towards Shasta and sat down on his haunches before him on the rock. For a minute or two neither of them spoke, except in that secret language of eye and nose which makes unnecessary so much of the jabber that we humans call speech. But presently Shasta began to ask questions in wolf-language and Gomposh made answers in the same. And the sense of what they said was as follows, though the actual words were not our human words at all, but deeper and sweeter in the meaning of them, and much nearer to the truth.

"Shall we be brothers, you and I?" Shasta asked, a little timidly, for he was feeling shy.

Gomposh looked at him kindly out of his little pig-like eyes.

"We are brothers," he said. "I am old Gomposh, brother to all the forest folk."

"I am brother to the wolves," Shasta replied.

"You will find yourself brother to many strange folk before you are much older," Gomposh said, and when he had finished he gave a slow wag with his head.

"Who are the folk?" Shasta asked wonderingly.

"Ah!" Gomposh said, looking even wiser than before. He looked so tremendously full of knowledge that Shasta felt very small and ignorant indeed.

"There are the lynxes and the foxes to begin with," Gomposh said after a pause. But Shasta shook his head.

"No," he said. "They are not brothers. We have no kinship with them, we of the wolves."

Gomposh looked at him for a minute or two without speaking, and Shasta felt uncomfortable.

"It is not for you to say who are not brothers," Gomposh said gravely. "You are not a wolf!"

Shasta blinked his eyes at that. It was the first time any one had told him that he was not a wolf.

"But I am!" he said. "Nitka and Shoomoo and the brothers—we are all of the wolf blood. I have many brothers," he added, as if to make the matter clearer. "They are all out in the world."

"I am aware of that," Gomposh said; "but many brothers do not make you different from what you are."

Shasta could not think of an answer to that, so he was

silent for a little time, while something which began to
be a question grew big within his head.

"If I am not a wolf, what am I?" he asked at last.

"You will find that out later on," Gomposh said with
aggravating calmness. "At present it is enough for you to
know what you are not."

"But I don't know it," Shasta said bravely, because he
was not going to give way weakly before a bear, if he were
never so old, and never so wise. "How do you know that
I am not a wolf?"

Gomposh blinked and did not answer for a moment or
two. He was taken by surprise, and was just a little
shocked. In all his long experience, reaching over many
years, no one had ever questioned his wisdom before, nor
asked him how he knew. The man-cub was very impudent. It would have been the easiest thing in the world,
with one cuff of his big black paw, to teach the man-cub
manners, and send him spinning from the rock. But although Gomposh had a great idea of his own importance,
he had also a kind heart, and there was something in him
which went out tenderly towards the little naked cub,
impudent though he was. So he contented himself with
being very stiff and stand-offish when he spoke again.

"I have eyes," he said. "I have also a nose. You are
not wolf to my eyes, and you are only half wolf to my
nose."

This was a knock-down blow to Shasta, and he didn't
know what to say.

"I am sorry if I don't smell nice," he said lamely after
a while.

"I didn't remark that you didn't smell nice," Gomposh
said. "Smell is a thing for everybody to decide on for
himself."

"What is the smell in me that isn't wolf?" Shasta
asked.

"That you will know later," Gomposh replied.

"But when?" Shasta asked. "Today, or tomorrow, or
when the moon is full?"

"That I do not tell you," Gomposh said. "When the time comes, you will know."

And that was all Shasta could get out of him. Gomposh either couldn't or wouldn't say more, and when he had sat for a little while longer he got up and slowly walked away.

Shasta watched him disappear into the chaparral thicket to the left, and heard him for some time afterwards as he knocked the rotten logs to pieces in his search for grubs.

For a long, long while Shasta sat where he was and gazed down the gorge. An odd feeling that was almost unhappiness was in his head and his stomach, and the feeling went rolling over and over inside him and knocking itself against the corners of his brain. "Not a wolf! Not a wolf!" the feeling kept rapping out. Then, if he was not a wolf, what was he? he asked himself. His memory, groping backwards into the dim beginnings of his life, worked hard to uncover the secret of what he really was; but, try as he would, he could remember nothing but the den and the wolf life that had its centre there, and the happenings of the mountain and of the forest, and the ways of their folk.

There was nothing else—no shapes of tall beings that carried bows in their fore-paws and walked always on their hind legs—nothing that told him of his Indian birth.

The morning slipped into the afternoon, and still Shasta sat motionless, humped upon the rock. His eyes were down the gorge, or on the opposite ridge where the tops of the spruces were jagged against the sky. Down below him, on the old run-ways that had threaded the thickets since the beginning of the world, the creatures came and went. Shasta knew them each by sight. He had known them all his life. Yet now, as their familiar forms came noiselessly like shadows over the grass, he had a peculiar feeling of being separated from them by the new knowledge that, somehow, he was of another world.

When the thin smell of the twilight came drifting through the trees, then, and not till then, Shasta slipped down noiselessly from his rock and stole homewards to the den.

But in the dark the odd feeling was still questioning: "If I am not a wolf, what am I?"

THE WOLVES AVENGE

Presently, at a given sign, the procession started. It was led by an old medicine-man, who moved slowly forward, singing a medicine-chant as he walked. He was extremely old and shrivelled and was smothered in paint and feathers. And he had a husky voice that cut the air like a saw. Behind him rode the chief on horseback, a splendid figure of a man, upright as a dart, and magnificently dressed. Immediately after him came Shasta on the travois. The braves followed in a long line.

Shasta's heart was heavy with fear. No one told him what was going to be done with him, yet a terrible foreboding made him shiver now and then. And yet the birds twittered, and the air was fragrant with the scent of the dew-drenched grass, and the sky blue between the trails of mist. All the world seemed full of life, and free, except himself only, bound and aching on the travois.

When the procession reached the top of a high ridge, the travois was stopped. The Indians lifted Shasta out and bound him to a stake driven into the ground. Around the stake they piled fagots of wood. When this was finished, the medicine-man sprinkled dried sweet grass over the pile so that when the flames rose up there might be a pleasant smell. During the preparations the braves arranged themselves in a large circle about the stake. As soon as the arrangements were completed, they waited for the medicine-man to light the fire, and sing the words which would be the signal for the opening of the dance. There was a pause. For a few moments nothing happened. It was one of those strange pieces of silence which drop sometimes even into the centre of civilized life, and people become uneasy—they could not tell you why.

Only the mist went on, trailing over the ridge, swaying weirdly as the air pushed. It was still cold with the freshness left by the dawn. And although the sun had already risen, his beams were not strong enough as yet to dispel the dense masses of mist that kept rising from all the lower grounds. Near or distant, so far as Shasta's keen ears could detect, nothing stirred. The fat blue grouse which had been feeding on the blueberries had fled at the Indians' approach. The old coyote who had made her den on the south side of the hill was out hunting with her young ones and had not yet returned. For any sight or sound that declared itself, the lonely ridge at the edge of the prairies was a dead lump of burnt-up summer grass where not a living creature stirred. In that tremendous pause when all the world seemed to be waiting, Shasta threw back his head and gave the long gathering-cry of the wolves.

That call for help went ringing out far from the summit of the ridge. The hollow places sucked it in, and gave back sobbing echoes of its desperate need. One long cry that was not an echo, came from the hills in answer. That was all. Then the silence of the Wild closed down, and you could hear your heart beat in your side. From the prairies, from the hills, from the mountains beyond, no sound came. The familiar shapes of things were there as before; but they were dumb, blind, motionless, strangled in the mist. Close by a small fire already burning, the medicine-man stood with a forked stick in his hand, ready to take the live coal which should light the fagots about the stake. And as he stood, he kept repeating to himself now and again the strange words of a world-old medicine-chant, so strange and old that even for him the original meaning of the words had departed, leaving crooked shapes and sounds behind. The eyes of all the assembled Indians were fastened intently upon him. When he should have finished the chant, he would take the live coal from the fire, and the great death dance would begin. It was the dance by which they would celebrate the burning of the evil spirit or "medicine" which they believed Shasta embodied, and which, once destroyed, would enable them to vanquish all their foes. And then, when the dance began, and became wilder and wilder as the flames mounted higher at the stake, the whole hill-top would be alive with Indian shapes that swayed madly in the mist.

But what shapes were those coming down from the foothills—those long, flowing shapes with tongues that lolled and eyes that shone? There was no warning sound that told of their coming. They flowed down the hillsides in a grey flood that rippled but did not break.

Down the hills, past the Indian camp, through the valley bottom, out on the prairie, it flowed uninterruptedly till it reached the foot of the ridge. And still, to all outward seeming, the world appeared exactly as it was before, as if the sun himself, with all the vast lonely spaces of sky and earth, and all the creatures they contained, were waiting for that terrible moment when the medicine-chant should cease.

As for Shasta himself, after that first despairing cry, he had not moved a muscle of his body. He felt that the end was near at hand; that nothing but a miracle could save him now.

The medicine-chant was drawing to a close. The medicine-man moved a pace or two nearer to the fire. Round the great circle of expectant braves there passed a thrill that went through them like swift flame. For a second or two Shasta felt as if his heart had stopped.

At that instant, a short, deep-throated bellow came up from the mist below. It was the signal for the attack. And there was no other warning. Yet there they all were— Nitka, Shoomoo, the foster-brothers who remembered Shasta, and the other brothers who did not, and many others besides, belonging to widely sundered packs, hundreds and hundreds of them, all united under the leadership of the giant Shoomoo for the one great purpose of rescuing Shasta from the hands of his cruel foes.

Up the sides of the ridge they bounded, those long, grey bodies that seemed buoyant like the mist.

When they reached the summit, there was not an instant's pause. In one ringing wolf-voice, the whole of the united packs gave tongue.

Already the medicine-man had taken the live coal on the stick and was just about to set it to the dried grass round the stake when he was hurled to the earth by the leaping form of a tremendous wolf—none other than Shoomoo himself!

As he fell, an Indian darted forward, intending to bury his tomahawk in the wolf. But before he could do so, Shoomoo had leaped away from the prostrate figure, and in an instant had thrown himself on his assailant. There was a gleam as the raised tomahawk caught the light. Yet though it descended it inflicted no fatal wound, and the Indian was borne helplessly to the ground, from which he never rose again.

The Indians fought desperately, but they were hopelessly outnumbered from the first. There were wolves everywhere. If one was killed or disabled, half-a-dozen more instantly filled his place. They came from all quarters, surging up from the lower ground in waves that seemed as if they would never end. On every hand the fight raged furiously. On all sides it was the same mass of dark, leaping bodies, gleaming eyes, and white fangs that tore and slashed. And everywhere it was Shoomoo, Nitka, and the wolf-brothers that did the deadliest work. Shoomoo, himself, seemed to be everywhere at once. Over and over again, Shasta, shivering, and frenzied with excitement as he watched the progress of the fight, saw the giant form of the great father wolf hurl itself through the air, and strike some struggling Indian to the ground.

Would the wolves win? Would the wolves win? That was the agonizing thought that made Shasta shake from head to foot. If they did, he was saved. If not—then all was lost. He would be doomed to die the terrible death by fire. He wrenched and strained in a vain attempt to loose his bonds. His utmost efforts were of no avail. Whatever was the result of the contest, he knew that he must remain helpless to the end.

Once or twice a wild despair seized him. There came a pause in the fight, as if the wolves wavered. Suppose, after all, the Indians were able to hold their own? In spite of their terrible losses, they had killed many of their wolfish foes. Numbers of them lay dead or dying. It would be small wonder if, after all, the rest should grow intimidated, and slink off. Yet after each temporary lull, there would be a fresh attack led by Shoomoo or Nitka, and again the air would ring with the terrible gathering cry of the packs.

At last the Indians could hold out no longer. Utterly unprepared as they were for this fearful horde of un-dreamed-of enemies; feeling, too, that their "medicine" had deserted them and that the Great Spirit, being offended, had abandoned them to their fate—the survivors lost their presence of mind and fled shrieking down the hill.

Few, very few, ever found their way back to camp. It was the wolf triumph, the wolf revenge. The ridge, from end to end, was strewn with Indian dead.

It was Nitka herself who released Shasta, and her famous teeth which tore the thongs from his arms and legs, and, after long and patient work, at last set him free. And when he lay on the ground, almost too dazed to understand, with his whole body feeling like one big bruise, it was her loving tongue that comforted him, caressing him back to life.

The sun was already high in the heavens before Shasta was strong enough to move. Then, with Nitka on one side and Shoomoo on the other, and the wolf-brothers all about on every hand, Shasta started for home. But it was not the home of his Indian kin. It was the cave upon the Bargloosh, far away from the tread of human feet; the old strange home whose rocky walls seemed to him to hold the beginnings of his life.

Did he go back to his people later? Did he say good-bye to the wolf-folk for ever, and forget the ways of the Wild? Perhaps. Who can say?

Perhaps Gomposh could tell you, or even Goohooperay. Or you might entice it out of Shoshawnee when his face goes red on the look-out butte towards the setting sun.

But *if* he went back, which is possible, I do not think he would ever forget. For the Wild, and the ways of its folk, are too great to be forgotten. And then, you see, he was Shasta of the Wolves!

Scream of the Condor

The pulp magazines of the '20s through the '40s
published many stories based on the feral human theme.
Argosy and Blue Book ran many short stories and novels
about Tarzan or Tarzan-like characters. A number of
pulp magazines featured serial characters about men or
women raised by beasts. One of these was the Ka-Zar
magazine, the main hero of which was Ka-Zar the Great,
a man who ran with lions. Lions, wolves, baboons,
chimpanzees, and leopards generally played the paternal
and maternal roles in these tales. Most were written in
the purple prose of the pulps, and the adventures did not
have much psychological or sociological value, but they
did what they were meant to. That is, entertain the
reader.

You wouldn't expect to find such a story in a magazine
devoted to stories of World War I aviators. However,
there was one, and here it is. It's a splendid example of
the type of prose and action and structure of plot so
prevalent, even obligatory, in the WW I air-war
magazines.

Besides, I could not resist the sheer audacity of a tale
of a child raised by condors. I would never have had the
nerve to try to pull this one off.

Scream of the Condor

BY GEORGE BRUCE

CHAPTER I   THE STORKS

THE first time any man of the 5th Squadron of the Second Pursuit Group, A. E. F., heard that terrible cry was on a sultry afternoon over Le Charmel in the Apremont sector on the Western Front. It penetrated the padded leather ear flaps of flying helmets and brought them a crawling sensation between the shoulders—a sensation engendered by horror and fear. The air was filled with the droning of six Hispano-Suiza motors. Added to this was the shrilling of flat wires, the rush of the slip stream through the center section, the faint drumming of wings, and the creaks and whispers which are a part of a Spad in flight.

Certainly, if one of them had attempted to call across the fifty feet which separated him from his flying mate, his voice would have been swept out of his mouth by the propeller blast and made as nothing in the midst of the sound of his own ship. That was why the cry brought a chill of apprehension to every man who heard it. They knew instinctively that it was a sound ripped from a living throat—and yet they knew that no human throat could utter a sound which could be heard over the racket of six Spads in flight.

Jimmy Powers, the sub-flight leader of B Flight of the 5th Squadron, turned his head quickly from right to left, consternation on his face, his bowels feeling suddenly constricted, goose-flesh prickling the flesh between his shoulders. He cast a quick glance over the tail of his gray Spad—toward the point from which danger always threatens. But there was nothing. No red tri-plane, no blue-black Hal, no warpish Pfalz, no shark-like Albatross was slashing down through the space which hung over him. The sky behind him was cobalt blue—cloudless, shadowless.

And yet the sensation which gripped him as he heard that sound was one of danger, of fury, of terror. His eyes, behind the mask and glass of his goggles, darted this way and that, as if trying to locate the source of that danger and to defend himself from its onslaught. The eyes were blue and filled with a cold light, narrowed. Sudden deep lines grew about his mouth and chin. His hand tensed upon the controls. His body was rigid in the seat.

But the source of the sound remained a mystery.

His position was five hundred feet above and between the last ships of the Flight. He was the lookout—the barometer which warned of the approach of a storm. No ship could flash down to attack the Spads below without first passing Jimmy Powers. His post was one of honor and responsibility. He had earned the post. He was a fighter and a finished pilot. There had been times when he had sent his Spad hurtling into the face of an entire enemy group, those cold blue eyes, narrow as they were now, the hand gripping the stick with the same strength, his brain just as alert and calculating.

And yet, the screaming sound had caused his heart to hammer, his muscles to knot, and his soul to shudder.

If it had been possible for a human voice to penetrate the eight thousand feet of space which separated the wheels of the Spads from the earth, he might have explained that sound. The cry might have been wrung from the mouth and throat of a man who had been thrust through the belly with a bayonet. It might have been torn from the chest of a warrior who writhed and twisted upon the ground in a delirium of agony with gas eating at the flesh of his body and at the mucous membranes of his eyes. It might have been the death cry of a horse gutted by the fragments of a bursting 5.9 high explosive. Such sounds did live upon the face of a war-torn earth—but they could not penetrate through eight thousand feet of space and make themselves heard over the sea of noise which surrounded the Spads.

Such a scream might have bubbled out of the mouth of a pilot. A man who felt himself swirling downward with the flame of burning gasoline, pouring in liquid torrent from shattered tanks, washing over his body. There would be time for one scream from a man in the midst of such an inferno—one last throat-bursting scream of exquisite suffering before death blotted every sound from his body.

But there were no burning ships. There were only the Spads, soaring serenely through space like great gray eagles, banded together in the search for a common prey, the line of the horizon, and the brown and green of the devastated earth.

Below, the five other ships of the flight flew together in a tight V. Harry Seymour flew at the point of that V. His ship seemed to fly without effort. Seymour was the leader of B Flight. He was the commander of the six Spads. He was a leather-faced, broad shouldered, deep chested, magnificent figure of a man. He walked and talked exactly as he flew. Confidently, softly, and with an air of complete authority. He had more hours in the air over the front than any man in the squadron, or, as a matter of fact, in the whole second group. The war for him was not an affair of a few months. He had no Kelly Field memories, he had no background of fond good-bys, cheering thousands lining the streets, the American colors floating from thousands of windows. No memory of the tooting of whistles and the ringing of bells.

Nine months after he had taken his first instruction in flying, Harry Seymour, with more than seven hundred hours of front line experience, was transferred to the Storks. It seemed that the Storks always had room for a man like Seymour. So he went from Spad two-seaters and

Hispano motors to Nieuport "27 bis" with Clergets and the blimper to the beautifully lined white wasps with the blistering sting, and to the Flying Stork painted under his cockpit.

The Storks were a proud lot. The eyes of all France were upon them. They ranged the front and threw their ships into whatever place the fighting was most intense. They were a wild flying, swashbuckling crew of boon companions and they rode the skies like the Four Horsemen, multiplied by ten.

Another man in Seymour's shoes would not have left the Storks when America cast her lot with the Allies. Being a Stork marked him as one of the chosen heroes of a specialized Valhalla. He had nothing to gain and everything to lose. He was going out of the company of seasoned veterans to take on the grief of teaching unschooled cubs how to kill and avoid being killed—and then to have them go out in a reckless spirit of bravado, and disregarding the voice of experience, get themselves killed. But he threw up his commission with the French and offered himself to America. Three years of fighting under the tricolor had washed none of his Americanism out of him.

He changed cockpits again. This time to the tight little seat of a new Spad—a single-seater with a Hisso—and two black Vickers firing between the banks and through the prop.

They offered him a squadron. He refused. He wanted no command, no authority. It was enough to have the red, white and blue cocarde of America under the wings of his ship, and to don a uniform marked with the eagles of the United States.

They forced him into a flight commander's job. He took it because he could not escape. When the 5th Squadron of the second group went to the Apremont Front, he led the vanguard; he stood watch over those gray fledglings. He hovered over them, scanning the skies with anxious wary eyes. He led them to the little field behind Gland. A little field ten miles south from an elbow in the muddy waters of the Marne. Screened by a fringe of trees, set in the center of a shallow depression between low rising hills. Green, fresh looking meadowland—untouched and unspoiled by the withering breath of conflict; unspoiled and unpitted by plunging shell fire.

He had led the way into the first combat at the head of his own B Flight. He had given his pilots a gentle baptism in the red flame of war, and because he was Harry Seymour, and because his fame had preceded him, they listened to him and lived. No man of B Flight had perished. If Harry Seymour needed any praises chanted in his favor, that one statement was more than sufficient.

And B Flight was the shock group of the 5th Squadron. Six weeks after it had first looked upon Harry Seymour, it had accounted for thirty enemy aircraft. Of that number, Seymour had dropped fourteen and Jim Powers had bagged eight.

But with his four years upon earth and in the air, in the midst of the most vicious war which had ever engulfed mankind, Harry Seymour had heard nothing like the cry which had risen over the drone of the ships of his command.

Powers knew that as he looked down upon the rest of the formation. He saw Seymour's head turning quickly from side to side as his own head had turned but an instant before. He saw him studying the skies, studying the air about his wings, glancing anxiously at each ship which flew in the tight formation.

Hanging above the formation, Powers could see what Seymour could not see. Every pilot in the unit was glancing about him nervously, was fidgeting in his seat. One of them, Juan Pinedo, had momentarily lost control of his ship. That was at the exact moment the cry had pierced through the motor drone and had reached the ears of the pilots. Juan's Spad had jerked spasmodically, its wings had bobbled dangerously. For a breathless instant it had edged toward number five in the formation—hung a hair's breadth from destruction—from collision—then it had been jerked back into its position.

So Powers from his position as Guardian Angel over

the flight knew that Juan Pinedo had heard the screech—
and had been afraid—as Jim Powers had been afraid.

He did not know that Juan Pinedo was the only man
of the six of them flying that day who recognized the
sound and identified it. He could see that Pinedo's eyes
were scanning the heavens far overhead as if searching the
vast reaches of limitless space for the sources of the sound
—as if he expected to see a ship—a pin point floating at
twenty thousand feet—a pin point which screamed like a
shell-gutted horse; a sinister, high flying bird of prey,
waiting to pounce upon its victims.

How could he know that Pinedo was searching for exactly such a winged creature? How could he know that
Pinedo alone knew the meaning of the sound, was the
only man among them who had heard it before, and that
it had struck actual transports of terror into the soul of
that fiery-eyed Argentinian—exactly as it had struck re-
flections of that terror into the souls of the men who were
hearing it for the first time?

None of them saw the Fokker at the moment they
heard the scream. To ordinary eyes it was not yet visible.
It came boring through space a full minute after the
goose-flesh had formed on their backs. Then they saw it—
but they saw something else—and heard the scream again.

They saw number five of the formation suddenly whirl
out of line, nose up, fall away in a breathtaking wing over
and go diving like a flash of lightning. At the top of that
wing over, with the Spad's nose pointing for the heavens,
they heard the scream a second time. It was carried
through space by the sudden velocity of the diving gray
ship. They saw a face, distorted, like the face of a demon.
They saw a mouth opened wide like the jaws of a wild
animal. They saw a helmeted head reared above the
curved edges of the Spad's cockpit. There was something
terrible, uncanny, about the posture of that head. Then
it was gone with the plunge of the Spad. They drew a
deep breath. The pilot of number five was John Craig. He
was making his first flight as a member of B Flight.

Short hours ago he had flown in from the pool, ferrying

his own ship onto the 5th's field. Newt Clancy had gone over to a A Flight as sub-leader leaving a vacancy. Craig had filled the vacancy.

Something about that Spad as it dived. Something that caused them to follow it with wide eyes and with breathless concentration. Something about the manner in which it was handled, the grace of its position, the certainty of its course.

And then they saw the Fokker. It appeared out of the mists which hung close to the horizon. Just a shadow at first, then a shadow with wings and a spinning propeller. A shadow which developed the Maltese crosses of the enemy, and which flew at five thousand feet.

Seymour signaled for the outfit to go down. There was a viciousness about his command. They knew he must be burning at Craig's disobedience of the order to maintain the formation until ordered differently.

A thousand feet down, they pulled out of the spiraling descent. The gray lightning had struck the D-VII. Jagged tongues of flame had spurted from the beak of the Spad. There had been a wild churning of gray wings, twists and turns in a dozen different directions, executed with such terrific velocity and finish that even as they watched those maneuvers they were telling themselves that it was all impossible. But it was not impossible.

The Fokker discovered that. He tried to make a fight of it, but there was nothing to fight. There was merely the tearing sound of insane speed.

The reflection of the sunlight from wings which had already passed the point of vision. There was a raging gray thing—sensed rather than seen—striking at him. Twice that Jerry tried to line the gray wraith with his Spandaus. Once he flicked a short burst at it—but the tracers and steel cut through empty space—the Spad had changed course, had feinted him out of position. After that he merely clung to his controls like a man hypnotized, and stared—with wide eyes, with lax mouth, with shaking hands.

To the men of B Flight it seemed that Craig's Spad

had pounced upon the Fokker like an eagle tearing an
enemy to bits with steel talons. They saw the wings of the
gray ship cocked vertically, the nose dropping like a meteor. Saw it whirl out of the vertical and descend squarely
upon the back of the green enemy. In that instant they
were under the spell of a hallucination. The landing
wheels of the Spad took the form of the eagle's talons.
The wings were the wings of the fighting bird. The nose
of the Spad was the powerful, cruelly curved beak—and
the flare of the guns were red eyes. There was a moment
when landing wheels seemed to grasp the upper wing of
the Fokker.

Then the green ship was falling. It was ripped and torn
from tail to nose. Linen fluttered from the center of its
fuselage. There was a sinister cloud of black smoke seep-
ing from under its motor cowling. After another moment
it was spinning, a lolling, grotesque black ball rolling
about above the sides of the cockpit. An arm, leather clad,
dangling on the outside of the fuselage, swaying with
each motion of the ship.

A leaping, white centered flame, rising like a curtain,
gushed from the Fokker's tanks and blew back until it
covered all of the D-VII.

Out of the wall of flame a blasting explosion—then a
stream of wreckage floating down through space like
black embers and ashes rising from a fire, borne aloft by
heat eddies. After that—nothing.

Excepting that John Craig somehow was back in his
place in the formation. None of them were conscious of
his return. He was merely there—number five again,
holding his position easily, exhibiting no more nervous-
ness than if he had never left the tight V, or was merely
flying in a practice formation over some training field far
removed from any theatre of war.

They were a nervous group of men as they went winging toward the field south of Gland. Something had happened to them. A breath of horror had touched them—
had dripped into their souls. They flew along unable to
keep their eyes from drifting to Number Five.

And as they flew they heard the echoes of that scream which had sounded over the roaring of motors—the scream that preceded the death of that Fokker. And they were asking themselves—What kind of a man was this Craig? How had he seen the Fokker when none of them had seen it—minutes before it had appeared out of the mists?

Once Craig turned his head toward Pinedo—and Pinedo had felt a liquid flame mount his spine, and a shudder grip his body. Something about Craig's eyes—something so fierce, so intense, so primitive. Strange that Pinedo, who had a reputation for wild, reckless courage, should go livid because of a sound, and should feel flame in his blood because of a pair of eyes. Pinedo, who had left his Argentine to beg service with the Government of the United States.

CHAPTER II   CRAIG FLIES ALONE

Back on the field, they watched Seymour climb out of his cockpit, his eyes fixed upon Craig's face, and then, with deliberate steps and stiff arms, walk to the side of Craig's Spad. They turned their heads away. All of them had listened to the quiet, vibrant voice of the flight leader—a voice that cut with razor keen precision to the very heart. All of them had sensed the seething scorn, the sarcastic pity, the white anger of this man who led them.

And because they remembered a moment such as Craig was facing, they turned away. Once they had been like Craig—new, young, eager, reckless. They knew what was coming; they pitied Craig. They knew how he must feel. He had dropped an enemy on his first flight. Had dropped him with an exhibition of marvelous flying, of finished combat tactics—tactics such as they had never seen. But that would make no difference with Seymour. If Craig had downed ten Fokkers, it would have made no difference. Craig was guilty of disobedience of orders. And with Seymour, obedience to orders was the fetish out of which he conjured life and safety for his men.

At the side of John Craig's Spad Seymour had paused

for a moment and had glanced over the ship. It was un-marked. No black dot, drilled by Spandau slugs, pierced its surfacing. Craig sat quietly in his cockpit. He was looking down at Seymour's face. His helmet was still on his head. His hands were inside the cockpit. His leather coat was buttoned closely about his neck.

Seymour's soft voice cut through the silence.

"Listen, you!" Then he stopped suddenly, his eyes held by Craig's eyes. A confusion seemed to grip him. He stood with his mouth ready for the utterance of the next word, but no sound passed his lips. Something about Craig's face, something about the smoldering, fierce fire that glowed within the depths of Craig's eyes. Eyes that looked down at him as if from a great height and held a mocking challenge, a scorn, almost a boundless contempt.

Something about Craig's face that took Seymour's breath away. Pity! That was it—pity! This Craig, this newcomer was pitying him, was feeling sorrow for him—pity—an abstract pity which seemed to be stirring in his soul, and yet was expressed, faintly, by his face.

"Listen, you!" The words forced themselves from his mouth. He heard himself speaking them, but they were meaningless, confused before that face which stared down at him, before the eyes that held him in a semi-hypnosis.

And suddenly, Harry Seymour was afraid. There was a sensation between his shoulder blades such as a dog must feel as it ruffs its pelt and howls at the moon when possessed by the uncanny. He was afraid of this Craig—afraid of that sun-tanned almost black face; of the sharp nose and thin-lipped mouth; of the dominant pugnacious chin; of the aura of fierce expectancy which hung about the man; of his silence, of his contempt; of his pity.

But most of all he was afraid of those eyes.

Never had a man looked at him as Craig was looking. Without a movement of the lids, without a change in the pupils. Narrowed eyes—never leaving his face. Eyes in which the lights flickered and flamed, eyes like white-hot embers fanned by a gentle breeze.

There was a whispering voice within Seymour that

prompted him to turn—to run—anywhere, to escape the power and ferocity of Craig's eyes. He was fighting to co-ordinate the confusion within his brain. He was telling himself that he had to tell this man that he was a fool; that he had disobeyed orders; that in disobeying he had placed his flying mates in jeopardy. He had to tell him that in a war it is team work that counts—not individual effort. He had to make him understand that the path of individual glory leads to the grave.

To live, one must conform. How many times had he explained that to other men? How many lives had he pre-served by preaching that doctrine? This Craig was a new man—he must understand. There could not be a faulty cog in a perfect machine; the machine would be de-stroyed. And Seymour loved his machine, made of flesh and blood of men and of the wood and linen of the Spads with a fierce affection. More than an affection, it was a love for something he had created out of nothing.

But even as he fought to speak the words which were hot in his chest, there was a dim picture in his mind of the way this Craig had flown his ship. Of the miraculous grace of his flying; of the cold fury of his attack; of a gray winged thing, whistling through space, maneuvering as no Spad had ever been maneuvered—and then, a final picture of that instant when the wheels of Craig's ship had lashed out like the talons of a hawk, and had ripped the vitals out of that Fokker—had sent it spinning and gushing flame—down to death.

A sense of futility overcame the anger. How could he punish a man who flew like that? How could he instruct a man who in a space of three minutes had proved him-self invincible? How could he answer with words the fact that in those three minutes he had watched a man do things with a Spad which Harry Seymour had never at-tempted and could never duplicate.

For the first time he was possessed of a feeling of in-feriority. Perhaps it was born of the near pity in Craig's eyes. Something about the man—he licked his lips. They were suddenly dry as if ravaged by a fever. He listened to his voice—speaking words—meaningless words—not the words he intended to speak.

"Where did you learn to handle a Spad like that?"

And then, John Craig laughed. A hoarse, chattering sound. It cut through the silence. It brought to all the men about him the memory of that scream which had sounded above the roar of the motors—the scream which preceded the death of the Fokker. A laugh, and it flicked nerves which were still raw—brought them the same shuddering sensation, the same chill of apprehension.

Craig's eyes were still fixed on Seymour's face. There was a thin white line about his mouth. "Learn?" he asked. "Who could teach me? What does a Spad have that I must take lessons—?"

He stepped out of his cockpit. Watching him, all of those men were gripped by another hallucination. They were watching a creature of the heights shedding its wings. Watching a creature leave its natural element—for the earth—which was not its natural element or habitat.

Craig, walking across the field, his long legs moving stiffly, his hands hanging at his sides, his body bent forward from the hips—in an attitude of constant tension and readiness to attack—the picture of an eagle walking with its wings folded.

They drew a deep breath. They shifted eyes to Seymour. He was standing by the side of Craig's ship, and in his eyes there was incredulity, shock, stunned surprise, and harsh anger. Disobedience of orders—and for explanation, a type of insolence—a type of pity. He swallowed hard, a lump moving in his throat. He turned away, after a long moment and like a man who is awakened from a deep sleep, tossed his helmet and goggles into the seat of his own ship.

Harry Seymour was proud of his record, proud of his ability to handle anything that flew. It was a bitter realization. But this Craig? How about him? Where did he come from? Who had trained him? How many hours had he spent in pursuit types in order to handle a ship as he had handled that Spad?

In the orderly room Seymour took down the service records and flipped them through his fingers until he came to Craig's name. There was no information there. The man's service record merely added to the confusion and unrest within Seymour's brain. It might have been the service record of the greenest kaydet. A name, address, a place of birth, a person to be notified in the case of death. Then a few brief lines—"enlisted as a flying cadet"—and a date. The number of hours he had spent on primary instruction. That got a start of surprise from B Flight Leader. There was a notation—"soloed after first hour of dual—evidently a trained pilot although such is not stated on his record—sailed for France—"

Soloed after an hour—a trained pilot—?

He saw Craig passing the office. He beckoned to him to enter. There was a slow deliberation in Craig's answer to the summons—as if he were debating in his mind whether he should obey or not. He stood negligently close to the desk, waiting for Seymour to speak. There was a glint of humor, wicked humor in his eyes now. He seemed to have read the flight commander's mind, to anticipate the question. His eyes flicked for an instant to the service record under Seymour's fingers.

"Where did you learn to fly, boy?" asked Seymour. "It says here on your record that you soloed after one hour dual. How about it?"

"That's correct."

The hoarse, guttural tone was gone from his voice. At the moment it was musical, almost sweet.

"Where did you get training before you went into the service—where did you learn to fly?"

Craig thrust his hands into his pockets. "I'm not going to answer that," he said, almost defensively. "If I told you I should be marked down as a liar—one thing I will tell you—I was never in the seat of an airplane until I went to Kelly. I never held the controls in my hands be-

fore that hour you see marked on that service record."
He made the statement almost defiantly.

"Aw, quit it," Seymour growled. "I've heard all that
stuff before. I wonder why people think it adds cubits to
their stature to make people believe that they soloed in
less time than anyone else. I've had a lot of experience
in this air thing. I know the capabilities of the average
man. He may get up and down in six hours training—
but he can't fly—"

He stopped suddenly. Craig's eyes were burning into
his brain. The thin lips were strained over his white teeth.
The sun-blackened face was almost taut with resentment.

"You mean that I was a pilot before I offered myself—
that I lied—when I told them that I had had no experience with airplanes?"

Seymour nodded. He could not force words past his
throat.

"You are wrong, as all of them were wrong," he said,
a fierce, almost dangerous note in his voice.

"Men may be wise in their own callings, as wise as is
possible to a man—and yet be in ignorance of the essential facts of the calling in which they imagine themselves
experts. I am not trying to be personal, my friend, I am
not at all interested in your personal opinion of myself.
I came here for a purpose, to fly and to fight—and you
could not in any way prevent me from doing either of
those things. But at the same time, let us understand one
another. There was a time in my life, when I lived among
—people—who knew flying as you will never know it—and
as you never could learn it. If you spent all your days trying to perfect yourself in your profession, still you would
be an ignorant infant before the knowledge of those
people.

"I am not trying to be insolent, nor insulting. You
asked me questions, I am answering you. So far as I have
seen men flying in this war, you are the best, and approach more closely to my ideas of flight than any other.
But you are like an awkward fledgling, attempting for the
first time to use its wings. You are afraid of flight—I mean

your brain instinctively guards you against the dangers of flight—and so long as that image is in your brain you will only be a mechanical flyer. To fly—and to the ultimate as a flyer, you must take your wings as if they were a part of your body—you must fly as if it was an elemental part of your being, an existence and not an artificial thing to be utilized for certain purposes.

"You must use the heavens as your natural abiding place, and must return to earth because it pleases you to do so, and not because the earth represents safety—" He paused abruptly, seeing the crimson flooding into Seymour's face.

"I'm sorry," he said contritely. "I did not mean to be rude. You see, I forgot that, after all, you are a man."

"What in the name of God are you?" demanded Seymour hotly. "Who in the hell are you to give me instructions in flying—a damned kaydet—with an hour of service at the front, lecturing me on the theory of flight—"

A white, almost ghastly smile gathered about Craig's mouth. "I wonder?" he said, as if to himself

"You wonder what?"

"I wonder who in the hell I am, and what in the hell I am—"

"Now listen, get this straight," growled Seymour. "You pulled a boner out there today, and I let you get away with it—yes—I did—for a minute you buffaloed me out of giving you the bawling out you had coming to you. Well, you're going to get it now—and you're going to take it. A man with your experience—"

"What do you know about my experience?" asked Craig with the same smile.

Seymour clenched his fists. "You're here for the first time, aren't you—you made your first flight over the lines today, didn't you?"

"Didn't I prove in that first flight as you call it, that I have sufficient experience to take care of myself?"

"That's beside the point," snapped Seymour. "A man who pulls out of a formation as you did, endangers the lives and ships of his whole outfit. You were lucky, you dived on some chump of a Fokker, and you knocked him down. So right now you have a head swelled like a melon, and an ego that is going to get punctured by the next Jerry you bump into. You're ripe for the cleaners, my boy. I've seen 'em, like you—too big for their pants—and they wind up by being the exact size for a pine box—"

"It's all so ridiculous," said Craig with a weary shrug of the shoulders. "I'm not at all interested in the morale of an outfit, nor in keeping herded together like a bunch of sheep passing through wolf country. I don't need such protection. I don't want it. I want to be left alone. I want to fly—can't you understand—I want to fly—"

Something poignant in that "I want to fly—" struck at the depths of Seymour's soul. He stared at the tense face before him—and again the little chills were running up and down his spine. There was a hungriness and a tenseness about Craig's face that was like being struck in the face with ice cold water. That flickering, dancing flame was back in his eyes. His nostrils were distended and moved with each deeply drawn breath. There was the atmosphere of wildness, of the untamed animal about him.

"You can't do it," Seymour said hollowly. "Maybe I understand the way you feel—maybe I don't. I know—all of you are eager to fly and fight when you come here—but you have to learn the rules of the game before you're fit to be trusted with your own lives. You don't learn them in a day—nor a week, nor a month—"

"You don't understand," assured Craig with the same weary shrug of the shoulders—"no one understands—no man—"

"Well, maybe I don't understand—but you'll understand me. You'll fly and fight my way—until you hear differently."

"I couldn't," said Craig. "I couldn't—not even the children of the people with whom I lived flew as badly as you fly—it would have meant death—and worse. Their elders would have destroyed them rather than to see them making fools of themselves."

"You're a nut," said Seymour gravely. "You're a damned nut. You belong in the bug house. A few more cracks like that and I'll see that you get into the bug house."

"Wouldn't it be better to see whether I can demonstrate the truth of what I have been saying?" asked Craig.

"So you want to fly, and you want to fight?" demanded Seymour. He was white with anger, his hands were trembling, his mouth working, his eyes blazing. "You want to show the boys what a sweet little pilot you are—what a wise guy—what a Scourge of God? Well, I'll let you. The sooner a guy like you gets himself killed off, the better it is for him and everybody around him. Go ahead—fly your own course. I wash my hands of you. But mark my words. You'll come back—if you're able to come back—and you'll show yourself up for a big bag of wind. I've seen guys like you take it on the chin before. You're just another in the crowd—that's all. It's a tough way to teach a man his lesson, ordinarily I wouldn't do it—but you have to be taught sooner or later. Go ahead—you have my permission to fly alone—anytime—anywhere. You'll fly alone until you get a belly full of it, or get yourself killed. But if you manage to get away with it, and you decide that you'd like to come back with the flight—I'm going to ground you for two weeks to take the conceit out of you, and then you can request me to return you to duty with the outfit."

"I've got a better plan," said Craig ignoring completely the anger and sarcasm in Seymour's voice. "Why don't you let me fly where the sub-flight leader flies. Being there I could watch and could fight off anything that attacked the flight by surprise—could halt them until all of you had a chance—"

"In Powers' plane?" stormed Seymour. "Cripes—you are a nut—you're worse than a nut—you're an insufferable ass. Listen, Jim Powers is the most valuable man in this squadron—you—"

"But he didn't see that Fokker I attacked this morning," insisted Craig. "I did—I attacked it. I beat it. I would have seen it sooner had I been in his station."

"Get out!" snapped Seymour. "Get out, you big mouthed, empty headed drum. You chattering monkey —Powers—Cripes—"

For a moment Craig towered over him and his hands opened and closed spasmodically. Flecks of flame danced in his eyes like coals of fire burning through saddle leather. "All of you—all of you so-called flyers—all of you, as flyers, are like scarecrows in comparison with living human beings. You have my pity for your affectations, and my disgust for your attainments."

He whirled about on his heels and thrust his body angrily through the door. Seymour sat in his chair, staring after him—remembering how his eyes had caused a burning sensation in the pit of the stomach—and how the fear signals had flashed along his nerves at the sight of the hands clutching and unclutching. He drew a deep breath and shook his head.

That night Craig did not enter the mess hall. It was just as well. There was a tension there—men waiting— for what, none of them knew. There was a tightness within their chests. A silence hung over them. Seymour sensed it and sat among them cursing in his heart. They had been a happy-go-lucky, carefree gang. Now they sat like tongue-tied dummies. It was not good for men to have such a psychology. But as he sat with them, he sensed the same uneasiness, the same tightness. It increased each time his eyes went to the empty chair in which Craig would sit when he made his first appearance at mess. The longer he delayed in making an appearance, the tighter grew the tension.

At last, when they had finished—had almost crammed the food down their throats, they left the table like men escaping from a term in prison.

"Pouting," said Seymour fiercely to himself. "Playing the little boy who has been spanked. Well, let him pout, he'll eat when he gets good and ready"

He was both wrong and right.

Neither did he appear the next morning for the hurried breakfast. Someone mentioned that he had been on the field, late at night, squatting on his heels as if brooding over the line of the night skies—a line that was stained a crimson by the flashes of the guns further to the north. Once, when a flight of D. H. 9's had returned from a bombing expedition and had crossed the field at a height of five thousand feet, Craig had leaped to his feet and had paced nervously back and forth, his head cocked upward, following the noise with his eyes, and acting as if he could see the D. H. through the blackness of the night. But if he had spent a sleepless night, holding vigil over the deserted, still field, he gave no hint of it in the light of morning. He came swinging out of his quarters, his goggles hanging from his wrist, his helmet jammed down over his head, his black flying coat buttoned tightly under his chin.

He had no greeting for any of them. He strode straight up to Seymour.

"Did you mean what you said last night?" he demanded. "That I could fly alone?"

"Oh, hello, Big Hero," greeted Seymour, with pointed sarcasm. "Say, I wouldn't change that for the world. Can you fly alone?—why I even encourage it. Go to it, Big Boy. Hell isn't half full—"

Craig turned away abruptly and walked toward his ship. He did not so much as glance at the mechanics nor listen to the beat of the warming motor. He merely climbed into the seat, buckled the belt around his middle, and called for the blocks to be pulled. Then his Spad was ruddering away from the line, pointing down field, swinging easily without effort, almost without guidance. The roar of the Hisso startled the quiet of the field, blasted out the sound of idling motors. There was a gray streak nosing through space, its wheels rising with a rush, climbing, climbing—while the men on the ground waited for it to fall off into a stall. But it disappointed them—it continued to climb, until it was a speck in the heights.

"I'm going to see this," Seymour announced to B

Flight. "This is going to be good. Craig, the Hun Killer, with the staggering total of one victory over an enemy aircraft, is about to go out and win the war single handed. I want to be on the spot when he gets disillusioned—"

"I don't know," said Powers slowly, "there's something about that guy. He gives me the creeps—frankly, I wouldn't want him smashing down on my tail the way he jumped on that Jerry yesterday—"

"Fools and drunken men are watched over by a particular Providence," said Seymour gruffly.

"But that guy is neither drunk nor a fool," assured Powers. "I have a kind of crawly feeling in the middle of my back that before he's finished with this outfit he's going to make us feel sorry for ourselves."

Seymour's ideas were too deeply ground into his soul to be shattered by any man. "Wait and see!"

Pinedo joined the group. "This Craig," he asked strangely. "Where he come from, eh? Where you get him?" There was a worried frown between his eyes. The eternal cigarette was hanging from his mouth. His hands were playing nervously with the strap of his goggles.

"I don't know and I don't give a damn," answered Seymour. "He may be a skyrocket to some of you guys, but he's just another swell-headed kaydet to me."

Powers was studying Pinedo's face. "Say, I meant to ask you something last night, Juan," he said. "I got the idea in the air. You remember when we heard that kind of a screech—while we were flying—just before Craig went out and knocked that Fokker flat. Well, I was looking at you—it seemed to bother you a lot more than it bothered the rest of us. I had the idea that maybe you recognized that sound. Did you? Where did it come from?"

Pinedo's eyes lifted to Powers' face. "I recognized it all right," he said grimly. "Many times I have heard that same sound. If you heard it one time you never forget. Also I know where it came from—it was closest to me. It came from Craig. I saw him. He sat up straight in his scat—quick like—he look over the top of his motor—at the horizon—remember we had black mists ahead of us.

And he open his mouth—and give that cry—" He stopped quickly. There was a pallor crawling under the olive of his skin. His black eyes were like liquid pools of jet.

"Craig, eh?" said Powers musingly. "You know, I had the same idea—but I didn't see him yell—I only heard it. Listen—you must be crazy—we all must be crazy. No man could let out a screech like that and make it heard over those motors."

Pinedo shook his head gloomily. "Craig made that cry," he repeated. "And he made it sound over the motors —it would have sounded over everything. In my country, when the people who live in the mountains—and on the slopes of the mountains hear that sound, they cross themselves and say an Ave Maria—and they run inside their houses—and get out of the fields—"

"Say, what is this, a ghost story?" asked Powers with a nervous laugh. "You've got me having the jitters. What the hell is this sound, anyhow—"

"It is the scream of the condor," answered Pinedo. "You hear it in the mountains— where the condors fly— where they live—where they fight. Once I saw two of them fighting. As they went diving toward each other —with their wings closed—with their beaks wide open, ready to tear each other apart, both of them made that scream—it echoed from the peaks—seemed to split the sky. Then they were locked together, blood fell out of the skies—their talons were tearing at each other's breasts— they both fell, still locked together—both dead.

"In my country, when people hear that sound—they think of death—"

"Condor?" said Powers in the same nervous voice. "That's all right for you, you live in that country. But how about Craig, he's an American—what the hell does he know about condors?"

"I do not know," shrugged Pinedo. "Only I know that he gave the scream of the condor, just before he went down to attack that Fokker—and watching him go— watching him fly and attack and kill—it gave me the hor- rors—for that is the way condors fly and fight—their wings

beating the air—shifting, feinting, like black lightning—
striking, until they get into position for the kill. Then,
one stroke with those steel claws—one tear from a great,
hooked, steel beak—and death strikes whatever they
attack.

"Watching him—I had pictures of condors in my mind
—coming down from the air on top of the highest peaks—
striking at things walking on earth—"

"Aw nuts!" Seymour snapped. "Stop that stuff—you'll
have the whole gang dreaming about being birds and all
that bunk—get into those crates—get going—if this Craig
guy is a condor he'll have a chance to prove it this morning. I want to be out there where I can keep an eye on
him. No use letting him get himself bumped off, just on
account of a swell head and a superiority complex."

They piled into the ships and swung them away from
the line. But somehow they were nervous and on edge,
and hands shook a trifle as they handled the controls.

They had one glimpse of John Craig that morning.
They learned the rest of the saga from observers in the
front line who telephoned the tidings back to the field.
They were far to the east of Le Charmel, cruising about,
with Seymour scanning the horizon with anxious eyes.
Guilt was weighing down his soul. He had been a fool to
let Craig fly out alone. After all, he was the Flight Leader,
responsible to his superiors. He could have ordered Craig
into formation and forced him to fly in that formation.
He could have disciplined him—grounded him for a second disobedience of orders. He had been lax in his duty.
He was contributing to disaster—even death.

And then they sighted Craig. At first they had no idea
that it was Craig. It was merely a crazy man, flying a crazy
ship that wheeled and circled at such a tremendous
height it was almost invisible even with the unlimited
visibility of the morning. Swung about in wide, easy,
graceful banks and turns. No propeller churned in front
of its nose—no glistening sheen of light to mark the position of a propeller. Just the ship, alone, flying at a height
impossible to man who does not carry his own oxygen.

Riding the up-drafts—a Spad! It was simply impossible. No Spad could soar like that. No Spad could maintain altitude without its motor. They wiped hands over goggles and stared again.

But it was a Spad, and it was soaring. It hung over them like a shadow even after they had forced their own ships up as high as the motors would take them. Until they were breathing white hot molten metal with each breath, until their ears were singing and the cold cut through leather coats and turned lips blue and mottled the flesh; until hands and feet were like lumps of ice, and the Hissos were panting and heating with the labor of keeping the gray ships aloft.

The lone Spad was under no such burdens—it rode the currents, cunningly, cleverly—turning this way and that, to face into the ever-changing gusts, rising two hundred feet, banking with the grace of an eagle, catching a new gust, riding that until it again changed direction.

The fear within humans who penetrate to great heights was hammering within them. The earth seemed lost in the vastness of the universe. Whispering voices were telling them that they had lost the earth—that they could never return—they were like ghosts—doomed to wander in the midst of space for an eternity. There was a jagged impulse within them to push sticks against the firewall and to send the Spad plunging downward.

But the lone Spad soared, sustained by its own ecstasy.

Seymour led them down out of the heights. His teeth were chattering loudly. There was a trickle of blood running from the flange of his right nostril. His eyes were bloodshot. There was a roaring sound in his ears as the Flight lost altitude with a rush—the Spads seemed like leaden images—the motors were cut. They fell like meteors.

But the gray shape above them hung in its place and seemed to mock them as they sped toward the friendly earth.

None of them had ever carried a ship above fourteen thousand feet—not even Seymour. That morning the altimeters had registered eighteen thousand and had refused to move further. They had flown to the ceiling. They were suffering the consequences of such foolhardiness. But that lone Spad, soaring about! It had been a bait, a challenge, a dare. None of them were in doubt as to the identity of the pilot of that lone Spad. The same thought possessed them all—Craig.

They piled into a group of Hals directly north of Le Charmel. There was some kind of an artillery strafe on the ground. Behind the ruined town a tide of bursting shells searched every nook and cranny of the terrain. A drum fire that covered the earth with a shifting curtain of white. Evidently the Hals were trying to prevent Allied ships from interfering with the target practice of Jerry gunners. There was no sparring for position or advantage. The Hals attacked with no more formality than the pointing of blue-black noses for the gray wings.

In the midst of that clattering, rushing confusion, the pilots of B Flight lost the picture of John Craig and his soaring ship. They were hard pressed to hold their own. There were eight Hals in the group—a full echelon, and five Spads. Just enough to give the Jerries a free hand in dictating the nature of the argument. The blue-black torpedoes whipped through space, B.M.W.'s whining nastily. Fumes of burning powder mixed with the smell of raw gasoline and hot oil. Tracers flicked a dainty way against the blue of the sky and pinged through the taut surfacings of black winged and gray winged ships alike.

The Spads had maintained formation until Seymour knew that they were cramping themselves and offering too large a target for the Hals darting about them. He gave the "break up" signal. Then the combat became a wild welter of flashing wings and the ferocious barking of motors. A bedlam stabbed through by the chattering staccato of Vickers and Spads. Pilots turning and twisting in seats, kept close watch over the empennage for an enemy in a position to make a kill; or leaning forward, with foreheads almost touching the crash pads, eyes like slits of flesh over white coals, concentrated on a winged shape lined on the cross wires of a ring sight. Seymour cut the odds from seven to five in the first three minutes of that combat. He rode the tail of a blue torpedo, carried his ship to within fifty feet of its rudder, and cut in his guns. The pilot of the Hal, hearing the crackling of whiplashes about his head, and feeling the fuselage of his ship shuddering under the impact of slugs, cocked the dark wings straight up and attempted to power slip out of range.

But there was one instant when Seymour's guns were on direct line with the Hal's cockpit—and they were spitting flame and smoke at that instant. A tracer smacked viciously against a leather coat, broke into dull fragments of burning chemicals. The pilot of the Hal twisted and squirmed in his seat. Then the Hal, with top rudder released by a suddenly inert foot, fell away on one wing, motor still roaring, went plunging down out of the action.

After that the pace was too swift to follow. The gray Spads were raging like demons. They maneuvered with such speed that unless one counted the black wings and the gray it seemed that the Spads outnumbered the Hals. Gray ships slinging grimly to black targets—riding the targets down through three or four thousand feet of space. And in quick succession the rivet hammer banging of short bursts from Vickers muzzles.

There were two more Hals down before a Spad went limping out of the fight. Black oil poured from a broken oil line, smeared the body of the Spad. Seymour saw it pull out of the fight, hard pressed by an enemy. He whirled his ship around on one wing and dived after the enemy. He drove it away. The Spad, with a dead stick, glided shallowly toward friendly territory on the south side of the lines. Seymour hung over it until it was safe, then he converted the velocity of his dive into climb and went winging back up to the madhouse in the heights.

But there was nothing further for him to do. Four Hals were making a slow retreat. They retired sullenly, reluctantly, as if inviting B Flight to interfere with their

going. Far below, a fifth Hal was spinning into the barbed
wire between the lines. But B Flight had listened too
often to the counsel of Harry Seymour's experience.

"Never fight until you have to," Seymour had repeated
a hundred times. "Then you pick the spot where the
fighting is to be done—and tear in like hell."

So the pilots of B Flight, sat back and mopped goggles,
and watched the four Hals circle back toward the north.

That was when they caught the fleeting glimpse of
John Craig in action for the second time.

They heard the rising scream of a Hisso. It was a stri-
dent, soul twisting sound as it mounted over the droning
of their own motors. They seemed all moved by the same
set of nerves. Heads lifted, hands rested upon the controls, the direction of their own ships forgotten in the
midst of that screeching tornado that plunged out of the
heights. The red, white and blue circles on the Spad were
blurred streaks of color. They shuddered. No wings could
stand that plunge. There would be a rending sound, a
crumpled mass of linen bellying in the force of the slip
stream. Slivers of woodwork from ribs and beams gouging
through the linen—and then a fuselage hurtling earth-
ward.

No man could live in the midst of such speed. No man
could pull a Spad out of such a dive and escape.

But John Craig did. How he did it none of them knew.
They had a series of disconnected pictures of what hap-
pened. The gray meteor fell into the center of the four
Hals. They heard the faint, far off sound of Vickers, saw
angry red tongues of flame lashing from Craig's guns.
Saw the Spad twist its wings this way and that. So close
to the blue black shapes that at times it seemed that the
Spad was rolling its wheels on the wings of the Hals.

The instant after that gray thunderbolt struck for the
first time there were two of the Cross-marked ships flut-
tering weakly, making frantic attempts to stay aloft, to
recover from a shock which seemed to have numbed
them; left them helpless and nerveless.

And the Spad had lunged upward, its wings spread

stiffly, its nose tilted toward the arc of the heavens, while its guns raked the bellies of the two remaining Hals attempting to escape the terrible onslaught. One of them did escape. It dived for the earth under full gun and never leveled until it was hedgehopping over the trees, flying like a frightened shadow, hugging the earth.

But the other three—they were down. One, with its belly gutted by tracers and steel, turned over on its back and burned. The other two went squashing down into the space between the lines.

The Spad, seeming to lose none of its speed, whirled into the south and disappeared over the horizon line. It was in a canvas hanger with a mechanic administering to it when B Flight taxied up to the line. All of them walked toward Craig's ship and examined wires and fittings with unbelieving eyes and hands. They felt that some hoax was being played upon them. They had expected to see that Craig's ship was out of rig, that it had a twisted fuselage—but it exhibited nothing of the sort. It was as trim and fit as it had been before Craig had taken it off the field earlier in the morning.

The telephone was ringing when Seymour entered the operations tent. He did not talk. Now and then he gave a grunt of understanding. He wrote words on a pad of paper upon the desk as he listened.

"Spad 2673, identified as belonging to the 5th Squadron, 2nd Pursuit Group," chanted the voice. "Directly over the Bois de Grimpettes. Attacked and forced down a Pfalz two-seater. Killed the observer and wounded the pilot. Plane washed out in landing. Eight minutes later, at St. Gillis, same Spad attacked a D-VII flying a solo patrol. Dived on it from a thousand feet above. Fired one short burst. The D-VII burst into flames and fell half a kilometre west of St. Gilles. Spad 2673 then circled and gained altitude. It encountered a group of D-VIII Albatross monoplanes flying at a high altitude. Observers counted six in the enemy group. Pilot of Spad 2673 attacked the group. Shot down one Albatross and forced remainder of high flying patrol to turn back toward the

enemy lines. After which Spad 2673 continued climbing
until lost to view of observers. This information will be
contained in the official order of the army for tomorrow.
For this purpose the Commanding General, Third Division, A. E. F., directs that the Commanding Officer of
the 5th Squadron supply him with the name and rank of
the pilot who flew Spad 2673."

"This is Harry Seymour talking," said Seymour in a
queer voice. "Leader of B Flight, 5th Squadron. The
Skipper isn't here at this present moment, but I can give
you the man's name. Lieutenant John Craig, of this outfit. The number of his ship is correct. And, if it means
anything to you, you can add to that information the fact
that the same bird chucked himself into the middle of
four Hals about half an hour ago over Le Charmel, and
downed three of them, one a flamer, and the other two
total washouts—"

"Some bird!" chuckled the voice on the other end of
the wire. "What's the matter—he didn't get them all—
for that guy three out of four is only warming up for a
real scrap. No kidding, Harry, the Old Man is tickled
pink, and it looks like a nice little citation and a couple
of chest weights for the guy in question—Craig, you said
is his name?"

"Yeah, Craig," repeated Seymour in the same queer
voice.

"Well, if he lives long enough he should get himself a reputation. Where do you get hold of guys like
him? Draw him in a lottery—?"

But Seymour had replaced the receiver. He was staring out through the flap of the tent. For the first time in
his life he was without thought, without speech.

Again that night Craig did not make his appearance
in the mess hall.

"What are you doing, running a hotel business on the
side?" asked Seymour of the mess sergeant. "Got a cash
customer—or are you just spreading out and putting room
service on the list of accommodations?"

The mess-sergeant stared at him blankly. "I don't get you?" he said.

"Craig—the new pilot—where's he getting his chuck? He hasn't been at table for a single meal since he came here—what's the matter?"

The non-com shook his head. "I don't sabe it either," he said with a worried expression. "I twice went out to ask him if he wanted something to eat, but he just sat and stared at me—and didn't say a damned word. I don't get him at all, sir. Is he sick?"

"You mean to say that he hasn't had anything to eat?" exploded Seymour. He was conscious of the staring eyes of the other pilots on his face.

"Not unless he's being fed manna from heaven," said the mess-sergeant grimly.

"I got that kitchen under my finger tips. I can swear that nobody gets any handouts at the back door—and he hasn't been here—and I haven't fed him myself. So what's the answer?"

"Well, for Cripes sake!" whispered Seymour. There was no anger or sarcasm in his voice this time. There was only stunned surprise and utter consternation.

But that was only the beginning. It was nearly ten days before John Craig entered the mess hall of the 5th.

And his coming was a greater shock than his absence.

During those ten days B Flight on three separate occasions had heard that hoarse, nerve paralyzing scream break from his throat, and had watched him send his ship smashing at new enemies, rending them, tearing them, clawing them to bits with sharp, stinging bursts of lead and flame.

"Por Dios!" Pinedo had said over and over. "Por Dios!" With white spots showing under the olive of his flesh. He said nothing more, but his hands shook as he rolled his cigarettes, and there were times when he looked at Craig's face as one might look at an apparition.

Days when Craig did no flying at all but sat hunched under the brown canvas that sheltered him. Hunched, with his head seemingly resting upon his shoulders, his narrow lidded eyes moving sluggishly, as if he slept with his eyes open. Days when it seemed that he lived in the midst of dreams and visions—and saturated his soul with memories which no man could share. Days when he was gripped by a complete lethargy.

Sometimes queer, unjointed, guttural sounds passed his lips. Sounds that had no meaning, and were formed by the back of a harsh, hard throat. There were times when he made movements with his body that suggested some great bird preening its wings.

There was no mistake about it, no imagination, no hypnosis. John Craig was a man with the mannerisms of a creature of the upper spaces. His very presence among humans was incongruous—awkward. It was only when he arose upon wings of linen and wood that he entered his element. When he became a thing of poetic beauty and at the same time a thing of primitive savagery.

None of the men of the 5th knew it, but it all began on that day when Kark, who ruled over a wind-swept mass of great peaks and thin air, sat perched upon his pinnacle and looked down upon the mourning, huddled figure of his mate and the cadaver of his first-born.

CHAPTER III   KARK THE MIGHTY

Kark was magnificent. He had the posture and the regal bearing of a true king and ruler. Standing upon his talons, which were like flexible bars of steel, and which grew out of legs which were almost as thick as the legs of a man, his graceful body reared upward to a height of five feet two inches. He was a giant even among his own kind. He was almost as large as a man. His body, excepting for the tremendous breast which housed his inexhaustible lungs, was like the torso of a trained athlete.

His neck was thick and corded with heavy muscles. He was black, tinged with brown—like a statue of jet which has been splashed with iridescent copper. There was a line of white encircling his neck—pure white fluffy down which made vivid contrast with the darkness of his feathers and gave him the appearance of wearing a decoration about his shoulders.

His eyes were fierce and splashed with an ever-burning flame. His beak was six inches in length, with the lower mandible straight and the upper curved like a scimitar. Crowning his head was a blood-red comb.

His wings, folded about him, were like the mantle of a warrior, covering him as he sleeps. When those wings were extended in flight they stretched over a space of fifteen feet. There were times when Kark looked down at his shadow soaring over the faces of the rocks, and his heart glowed with pride, for among his kind, Kark was the greatest, and his wings were the mightiest. Wings capable of maintaining him at heights of eighteen thousand feet without movement. Exquisite things which circled and swooped and soared until they caused even Kark's heart to experience a delirious suffocation because of the sheer beauty of their passage through the heavens.

But there was no beauty in Kark's soul as he looked down upon the huddled, sorrowful figure of his mate. His talons clutched at the crag upon which he sat; held his weight like steel clamps driven into the living stone. Even in her sorrow she was magnificent as Kark—magnificent. There were times when Kark, swinging his great hulk upon his very pinnacle which hung fifteen feet over the shelf in the side of the cliff which they had taken for an abiding place, had paused to look down on her, a fierce gladness churning within himself stirring within him so hotly that his chest swelled and his great throat strained and sent his battle cry and challenge reverberating among the peaks—echoing up to heaven—floating down to the earth that was wrapped in the eternal mists. A battle cry that was given an added ferocity by the sound of his wings beating against his body and the rocks about him.

Kark was young and the zest of life coursed through his body. Less than a year ago he had arrived at his full heritage and an understanding of his terrific strength and size. Less than a year ago he had been a youth, floating above the menacing, snow-covered peaks of the high

Andes, alone, and in full possession of the ecstasy of existence. And then, suddenly he had become a male, and had known loneliness. The great loneliness of the far places—of limitless space. An unrest had seized him, an emptiness within his body that cried aloud for something he had never known. At first he had thought the emptiness to mean hunger but the emptiness was not hunger. He did not understand what it was until he had seen Sa who was of the family of the Lord of the Peaks—Old Kaw who had but one eye, and whose left leg was broken and twisted, and whose wings were flecked with white, which was the sign of great age.

There had been a single faltering motion in Kark's flight when he had first looked upon Sa. Something had exploded within his soul. He wheeled about the crag upon which she rested for endless hours, looking down at the sheen of her body and the proud carriage of her head, at the graceful lines of her chest. For the first time he wanted another creature to notice him. He wanted her to see how great his wings were and how rigidly he maintained flight, and with what delicacy his great body responded to the slightest breath of wind and went lifting to new heights.

Half a dozen times he had folded his wings and had fallen like a black meteorite, against the face of the cliff, passing within a foot of the point upon which she rested. Falling until his descent was like the passage of a projectile, and then checking himself abruptly by unfolding the tremendous wings and transforming the dive into forward speed—speed which caused him to appear like a black blur against the faint tracery of high flung clouds.

If she saw him she gave no sign. The red of the setting sun was changing to purple when she opened her wings and permitted her body to drop from her perch. She soared up to him, and hung in space a dozen feet from him. He circled with her for a moment, a fierce throbbing causing his wings to feel weak and incapable of sustaining his weight. Then they both floated down

into the fastnesses of the mountains, to where Old Kaw
ruled his family.

Perhaps it was his delight in her discovery that blunted
his senses. The first warning of attack sounded from over
his head. A black fury struck at him. Talons ripped at his
head. He folded his wings and dived. Down and down,
through countless thousands of feet of space, with Kark
desperate in the attempt to escape the death that was
diving with him.

Blood ran from half a dozen wounds on his body. He
whirled with frenzied beating of wings. Through the red
curtain hung before his eyes he saw that he was attacked
by Kaw. He struck with one of his great wings. A single
blow, as rapid as the head of a striking snake. He saw
Kaw recoil before the force of that blow. He struck with
the other wing. It smashed against Kaw's body. His talons
sank into Kaw's back—ripped at flesh. He wondered why
Kaw had not killed him—Kaw—who was the mighty warrior—who was Death in battle. And suddenly he understood that he struck harder than Kaw—that his body was
more powerful, and that his wings could smash against a
body with a stunning force.

A hot exultation swelled his soul. Kaw on the defen-
sive. He was not attacking now—merely trying to escape
further punishment.

And because he was the father of Sa—and a King—Kark
did not kill him. He merely spread his wings proudly and
soared upward into the gathering darkness.

CHAPTER IV THE WHITE, WINGLESS CONDOR

One day Kark's heart contracted sharply as he made a
landing upon his terrace. Contracted with a tinge of exquisite happiness. He stared at the person of his mate for
a long moment before he stepped toward her. There was
an attitude of expectancy about her, a half-shy, half-fierce
expectancy.

He moved forward slowly, his spurs ticking as he
walked. She was shielding something with her wings.

Then he saw. Then a knife of exquisite joy pierced his chest.

On the bare floor terrace were two white eggs. Pure white—large—side by side. They were still warm with the heat of her body. Kark stared down at them, lost in his admiration. She made soft sounds in her throat. He touched her with his wings—gently. But he did not dare to go near those white eggs. He walked about gingerly, like a man on his tiptoes, holding his breath, fearing to jar them or to disturb them, and after a moment, Sa covered them again with her body and looked up at him with soft eyes.

Days—endless stretches of time—seven weeks as men measure the age of the universe, and one day the white shell of the egg stirred strangely and cracked, and a taloned foot was thrust through the crack. A foot that became a leg, and then a body and a head, while Kark stood aloof and watched, a queer tightness within his chest.

A strange, white, almost naked thing, this offspring of his mighty strength and the warmth and mystery of Sa's body. A thing—gangling, helpless, blind. A thing that opened its mouth, and, with its first breath, raised the cry for food, and attacked voraciously the still warm meat which Sa dropped into its beak.

The second egg did not hatch. Something had gone wrong with it. For another day Sa warmed it and watched over it, and then she pushed it over the edge of the cliff and gave all of her attention to the living son.

So there were three of them on the terrace. And Kark hunted more fiercely than ever, for his first born was ravenous, and a sheep did not last them more than a single meal. Rabbits, young kids, fawns, full-grown does, calves—everything that was flesh, and fresh meat came up from the earth in the clutch of Kark's steel claws and disappeared down the throats of Sa and her white baby.

Kark wondered why his son was not the brilliant black and copper of his father, and why he could not lift his heavy body on wings and soar through space with him, so that the People might see the King and the Prince side by side, hanging in the heights. But Sa looked at him angrily when he attempted to urge the young Kark to fly, and she was abashed and filled with wonder.

Days—endless stretch of time—with the first born changing not one whit, excepting that he grew hungrier and hungrier, and his voice was stronger and more insistent.

Then one day Kark flew up from the earth below. There was a sheep clutched in his talons, its white fleece making vivid contrast with the black of Kark's body. Its blood dripped sluggishly from a dozen wounds and fell back to the earth from which it had been seized.

He sensed disaster when he was yet far distant from the castle of rocks. There was a queer scent in the air. His battle sense flamed—for it was the scent of Rurk, the jelly-bodied scavenger of dead things. He increased the speed of his climb and flight. He burst upon the terrace like a black thunder cloud. He saw Sa huddled, forlorn, grieving, her body pressing against the wall of rock, her eyes fixed upon a torn white thing that lay in the center of the terrace. A torn, pitiful thing, resting in a pool of its own blood. The sheep dropped unnoticed from Kark's talons. A sickness entered his soul.

It required a single glance—the heir to the House of Kark was dead. His body was still warm. The blood which stained the rock was still liquid. Dead—killed—torn by beak and talon—and Sa was weaving weakly upon her legs in the utter misery of her grief. Her eyes were closed and her head drooped. Her feathers seemed to have suddenly lost the gloss and luster.

And after a while Kark came to understand. She had left the terrace for an hour, to exercise her stiff wings. She had floated about in space and had returned for just a little while to the house of her father, Kaw. And upon her return—this—and the scent of Rurk.

But Kaw's vengeance was swifter than the vengeance of Kark. The old warrior had pounced upon the scavenger out of the heights, had struck him with his one good leg —had buried the steel claws of his talons in Rurk's back—

and had slowly and relentlessly shaken him—until he had torn a great mass of flesh from Rurk's spine—then he had released him, and, falling beside him, had struck his scarred and blunted beak into Rurk's heart, so that the scavenger fell a lifeless mass of lacerations, to become himself carrion upon the face of the distant earth.

But Kaw's vengeance did nothing to assuage the grief of his daughter, nor to fill the emptiness in Kark's heart. It could not give him back the dreams of his son flying with him—straight up, into the blazing pathway of glory —up above the clouds, where only the rulers of the Universe might penetrate.

Kark grew desperate. All his heavens and all his earth and all of his life itself were centered in the person of Sa —and all of those things were slipping away from him— being reduced to ashes day by day, while Sa shut herself up with her grief, and sat with drooping head looking out upon space.

It was a fledgling she needed to bring back the color of her plumage and to restore the beating of her heart. A little white thing—so tiny, so helpless—and Kark with all of his might, with all of his strength, was helpless to fill her needs.

But the days went by and Sa descended more deeply into her despondency. He searched the earth for choice morsels of food and mounted into the heavens with it so swiftly that it was still living when he placed it before her, but she would not eat and the sight of food seemed to sicken her.

And then one day, as he swooped low over the earth, flying with his blurring speed in his eagerness to be back in the heights, he saw a strange sight. He checked himself with his great wings and circled the spot. Several times before he had seen similar creatures. They were always fascinating. These were creatures that walked upon two legs, and rode upon beasts which were strange to Kark but which had four legs like the goats and other animals he knew. The two-legged creatures were never seen without the company of the four-legged beasts they bestrode and which carried them over the earth.

A strange sound came up to him. He cocked his head and listened. A thrill raced through him for an instant. A quivering weak little cry, like the dead son of Kark had uttered when he had lived. A hoarse, frightened cry—fright mixed with the hunger sound. The nerves in Kark's body went taut. His fiery eyes were fixed upon one of the two-legged creatures. The sound came from her. After a moment he saw and heard that the sound did not come from her mouth, but rather from something which she carried in her arms. He dropped lower and circled the spot.

Then his heart did leap. There was something white in her arms—something with a voice that was like the voice of Kark's son—the son for whom Sa mourned herself to death. And the voice of this little white thing called for food—and the two-legged she creature was not giving it food—merely holding it close to her breast as if to smother the cries.

A cunning came into Kark's brain and whispered to him. "It is a fledgling," said the whisper. "A fledgling in the arms of a two-legged she creature who knows nothing about fledglings. It is like the little Kark who is dead, and seeing it, and having it under her wings, Sa would be comforted and her heart would know peace. You are strong and mighty—yea—even the Ruler among your people, and here are these two-legged animals, who ride upon beasts, with a fledgling and Kark the Mighty has nothing but an empty castle—and the empty hearted body of his mate. Seeing this white fledgling, Sa would take it to her heart and the end of life would not come to her."

So he circled and circled, and the hot smells of burned flesh came up to him, and his eyes grew brilliant and his heart raced strangely. Circled until he saw that the she creature had placed the fledgling upon the soft grass so that she might handle strange shining things with the two short, ridiculous looking legs that grew out of her shoul-

ders—Kark experienced a sense of disgust. Two-legged
creatures who stood upright and yet had no wings. Creatures who were not like the animals and not like the
People of the Upper Spaces.

He listened to the cries of the fledgling and the blood
was pumping in his throat. He saw that it was wrapped
in something. Something white, like the soft, woolly pelt
of a sheep. He could see the fledgling moving within the
woolly covering and wondered why it should have two
skins. But he saw that the covering was loose and not connected with the body of the fledgling.

The whisper was in his brain again. "One instant," it
said. "It weighs no more than a few feathers—less than
the wind itself. You could grasp that soft covering with
your talons. The fledgling is hungry and cries for food,
and the two-legged fools do not know enough to feed
him. Sa would mother him and fill his belly—"

Then his wings were folding and he was dropping like
a black stone. Straight in the smoke of the fire. His heart
was bursting, his lungs sucking air in his excitement. He
screamed once—when he knew that he was successful,
that nothing could stop him from snatching the bundle
of fluff from off the green grass. Screamed, with the full
power of his throat, just before he lifted the bundle in
his talons and hurtled upward like a black shadow racing
across the descending sun. One scream. He heard that
scream echoed from the mouth of the she creature, a
scream of fright and of fear. He heard the hoarse voice of
the he creature. Out of the corner of his eye he saw a
hand of the he creature grasp the black branch in his
hand and lift it to his shoulder. There was a loud sound,
like thunder among the peaks. A flash of lightning leaped
from the end of the stick. Something hot struck Kark
across the back and caused him to waver for an instant
in his flight, but he tightened his grip upon the feather-
like bundle in his talons, and his wings beat the air until
he was rising upward with a breath-taking surge of
motion.

High above the earth his wings became stationary and

he soared, borne upward upon the gust which swept down through the peaks.

Up and up, into the biting cold of the upper spaces made frigid by the eternal snow. Up and up until there was only barren rock rearing into the blue of the sky. Barren rock—

And when the purple light was on the snow, and the sun had flown down behind the line of the mountains, and when the stillness of the dusk brooded over the world, Kark made a landing upon his terrace and stood before his mate.

He walked forward slowly, pushing the woolly bundle before him, making no sound. When it was close to Sa he stopped and waited for her to notice it. But her eyes were closed and her head rested beneath a wing. He saw that the flesh of the fledgling was purple, and that its eyes were closed, and that it was breathing in dry shallow bursts. And he grew afraid, for the flesh under the white down of his first born had been purple—as it stiffened in death.

And yet Sa remained motionless, her eyes closed, her body drooping.

Then a wailing cry from the young one cracked the stillness which hung like a blanket over the heights. A gasping, gurgling cry. It came so suddenly that Kark leaped backward a step in alarm and the white ruff about his neck stood up stiffly.

But the electric shock had coursed through Sa's body. Her head snapped from beneath her wings. Her dull eyes flashed for the first time in days. Her body straightened, and Kark holding his breath, moving the woolly bundle a little closer to her—and the hunger and fear of the young one echoed from the cliff.

Very slowly, Sa stepped from her perch and looked at the bundle which Kark had carried up from the earth. She examined it closely, while Kark, his heart hammering and his breathing stopped, watched her. Then she turned away from it. Ignored it completely, and returned to her perch. And Kark's heart was heavy, and for an instant he was so sick with his disappointment that he was on the verge of pushing the fledgling over the edge of the cliff. But the voice was whispering in his brain again: "She knows that it is not her own first born. But her heart is hungry and her love is great. Be patient, and she will take this young one to her heart—for the ways of the females are strange and the manner of their affections are beyond knowledge. Be patient—be patient—"

And so because the cry of cold was in the wail of the fledgling from earth, Kark covered it with his wings and warmed it with his body through the hours of the night until the sun again brought heat and life to the upper spaces.

And with the sun the young one stirred and his voice sounded again—and this time it was the hunger cry. Over and over, until Sa stirred nervously, and, leaving her perch, walked back and forth along the edge of the terrace.

Out of the corner of his eye Kark watched her, and his spirits rose and a song came into his heart, for he knew that the mother in Sa was stirring and would not be denied.

And after a long time, when the sun was hanging in the sky, and when the cries of the young man were constant, and urgent, Kark unfolded his wings from about its body and walked to the edge of the cliff. He hung there for a moment, poised for the leap into space —until he saw that Sa had covered the fledgling with her wings and was making soft sounds in her throat—and then he threw himself far out into space, and the delirious happiness rose up within him again.

In the green valley he killed a kid with a single sweep of his steel claws. Then he grasped his kill in his talons and rose swiftly. On the terrace he tore his kill to shreds and put tender chunks of warm meat down before Sa. And Sa, taking the meat in her beak, searched until she found the mouth of the fledgling. And the fledgling sucked noisily—sucked the blood from the meat, and its cries were stilled.

And Kark smiled within himself, for this young one was even more ridiculous than the other, for it had not as yet grown a beak, and its wings were unformed. But it was white, as the young Kark had been white—and it was hungry. Later, Sa, using her talons with delicate care, ripped the woolly covering from the body of the fledgling. The air was heavy with a strange scent—the scent of the two-legged creatures, and Kark felt the ruff rising upon his neck without knowing why it should rise.

Days—unending stretch of time—the sun and the darkness. And Kark roamed the earth and the upper spaces as he hunted for food in days past, and he brought his kills to Sa, and Sa fed the young one. And it grew, rapidly—more rapidly than the first Kark had grown, and its cries were lustier, and its body was filled with a strange strength—but it remained white—strangely white, and it grew no down, and no feathers covered it, and Kark marveled, for here was a miracle.

But as the time went on and on, and there was not the sign of a wing, not the sign of a feather, he wondered in his heart if he had injured the young one in seizing it from the earth, and if because of the injury it would never have wings, and would grow no feathers.

Of course he did not expect it to fly—not for a long time, for some of the young of his people do not fly for two years as men measure time, and none ever fly before a year. But Kark was impatient to have this son of his house take to the air and to wing through space with him, so that he might be taught the lore of a warrior, and know the secrets of the kill and the chase and the free, wild ecstasy of flight, of being borne aloft by the cold, clean gusts which clung to the peaks, and to float on great wings and to look down upon the soft, billowy clouds, tinted in brilliant colors by the sun.

But the young of the families about him took to the air, and other young were being born, and yet the white fledgling in the House of Kark developed no wings, and no feathers. It merely learned to walk about on its little legs, and Sa was fierce on the watch so that it might not

topple from the terrace and fall down to death. Time
after time, as Kark watched, and with infinite patience,
Sa reached out her wing when the young one ventured
too near to the edge, and pushed it out of danger. Now
and then she gave it a buffet and a quick note of warning.
And the young one would cry out in pain—but after a
time it no longer attempted to step off into space, but
stayed on the terrace, and played with the broken fragments of stone which had fallen from the cliffs, or clung
with its queer, wingless, funny little legs which grew from
its shoulders, to Sa's neck and caressed the feathers which
grew upon Sa's back, and spoke to her in soft gutturals.

But Kark's heart was hungry. This strange foster son,
who had no wings and would never know the joy of flight
—who would never mount with his father into the blue
of the sky—this poor, unfortunate fledgling who was
doomed to cling to the terrace of Kark's abiding place!
And Kark's heart was filled with a great pity and a great
affection, and he was gentle with the young one and
killed only the youngest of kids to feed it.

Until one day he had a great inspiration. The white,
featherless fledgling could fly! Were not the wings of
Kark the greatest among his people? Was not his strength
greater than the strength of any two warriors? Was not
his body bigger and heavier? Well then, Kark would give
this poor little fledgling wings—he would make it possible
for him to know the happiness of wheeling aloft, hour
after hour and looking down upon the poor earth creatures who could not fly.

His heart was pumping madly at the pleasure the inspiration gave to him. He would lift him, careful not to
gouge him with the cruel talons. He would hold him carefully so that he would not tear the soft flesh of the young
one. He would carry him up into the skies—up into the
unspoiled light of the sun—where nothing could live but
Kark the Mighty. And the son of Kark would fly on the
wings of his father.

But Sa attacked him strongly when he attempted to
take hold of the young one with his talons. She threw

herself at the breast of her mate screaming loudly and striking furious blows with her beak, while Kark patiently defended himself from her anger and her fears, until he could explain that he meant the youngster no harm and that he wished to give the boy flight. And even then Sa was dubious and nervous and watched with anxious eyes as Kark lifted the white fledgling cautiously and beat with his wings to lift him from the terrace.

It was awkward taking off with the precious burden, but once Kark was clear of the ledge he rose swiftly, the soft body held firmly, and Sa, clucking fear sounds in her throat followed after them and flew wing to wing with Kark, hovering nervously all the while Kark soared over the peaks.

And the young one made pleasure sounds in his throat and gurgled and clutched at Kark's steel hard legs with his hands.

Kark's chest swelled with pride when he returned to the abiding place and touched the white fledgling to the stone terrace. There were blue welts on the young one's body where Kark's talons had gripped him, but he wailed lustily and gestured toward the top of the world with his two queer legs which grew out of his shoulders. And Kark knew satisfaction, for this foster son was a creature of the upper air and yearned for flight.

Days—unending stretch of time.

The son of Kark became a warrior who needed no wings to wage warfare. They were a terrible team, Kark and his son, for if there was punishment to be meted out, or vengeance to be taken, Kark lifted his son and carried him through space and landed him upon the terrace of the enemy or recalcitrant. And the sun-blackened son of Kark, with his mighty muscles moving under his flesh, fell upon the family which had incurred the displeasure or hatred of his father, and destroyed them or defeated them utterly. For even the strongest of the warriors among the People of the Sky were helpless before the strength of the son of Kark.

And from his father, through those years, the son of

Kark knew all of the secrets and cunning tricks of flight. Wings he had none, but he flew with the wings of his father and became a part of the body of his father while in flight—and he might have been the equal of his father in cunning and strategy if he had had wings of his own.

But in his heart, even though he was a mighty warrior and a killer among his own people, the son of Kark was ashamed of himself, for he knew that he was a poor, crippled thing who could never rise upon his own wings, and that even the weakest of the fledglings which tottered about through the air was more blessed than the son of Kark.

The son of Kark grieved, for he could not fly, except upon the wings of his father.

CHAPTER V

THE SON OF KARK RETURNS TO THE HEAVENS

But of course none of the men of the 5th knew that the man who was listed as John Craig and was one of their number was the son of Kark. They knew nothing of the struggle which had gone on in John Craig's soul after he had been taken down from the heights of the distant Andes, and like a captive led back into the reaches of civilization. Neither did they know of the infinite patience and kindliness of another John Craig who had been the leader of the expedition which had gone into the Andes country, and who had been the strange two-legged creature whose thunder and lightning from a black stick had struck Kark and Sa and done them to death.

This older John Craig who was a famed scientist and explorer, had given the son of Kark his name—the name by which he was to be known among men, and had slowly transformed him from a wild, fighting animal, into something which resembled a youth born of humans and who has lived among human environment.

But after ten years the elder John Craig had shaken his nead and sighed deeply. For he knew that no amount of "civilization" would ever completely "tame" the son of Kark, and that men had nothing to offer him for the purpose of obliterating completely the memory of the Condors and of the free wild life above the clouds and above the snow-capped peaks of the spires of creation. In his heart the elder John Craig, who had brought the screaming, frenzied son of Kark down from the mountains, who had torn him from the dead bodies of his foster parents whom he, the older John Craig, had been forced to kill, knew a sorrow and a great doubt.

There were times when the elder John Craig considered that he had committed a great wrong. It would have been better to have left the son of Kark to his condor parents and the vastnesses of space. He knew in his heart that so long as the son of Kark should live, the memory of those days when he had been borne aloft on great wings, would rise up within him, and burn his soul and cause him to cry out at the shackles of mere human existence.

Neither did the 5th know that John Craig, as they knew him, had been completely lost to civilization during the first months of the great war. He was lost in that minute when his eyes had first beheld an airplane in flight. He had stood spellbound, breathless, his eyes glittered, his heart hammering, his soul suffocated with the magnitude of his discovery.

Wings! Flight! Glory! Freedom! That poor, almost helpless airplane meant all of those things to the boy who had ridden the heights with his mighty foster father. He smiled contemptuously at the gyrations of the poor airplanes and thought of the graceful maneuvers and blinding speed of Kark his father, but it was the key to freedom. Wings—for the white fledgling who had never been able to fly alone.

The fact that the wings were meant to use in combat meant nothing to him. For combat was a part of life, an element of existence.

There was a day when he disappeared from the home of John Craig, the elder, and appeared upon the field where the United States was training pilots for service abroad. When John Craig discovered the whereabouts of the son of Kark, he was troubled, and his dreams were filled with visions in which a black-plumaged devil with the face of a human slashed and roared through the heavens, striking with great, steel-shot talons, and taking vengeance upon all human kind for the murder of Kark and Sa, and for the years of his captivity and confinement. John Craig, who had been the ruler of the terrace which was Kark's abiding place, who was a university student, and who walked, talked and pretended at being a polished gentleman of the human world, found wings! And John Craig who was responsible for all this, trembled.

But the men of the 5th knew nothing of this. They only knew that this John Craig who flew and fought with the cunning and the skill and ferocity of an eagle, had a sun-blackened face and black, piercing, dangerous looking eyes, and that he wanted the companionship of no man. They knew that after a long period he had submitted to the association of their company and had sometimes taken meals with them at the mess table. And they knew a sense of shock and almost disgust, for in moments when he was not on guard against his impulses, John Craig snatched at the food before him with his hands and crammed it into his mouth like a starving man—all the while he glared about him as if daring any of those present to interfere with his eating.

And Pinedo—he would hardly look John Craig in the eyes, and it was easy to see that he was afraid of him, not physically, nor superstitiously, but afraid because a whisper in his soul bade him be afraid. The same sensation that was the motive behind his countrymen running into their houses and bolting the doors when the scream of the condor and the beating of black wings came down from the heights.

And so, John Craig, who was the son of Kark, rode the spaces above the earth in man-made wings, and for talons had the dead black bulks of his machine-guns. And he struck dismay and confusion among his enemies, until at last groups of them banded together to kill him, but he laughed that wild and reckless laugh, and went out to meet them, as Kark had gone out in his arrogance and pride to battle with the youths of the sky people who dared to dispute his rule, and his fame increased and the lists of his victories grew and grew until the 5th Squadron believed they lived in the presence of a dream which was filled with impossible happenings.

The division general came to see him and brought him a glittering bauble in a black case of Morocco leather. A glittering bauble strung upon a brilliant ribbon. John Craig had examined it casually and had handed it back to the general. There were stares of surprise—until John Craig understood that he was being honored and that the bauble was a materialization of the applause of a nation. Then he stuffed it negligently in his pocket, and never wore it upon his tunic. It was the same with a French general, and a Belgian, and an Italian, for the fame of John Craig had been bruited below the Alps. But he smiled at them, as a savant might have smiled at the antics of children. The decorations were meaningless.

And he continued to fly his wild course through the war-lit skies. And as he flew, the tension upon the field of the 5th increased until men were wound up inside like steel springs. They knew that in the code of John Craig there could never be defeat; that defeat to John Craig meant one thing—death. And they knew that no man could fly as he flew, without coming face to face with defeat sooner or later.

It was dark and there was no moon. High over the earth tiny points of light, the stars, twinkled and went out, or disappeared as flying masses of scud flew under them. And there had been the sound of motors from the heights. Far off and droning—enemy motors. John Craig had walked into the blackness hanging over the field and had turned his head up to the night skies. His keen nostrils sniffed the winds as if he scented the enemy, and his body quivered and his hands clutched into knots at his sides.

A telephone jangled in the operations tent, and Seymour barked into the transmitter.

"I know," he said angrily. "What are we supposed to do about it? We're not owls, you know, and you can't play hide and seek with a gang of Gothas surrounded by a crew of Fokkers. It's like trying to fly blindfolded. Pick the damned things up with the lights and give us half a crack at them and we'll do business for you, but for Cripes' sake give us half a chance—"

A tinny voice spoke words into Seymour's ear.

"I can't help it," snapped the leader of B Flight. "It doesn't help us to know that the tin ears have picked them up crossing the lines. They'll be miles away and traveling like bats out of hell before we can get started—and we can't hear what the tin ears hear, once we get going. Pick 'em up with the lights, or take pot shots at them with the a. a.—maybe you'll get lucky—" He put the receiver back on the phone.

"Damn fools," he muttered to himself. "Raising hell because we aren't going flying after a bunch of Gothas at midnight. What chance would we have? We'd do ourselves more damage than we'd do the Gothas—" He stopped abruptly, there was the sound of a motor bursting into a staccato beat from across the field. He shrieked toward the noise.

"Who's that?" he demanded. But no answering voice came back to him—merely the steady beat of the Hisso. He trotted across the field, in time to meet the blast of a slip stream as a gray shadow in the darkness ruddered away from the line and moved to the head of the field. He shrieked his question into the ears of John Craig's mechanic.

"Who's that?"

"Craig!" yelled the voice in his ears. "No helmet or goggles or nothing. Gas for an hour, and his chest full of ammunition. And with a funny little cold grin on his mouth—and his eyes—Cripes—you should have seen him. Came walking over here like a damned ghost—nearly made me bite my heart in two—and ordered his ship out."

There was a roar from the end of the field. The sound of

wheels moving rapidly over the sod. Then flight—with the gray shadow mounting into the upper darkness.

And Craig, who was the son of Kark, sat in the cockpit, his keen, narrowed eyes peering upward through the darkness of the night, dancing pictures before his eyes. Once he had walked through a town which had been bombed by Gothas. The buildings were shattered and ripped asunder. There was blood spattered on the sides of the bricks and windows. There were great gaps torn in the streets, and gutted horses lay starkly, with stiff legs thrust upward—bowels strewn over the blood-soaked cobblestones. And there were bodies—blasted and torn— where they had fallen, for there were none left to give them burial.

And somehow, as he looked at the blood-soaked ruin of death, a picture grew up in his mind of Kark and Sa, stiff and going cold, with the rocks about them slippery with the blood gushing from their chests. His face had gone white and his breath had whistled through his teeth —and he had turned his eyes toward the heavens—implacable, swirling eyes, and he had cursed the Gothas in his heart—black, lumbering cowardly things who fed upon such carrion as littered the streets about him.

So, as he flew off the field into the darkness, he was remembering Kark and Sa—and the death which had rained down out of the night upon the defenseless town—and he was searching for Gothas.

How he found them no one ever knew, for it was black as the interior of the caves of Souk in the skies. Perhaps his condor eyes penetrated that blackness or, perhaps, he made out the ruddy glow of exhaust from the B.M.W.'s in the Gothas—ruddy glowings like tiny fireflies in the midst of space. No matter. He rose until the winds of the upper spaces blew his thick black hair and stung his cheeks. He spent a long moment looking downward, studying something which had no existence for normal human eyes. Once he cocked his head and listened. Over the droning of the enemy motors he made out the sharper explosions of Hissos, and he smiled—a single movement of his mouth. The 5th was coming up. In spite of Seymour's grouching, in spite of the danger, the 5th was rising to the attack.

Suddenly he pushed the stick against the firewall. And the son of Kark, who had gained a score of victories over the humans who rose upon man-made wings, was falling like a gray meteor through space. The whine of the wires increased with the blare of the Hisso. The struts drummed a strange cadence, like the beating of war drums. The soul of John Craig was flooded with an intense ecstasy, and his hand gripped the controls, and his body crouched forward in the seat, and his eyes, like glowing points of flame, stared into the darkness over the nose of his ship.

Once he veered slightly to the left—two thousand feet after the beginning of that dive—and sharp bursts of flame spat from the unseen muzzles of his guns. Something black curled up like a punctured balloon and burst into flame. The glare illuminated the white face of a human, framed by a black helmet. It called a white Maltese cross out of the Stygian depths of the heavens. A white cross painted upon the dull green sides of a Fokker.

Again and again the Vickers mounted before Craig's face flamed venomously, and each time some target, lost in the darkness, or touched by the flickering glare of the burning ship, leaped as if stung by barbed whiplashes, or rolled as if felled by a club. White tracery of tracers darting through space.

It was not until he hung over the first of the Gothas that he discovered himself to be suddenly helpless. The great winged shape loomed before the nose of his Spad. Instinctively his thumb pressed against the trips, but no sound came from the deadly guns. He clawed at the breeches to clear the stoppage, but there was no time. The Gotha was as large as the whole of creation. There was a cluster of Fokkers diving at his tail.

If he fell there in the darkness the Gothas would go on. There would be another town, and other streets, and other stark bodies staring up at the sun with sightless eyes. Over the din of motors came the sound of the Hissos in the Spads of the 5th. They were climbing rapidly; they were ready to come smashing into the fight . . . but they could not see . . . if they could see, the Gotha would not unloose the flood of lightning and thunder from the heavens.

There was a picture of Sa and Kark before John Craig's eyes. Blood gushing from shattered chests.

And then, in the night skies, the shrill blood-curdling scream of the son of Kark rose over the sound of those racing motors—over the chattering of Spandaus, over the whining of wires and the drumming of struts.

In his seat, half standing, John Craig opened his mouth and closed his eyes, and his throat swelled until it seemed on the point of bursting asunder.

And then the nose of his Spad crashed through the center of a Gotha's fuselage. Crashed with the propeller cutting a terrible pathway through flesh and linen and light woods. With the Hisso still turning, with the gas churning in the carburetor—gas which suddenly became liquid flame and gushed over all of the Gotha, kindling it like a torch plunged into a barrel of explosives.

From out of the welter of destruction, the pilots of the 5th heard that screaming challenge and battle cry—then they saw the gray shadow go plunging into the heart of the great black shape. Flame leaped upward—columns of flame—roaring, dancing, billowing black smoke. The gray tail of the Spad sticking out of the heart of the flame. And the Gotha, with the Spad locked in an embrace of death, began a slow, weaving fall from the heights, Flying embers gushed up from the core of the flame and hung over the spot like a magnificent display of pyrotechnic—and then went cold and dead.

And the gray wolves of the 5th nosed in and out of the red shadows of that flaming beacon, and Vickers burst into frenzied hammerings—at great winged targets made plain in the red glare of Death. In and out, weaving and slashing, evading the attempts of the escorting

Fokkers to stop them—ripped the vitals out of the bombers with vicious bursts driven home at point blank range.

Below, falling in ever faster circles, the ball of flame, fanned by the winds of the heights.

The son of Kark, his talons sunk into the heart of his enemy, falling in death through the space which was his element, and according to the code of the people of the sky. And if Kark could have watched that descent, he would have smiled proudly, and his fierce scream would have sounded through the heights, and there would have been no sorrow in his heart, for such would have been his own end; and in so dying, this white foster son, who was a mighty warrior, proved himself a princeling and a fit scion of the House of Kark, Ruler of the Sky People.

Flickering shadows, and then a great umbrella of sparks as the burning wreckage struck the earth.

And somehow, the pilots of the 5th, as they flew down from the heights, wings scorched and drilled through by black dots, could hear from the wires and the struts, echoing cries such as they had heard from John Craig in life and in flight, and they flew over the glowing embers upon the ground.

It was the son of Kark the Mighty who had died.

And in a little village of France, two fledglings of the two-legged creatures the son of Kark had despised, walked hand in hand along the tree-shaded streets, and breathed of the sunshine and the soft air. Not knowing that upon the table within the pilot's cockpit of a Gotha, which had gone down in flame fifty miles to the north, was a map upon which a circle had been drawn about the name of that little village.

Walked along hand in hand, and stopped to look with wide eyes at the columns of troops which passed through the cobblestone streets of the little village . . . hand in hand, breathing the soft air and scarcely seeing the blue of the sky which stretched above them.

And on the field of the 5th, men labored over a mound dug into the earth, and placed about the mound a cross made of the fire-blackened remnants of a pursuit Spad. And upon the board which was the headstone of a grave they wrote:

JOHN CRAIG, LIEUTENANT
FIRST 5TH SQUADRON
SECOND PURSUIT GROUP
A. E. F.
R. I. P.

And in a far distant country, where the white heads of the mountains reared themselves up as if yearning to touch the blue vastness of the skies, great winged People of the Sky soared and floated in the upper spaces, and looked down upon earth with pity and scorn.

And if, as it is said, the soul escapes from the body when the body dies, the soul of John Craig, who was the son of Kark, escaped from the fire-swept wreckage of his Spad, and returned to the terrace in the side of the cliff which was the abiding place of Kark the Mighty—and became a soul at peace. And none of him was imprisoned in the earth which formed his grave upon the field of the 5th.

And his spirit returned to the upper spaces and sought the spirits of Kark and Sa, who was his mother.

FOREWORD to
The Man Who
Really Was... Tarzan

This article appeared in the March 1959 issue of
Man's Adventure magazine, Stanley Publications, Inc.,
New York. The accompanying blurb was: This incredible
but true saga of William Mildin who lived for 15
years as ape-man and jungle king!

As you will see, the writer claims that it was
William Mildin who was the basis for the Tarzan
stories by Edgar Rice Burroughs. The article aroused a
furore in the Burroughsphile circles. Was it authentic
or a hoax? My own conclusions are presented in
the Afterword.

The Man Who
Really Was... Tarzan

by THOMAS LLEWELLAN JONES

ID you ever grab hold of a treeborne rope, give yourself a mighty swing, drop down 20 or 30 feet away, right in front of where your kid sister was playing, pummel yourself on the chest, letting out a ululating howl to announce: "Me Tarzan, you Jane," an act of bravura which brought your mother on the run to restore a semblance of peace and quiet to the neighborhood?

You did? Good. So did I and a million other young 'uns in the past 30 years or so. And like countless other boys and young adults, we were 100% fans of Edgar Rice Burroughs' fabulous hero, Tarzan of the Apes. We followed him through innumerable adventures with his horde of friendly anthropoid apes, his indomitable sidekick, the elephant, and other assorted denizens of the jungle; he wreaked his fury on the endless chain of villains who were attempting to interfere with normal jungle fun and games.

Tarzan, as Mr. Burroughs portrayed him, was a young English nobleman, a certain Lord Greystoke, who was lost in the jungle as an infant and grew up among the apes. As he appeared in print, there was no doubt in anyone's mind that he was a fictional character—a literary invention—pure and simple.

There never was a Lord "Greystoke." That particular name was made up; pulled right out of the air.

But the actual character, the person on whom the en-

217

tire series was based, did live. There really was a man,
an English nobleman, who, shipwrecked on the jungle
coast of Africa, was cared for by the apes, grew up with
them and eventually survived a thousand adventures before returning to London to assume his rightful title and
position. The man was William Charles Mildin, 14th
Earl of Streatham. For 15 years, between 1868 and 1883,
his life was the prototype of Tarzan.

Although many of the details were unknown at the
time, the broad outlines of his story were fully known to
the public. The London *Times* published several articles
on the noble Earl. And more romanticized versions of
his adventures appeared in several of the English illus-
trated papers and magazines of the late 19th century.

Edgar Rice Burroughs had ample opportunity to study
these stories before creating his own character. And the
similarities between Lord Streatham's sojourn in Africa
and Tarzan's are too many to be merely coincidental. All
this came to light rather recently. For the existence of a
50-year-old story in the files of old newspapers was not
even noticed when the first Tarzan novels appeared.

It wasn't until late 1957, some 74 years after the event,
that the spotlight was first thrown on the entire affair. It
came about almost accidentally. And since that time, the
family solicitors of the Mildins have made every effort
to hush the story up.

There was no hint of the unusual when Lord Edwin
George Mildin, the 15th Earl, died in September 1937.
His Lordship had no heirs and so it was not considered
surprising when the huge family estate was bequeathed
largely to charity.

There was a proviso in the testament requiring that all
family papers be kept secret, under lock and key, 20 years
following the Earl's death. But that was normal too.
Many people prefer to keep details of family history quiet
until all living participants have passed away. It avoids
a lot of unpleasantness.

To a solicitor, the commands of a client are ironclad.
And so, right after the Earl of Streatham had died, a

formal notice appeared among the day's legal advertisements, advising all interested parties that the papers of the Mildin family would be unsealed.

The ad attracted the scant attention that usually follows any legal notice. For at the appointed hour, there were present in the offices—Mr Edmund Bennet, the solicitor who handled the case, and two clerks of his office. No one else showed up.

The boxes and chests containing the memorabilia lay on a broad table. At precisely 11 A.M., Mr. Bennet picked up the certified copy of the will, read the applicable paragraph, asked formally it there were any objections to carrying out the proviso. Naturally, since no outsider was present, there were none. Forthwith, the seals were broken and the boxes opened.

Most of the material was typical of that collected by old English families. There were account books and records dating back to the time of Henry the VIIIth. Stacked neatly in their containers were yellowing, crumbling, letters from kings, queens, dukes and earls.

"The old boy had some very distant relatives," one of the partners shrugged. "We might as well ask them if they want this stuff—if not, we'll just turn it all over to some museum. There's really nothing startling here. . . ."

The office staff began packing all the papers back into the boxes when one of the clerks, who had been rummaging through a brassbound chest, let out a sudden whoop of amazement.

"Good Lord!" the clerk exclaimed. "Look at this!"

He thrust forward a thick packet of papers that looked as though they made up a manuscript of some sort. Hand-printed neatly on the cover-page was the following:

"An account of the incredible adventures of Lord William Charles Mildin, the 14th Earl of Streatham, who lived for nearly 15 years among the apes and animals of the African jungle."

Astounded, the law clerks took the manuscript and began reading through it. They were still at the job more than three hours later—for the manuscript consisted of more than 1,500 pages of fine, tiny-charactered hand-writing.

"By God!" Henry Randolph, the senior partner of the firm, muttered. "I remember now—there was some story about Lord Edwin's father. I heard something strange and weird—years ago—when I was only a child. . . ."

The story that then unfolded was odder than odd—stranger than strange—and proved once again that truth can often put fiction to shame.

"I was only eleven," wrote Lord Mildin, the father of the Earl of Streatham who died in 1937, "when, in a boyish fit of anger and pique, I ran away from home and made my way to Bristol. There, using an assumed name, I sought and obtained a berth as cabin boy aboard the four-masted sailing vessel, *Antilla*, bound for India and the Orient via African ports-of-call and the Cape of Good Hope. . . ."

Lord William described the voyage from England and down the African Coast in great and meticulous detail. Then, he told of a violent storm which caught the *Antilla* in the Gulf of Guinea—a storm which, raging for over 72 hours, wrecked the vessel.

"When the wind subsided, I discovered, I was the only survivor. I was alone in the gulf water clinging to a piece of wreckage. Fortunately I was being borne toward shore—"

At this point, Bennet sent for old shipping records. Yes, the account checked through—at least that far. The four-masted sailing vessel *Antilla* had, indeed, sailed from Bristol, England, in 1868—and, according to Lloyd's *Register*, was lost, "with all hands" off the African coast in October 1868!

The document the solicitors held in their hands then told of how young William Mildin was washed ashore at a point probably about midway between what is now Pointe-Noire and Libreville in French Equatorial Africa.

The area was largely uninhabited when the child cast-away dragged himself upon the beach. The thick, interlaced jungle came down to within 30 yards of the water's edge—and the boy lay there on the sand, exhausted and terrified.

"I dared not search for natives, for I had always heard that they were savages—headhunters and cannibals," he wrote. "Instead, I waited until I had regained some strength and went directly into the jungle in the hopes of there finding food and water—"

It was on his very first foray into the jungle that William stumbled upon a colony of apes. Evidently the primates had never seen a white human before. Instead of running from him, they drew closer, chattering excitedly and with great interest.

"For some strange reason, I was not afraid of these strange creatures," he goes on. "They were hideous to look upon, but nonetheless seemed gentle and harmless."

Their initial surprise subsiding, the apes offered the castaway nuts, grubs and roots to eat, thrusting the food at him with their long grotesque arms and hands. Starved, the youngster smiled gratefully, took the food and ate it.

"I was terribly ill afterwards and the apes appeared to understand this. One ancient female hunched her way over to me and cradled me in her arms."

Lord William was, in fact, "adopted" by the apes. After he had recovered from his immersion, they led him to a clearing where they lived.

"I was unusually strong and agile for my age," he wrote. "Without too much difficulty, I gathered branches and saplings and managed to make myself a crude treehouse—"

He also obtained a knife, spear and bow and arrows by raiding a native village about two or three miles inland. The possession of these crude weapons made him feel more safe and secure, he declares. And, credibly enough, they also served to give him new stature and even power among the apes. With these weapons he obtained food of his own choice, hunting by moonlight.

The boy never gave up hope of rescue. He went often

to the beach and scanned the horizon for passing ships. He did this for nearly eight months, by his own reckon ing, without result.

Then in 1869, as can be verified by checking detailed histories of Africa (that of Edwin Pearsall and Marion Donamy for one), the tribes of Western French Equatorial Africa began a three-year-long, savage war of annihilation against each other. The jungle swarmed with bloodhungry groups of warring natives.

"My ape 'friends' and I were forced to remain fugitives during the entire time," he writes. "I knew that I did not dare show myself in the jungle whenever any of the rampaging blacks were nearby. They would have killed me instantly."

He stayed with the apes. They accepted him and allowed him to live among them. No, William Midlin did not "learn the language of the apes"—as did the fictional Tarzan several decades later in the books of Edgar Rice Burroughs. He did, however, manage to establish a primitive form of communication with the animals.

"After a time, I did pick up a number of basic, guttural sounds which meant specific things to the great beasts. There was even one sound that I eventually learned was a call or signal especially for me. It can hardly be rendered in English, but the nearest rendition would be: 'Okhugh.' This was my signal—or, if you prefer, my 'name' among the apes."

The great apes marvelled at the way their human ward hunted, that he ate meat—and above all that he could build fires. These apparently supernatural, flickering blazes they feared greatly at first, but then accepted and finally began to enjoy for their warmth.

"I built the fires with flint and steel I had stolen from a native village," Lord William admits. "The brutes came to look upon me, not as a leader—for I could not match their feats of strength and endurance—but as a sort of mute but well-intentioned and helpful counsellor. I found new and easy ways to root under rotten logs for grubs and could dig for roots more easily with a sharp-tipped stick than they could with their anthropoid hands.

"When one of their number was injured—accidentally or in a quarrel, of which the apes had many—I would wash the wound and do what I could to ease the pain, using cool moss or some wet mud. The beasts were numbly, almost pathetically grateful for these services and would make happy sounds, point to me and dance up and down in approving joy. . . ."

Bright, resourceful, industrious, William Mildin learned to make his own bows and arrows. Living in the open, with senses made keen by the purity of this natural life, he was able to pick up the faintest animal spoor and track his prey for miles through the jungle.

When the internecine conflict among the blacks finally subsided in 1872, he was almost 15, a lean, muscular youth who dressed himself in animal skins and roamed through the jungle as confidently as if he were strolling through Piccadilly.

"It was then that I entered a period during which I gave up all hope of rescue," he relates. "I resigned myself to remaining in Africa. I had no way of knowing how or where I could go to make contact with whites. I was aware of the enormous size of the African continent and the vast distances involved. Truth to tell, I even exaggerated the distances in my own mind so that I probably tripled or quadrupled them. . . ."

In 1874, he encountered his first human being face-to-face in more than six years. He approached a native village with the intention of raiding it, but was surprised in the act by a group of warriors.

"To my astonishment, they were friendly and made me welcome," Lord William wrote. "I stayed with them for that day and then went back to the jungle laden with gifts. I returned to the village about a month later and remained there for nearly five years."

The story he tells is astonishing. He remained with the blacks and lived as one of them, marrying, as was the custom of the tribe, five of their women and begetting children by four of them.

"To my sorrow, the headman, N'dunda, informed me that my barren wife would have to be killed by the elders of the tribe, in accordance with the time-honored tradition of their people," Lord William reveals.

The woman, he says, was speared to death as penalty for her sterility in a wild, ritual murder.

"In the meantime, while I lived with the tribe, I often visited with the apes who had saved my life and befriended me. They often came close to the village and announced their presence by calling and bellowing. As soon as I knew the language of my adopted tribe well enough, I told the elders the entire story. They saw some supernatural significance in it and decreed that henceforth no member of the tribe could kill an ape, save in self-defense."

In 1880, 12 years after the shipwreck, another internecine war began between the native tribes. Williams fought with "his" people and his nimble, European brain invented tactics which enabled them to score decisive victories against their enemies.

"I taught them how to make quiet, surprise attacks instead of rushing through the undergrowth announcing their onslaught by shouting and screaming," he states. "I showed them how to feint and make diversionary attacks. . . ."

He tired of the fighting, however. While accompanying the tribal warriors on a campaign several score miles to the north of the village, he decided to desert them. Soon thereafter, he made his way alone to a point some 250 miles further northeast.

There he encountered a tribe which spoke a dialect somewhat similar to the one he had already learned. Inquiring if these natives had seen any other whites and receiving a negative reply, he decided to stay with them.

"It was a repetition of my former experience. This tribe, the Lunugalas, was even friendlier and more hospitable than the first one. I 'married' again—but this time I had only two wives, both handsome, strapping young virgins with coffee-colored skins and high, firm breasts. In a year, both were pregnant."

It was in 1884 that he finally learned of a trading post operated by white men in the Chari River, which feeds into Lake Chad.

"Hearing that there were whites in the vicinity, I did not wait one moment more than necessary. I left my wives and children and struck off toward the North. After a 22-day march, I finally reached the trading post, which was located 50 miles south of Fort Lamy."

To his amazement, William discovered on arriving there that he could hardly remember any English! The trading post was manned by Frenchmen, who stared increduously at the apparently tongue-tied, stammering young man who seemed to know no language of his own and whose skin was burned to a deep cocoa-brown.

Eventually, he managed to make himself understood after a fashion. After three months of delay, he was returned to British control in the coastal Anglo-Egyptian Sudan, from whence he took passage to England. That, however, was in 1885—the year that several thousand whites and General Gordon were massacred at Khartoum in the Sudan.

Lord Mildin's arrival in Great Britain and the amazing, confirmed stories that accompanied him, were buried under a mass of fervent, imperial patriotism. When a war is in progress, individual stories take a back seat. And it is suspected that the vast bulk of people paid no attention.

Some years later, when the popular magazines began to relate the tales, the very strict English laws of libel prevented them from too closely identifying the nobleman, or even mentioning the more bizarre details. It was only with his death, in 1919, that such restrictions were removed. By that time, nobody cared.

At any rate, Lord Mildin discovered on his return that his father had died some years before. In the interim he had succeeded to the title and family fortune.

Henry Randolph, Edmund Bennet's legal partner remembered the rest of the Mildin family story as he read the manuscript in his office in September 1957. Lord William had settled down on his ancestral estates, married a young girl of good—though untitled—family and had one son, Edwin George, born in 1889.

Lord William himself died in 1919. His son never married, living quite alone until his death in 1937.

Less than half a dozen people have had the opportunity of reading these diaries, including the two solicitors and the office staff. For a few weeks later, after consulting with the charitable organizations who were the Earl of Streatham's heirs, a solid wall of silence intervened between the office and the public.

So many new legal questions were involved as to threaten even the enormous size of the Mildin fortune.

For example, under British law, a significant portion of the Streatham property was entailed. That means that it must, of necessity, pass to the next direct male heir. If children existed, Earl Streatham had no right to will this property away, even to charity, because under the law it was not his.

In his own handwriting Lord William had admitted to marrying at least six native women. He had fathered several children by them. These children, and their offspring, might well and properly be considered his legitimate and legal heirs. Possibly one of them, rather than Lord Edwin, should be the recognized 15th Earl.

Publication and attestation of the diaries would be a direct invitation to one of the most exhaustive and expensive series of lawsuits in British history.

And so, there the matter lies. Independent inquiry to French authorities has unearthed confirmation of Lord William's story that he went to the trading post near Fort Lamy. French Army files for 1884 contain a report from the Fort Lamy commander to that effect.

French authorities in the area where Lord William Mildin was washed ashore also confirm the existence of a "white-man-who-lived-with-the-apes" legend there.

They also report many obviously part-white natives who could be Lord William's descendants.

Beyond that?

Well, there can no longer be any doubt that there was a Tarzan. But how Edgar Rice Burroughs heard of him —and whether or not he based his "Lord Greystoke" on the model of Lord William Mildin—well, that's a good question. Suppose you decide.

AFTERWORD

There are three ways of checking the authenticity of this article.

Write Lloyd's of London to determine if there was indeed an Antilla which sank off the coast of western Africa in 1868.

Check the London Times of 1885 for a story about Mildin's fifteen years in the jungles and his return.

Check Burke's Peerage under "Streatham."

As for the first, there was an Antilla which sank off the coast of French Equatorial Africa.

I haven't read the Times of 1885 because I haven't been able to get copies.

However, there never was an Earl of Streatham. Nor, as far as I can determine, was there any member of the nobility with the family name of Mildin. All one has to do is to refer to Burke's Extinct Peerage and Burke's Peerage.

But there is a Lord of Streatham. Baron Howland of Streatham, Surrey, is one of the lesser titles of the Duke of Bedford, whose family name is Russell. This would seem to indicate that the article is a hoax. Yet I have at hand a book titled Survivors, written by a Whitworth Russell and published by a private press, Rackham, in London in 1887. It contains an article entitled The Wreck of the Antilla; and it narrates the adventures of a William Hastings Russell, a distant relative of the Duke of Bedford. He had no title, being
228

a member of the landed gentry, though he was a descendant through the female line of the baronets of Strensham, the last one of whom died in 1705.

According to Whitworth Russell, his cousin, William Hastings Russell, was cast upon the shore of Gabon at a halfway point between Libreville and Point-Noire. This, by the way, would be in the same area in which the parents of "Lord Greystoke" were marooned and in which "Greystoke" was born. William Russell did live with a band of apes or at least claimed to have done so. Fifteen years later, after some adventures similar to those claimed for Mildin in this article, he appeared at a French trading post; but this was in Gabon, not on the Chari River which feeds into Lake Chad.

Whitworth Russell says that the Times did report briefly on the reappearance of William Russell. It also commented skeptically on his account of having lived with a band of apes. If Russell had been a long-lost peer, however, you can be sure that his story would have made a bigger splash than it did. William Russell disappeared three years later, presumably headed for South Africa. No one knows what happened to him after he boarded ship.

If Russell's story was true, what kind of apes did he associate with? Were they chimpanzees or gorillas? Or perhaps monkeys, since the Englishman of that day was careless about the distinction between the larger and the smaller primates?

We know now, from Goodall's and Schaller's accounts, that a human can establish fairly close relations with wild chimpanzees and gorillas. But this takes many months and vast patience and determination. No group of either type of ape would welcome a human at first sight and share its food with him. Monkeys, apparently, are just as shy.

Could the apes have been an unknown type, such as the agogwe which "Greystoke" speaks of in his memoirs and which have been described by Bernard

Heuvelmans in On the Track of Unknown Animals? *Or were they the n'k of "Greystoke," Burroughs' mangani, Paranthropoids or Australopithecoids? It doesn't seem likely that they were the latter, since Russell said that they had no language.*

Perhaps Russell made up the whole thing.

The question remains, where did Jones, the author of the article in Man's Adventure, *get material which is so strikingly similar to Russell's account? Did Jones come across a copy of the very rare* Survivors *and base his article on that? It seems probable. But then why did he modify a story that is striking enough as it is? Why give Russell a fictitious title and family name? Was it because he felt it necessary to gild the lily so that Russell's story would be much closer to that of "Greystoke's"?*

I don't know and may never know. Stanley Publications was long ago dissolved, and there is no chance of finding Jones unless he reads this book.

The Feral Human in Mythology and Fiction

A Brief Essay
BY PHILIP JOSÉ FARMER

VERY child learns at school the story of Romulus and Remus (at least, in my time he did). They were the twin sons of Rhea Silvia, the daughter of Numitor, king of Alba Longa, a city of ancient Italy. Numitor was deposed by his younger brother Amulius, who then forced Rhea Silvia to become vestal virgin. Numitor expected to keep Rhea Silvia from bearing children who would have claim to the throne, but Rhea Silvia fooled him. She bore twins whom she claimed were begotten by the god Mars. Amulius questioned both their paternity and their right to live. He had them set adrift in a boat or a trough of alderwood on the Tiber. Instead of dying of exposure, the twins drifted ashore at the site of the future Rome near the Ficus Ruminalis, a sacred fig tree. A she-wolf and a woodpecker adopted them and fed them until they were found by the herdsman Faustulus and his wife Acca Larentis.

Finally recognized as the grandson of Numitor, the twins slew Amulius, and Numitor became king again. The twins then founded the city of Rome. Romulus built a wall around the city and Remus jumped over it to show how contemptible it was. Romulus killed him for this and became the sole king of Rome. In his old age, Romulus disappeared during a storm. The Romans said that he had been changed into a god, whom they thereafter worshipped by the name of Quirinus.

Writers of the classical age rationalized that this story

evolved from a desire to explain the founding of Rome. Far from Rome being named after Romulus, Romulus was invented to explain the name of Rome. The wolf and the woodpecker were both sacred to Mars, which explains why the legend-makers chose them as the nurses of the twins. Moreover, Acca Larentia, according to Livy, had loose morals; and she may have been referred to as a *lupa*, which means both she-wolf and whore. And so on.

No doubt something like this is the truth. However, as Lucien Malson has shown, human infants have been suckled by wolves and some flourished and grew to a healthy adulthood.

Tales similar to that of Romulus' and Remus' feral childhood are common all over the world in folktale, legend, and myth. Stories of animals giving protection and food to lost, abandoned, or kidnapped children have appeared in such distant places as Ireland, Zanzibar, Brazil, China, Canada, Greece, Indonesia, India, and Ceylon.

Pindar recounts the Greek legend of Iamos who, abandoned by his mother Evadne, was fed honey by serpents. Ptolemy I or Soter, Pharaoh of Egypt, was raised by an eagle. (This is the literary precedent of George Bruce's *Scream of the Condor*, though Bruce may never have heard of the tale.) The Gros Ventre Indians (the Atsina of the Plains of North America) had a tale of a boy adopted by seven buffalo bulls. A medieval European story relates that a baby girl was placed in an egg shell and hatched by snakes. Alexander the Great decided to take her as a mistress, but Aristotle, suspicious of her, put her inside a ring of snake venom and she strangled on its fumes. A good thing, too, because her kisses were full of venom.

In Greco-Roman legends, Cycnus was fed by a swan; Hippothoos by a mare; Telephus, son of Hercules and Teuthras, by a deer; and in a Celtic tale, Lugaid MacCon is nourished by a dog. Since the names of each of these heroes is obviously derived from that of the creature which fed him, these tales are undoubtedly eponymous and based on totemic animals.

Cybele was fed by leopards, Atalanta by a she-bear, and the Tewa Indian deer-boy by a deer. Paris of Troy, abandoned as an infant, was suckled by a bear until found by some shepherds. Cyrus of ancient Persia was suckled by a cow. Goats nourished the infants Aegisthus, Aesculapius, Phylacides, and Philandrus. The baby Zeus was suckled by a goat, though Robert Graves claims that Amaltheia was, in the original form of the myth, a nymph (priestess) of a college associated with the goat totem.

These legends and myths come from very ancient times. They were probably popular for thousands of years in one form or another before they were written down. Preliterate man regarded animals as different species of human beings, or vice versa. He thought it a fact of Nature that beasts would be likely to adopt human children and that they should have speech as eloquent as his own.

Perhaps some of these tales were founded in reality. What can happen and has happened in modern times could just as easily have happened at the dawn of history.

The literary history of the feral theme is a surprisingly long and full one. Richard Lupoff, in his *Edgar Rice Burroughs: Master of Adventure*, describes a detailed and scholarly essay on this subject written by Professor Rudolph Altrocchi. Altrocchi was a professor of Italian at the University of California; his forty-five-page essay on feralism was included in his *Sleuthing the Stacks*, issued by the Harvard University Press in 1944. In this, Altrocchi refers to an essay on the history of feralism which appeared in 1603. He cites a twelfth-century Arabic story, *Hayy ibn Yaqzan*, in which a boy is raised by a deer. Altrocchi traces this work to a tale, *Salaman and Absal*, by the great Persian philosopher and physician, Avicenna (980-1037 A.D.). Altrocchi also notes a reference to feralism in Shakespeare's *The Winter's Tale*, Act II, Scene iii. The courtier Antigonus is required by King Leontes of Sicilia to take Queen Hermione's baby to some remote desert place and cast her to the crows. Leontes gives this cruel order because he believes his wife's baby is not his. Antigonus, a kind-hearted man, appeals to the animals to spare and to nourish her. (Part of this speech is quoted on the title page of this book.)

The baby, Perdita, is not adopted by the animals, though a bear does show up just as Antigonus places her on the seacoast of Bohemia. The bear chases and eats Antigonus. The baby is immediately found by a shepherd, who raises her as his daughter. Perdita, like so many foundlings (including Tarzan), eventually comes into her rightful inheritance and all ends happily.

It would be interesting to speculate the direction *The Winter's Tale* might have taken if Shakespeare had decided to portray a Perdita who had been raised by bears. He has given us the deepest of insights into humans raised by humans; what might this genius have done if he had probed into a mind which was half-infrahuman?

Altrocchi's essay demonstrates conclusively that man has always had an interest in feralism. It was, however, Rudyard Kipling who started the modern tradition of feral man stories, or at least gave it its main impetus and direction. In *The Jungle Book* (1894), he sparked off the flood of stories based on this theme. His hero, Mowgli, is an Asiatic Indian infant raised by wolves and tutored by Baloo, a honey-bear, and Bagheera, a black leopard.

This splendid and truly classical work makes no attempt to be realistic. It is as mythical in form as the tale of Romulus and Remus. Its beasts speak a common language; their societies, though simple, are even more rigidly regulated by custom than any human society. And Mowgli, like the Roman twins and Tarzan, eventually returns to human society and marries.

If Kipling is the spring from which the modern tales flowed, it is Edgar Rice Burroughs who provided the floodwaters further down the stream. A number of feral human stories owe their origin to Mowgli, but by far the greatest number have obviously been inspired by Tarzan. Many critics have claimed that the character of Tarzan was derived from Mowgli. Lupoff's study of Burroughs quotes a letter to Altrocchi (March 31, 1937) in which Burroughs says he himself has no clear memory of how he got the idea for Tarzan. He states that the story of Romulus and Remus may have been the main genesis. He also remembers vaguely reading a story about a shipwrecked sailor who had some hairy adventures with a band of apes on a South Pacific island. This was probably *Captured by the Apes*, Harry Prentice. Lupoff gives the date of publication as 1888 (the same year in which Tarzan was born). My copy gives the copyright year as 1892.

The truth is that Burroughs was purposely vague about the literary origins of Tarzan because there were none. Tarzan was based on a living person.

The fiction about feral humans can be put into three main categories. One type can be classified as pure fantasy for one reason or another. The second is in the category of realistic literature. The Tarzan novels are in neither and yet in both. They are founded on reality but contain many fantasy elements, such as talking monkeys and gorillas, animals which do not reside in the areas of Africa in which Burroughs has put them, genetic impossibilities, an incredible abundance of lost civilizations, a race of men eighteen inches high, and so on.

The third category is represented by a single short novel which is as yet unpublished in English and is almost unknown in Finland, where it originally appeared. This is *Karhun Tytär*.

I will ignore the many and varied short stories and comic books devoted to the theme of ferality. I will describe only modern novels, and I will not by any means cover the entire field.

The fantasy class can be broken down into two subgroups: the Mowgli-derived and the Tarzan-derived, though some contain elements of both.

Shasta of the Wolves by Olaf Baker is a Mowgli novel, as the reader knows.

Hathoo of the Elephants by Post Wheeler is an openly

Kiplingesque book. It takes place in India, Mowgli's locale; and its hero, Hathoo, is the son of an English noble. In this respect only, the novel is Tarzanic. Hathoo, or Charles Wilberforce Moncrief Armistead, is the infant grandson of Lord Bleyden. He is kidnapped by a tiger, Raj' Bagh, who turns him over to a herd of elephants. Though the tiger kidnaps goats to provide the baby with milk, many kinds of beasts have a hand (or paw) in raising him. In the end, Hathoo, like "Lord Greystoke," comes into his British inheritance. Post Wheeler was an elegant and poetic writer and a professional diplomat who knew and loved the jungles of India. He also believed that animals did speak some sort of language. I highly recommend this work.

In the second category, the Tarzanic, I recommend two novels by an Englishman, C. T. Stoneham. These are *The Lion's Way* and *Kaspa the Lion Man*. Stoneham was thoroughly acquainted with East Africa, loved lions, and writes in a realistic and convincing manner. The hero, Kaspa Starke, is half-Canadian, half-Danish. At the age of two or three, his parents were murdered in Africa. He wandered into the bushes, after having been hidden by an Arab servant, and was adopted by a lioness who had just lost her cubs. Stoneham maintains that an infant could be taken into a lion family and could survive to manhood. He makes a good case for his thesis in the novel.

Unfortunately, Kaspa, deprived of all contact with human beings for eighteen years or so, would have been linguistically retarded.

Lord of the Leopards by F. A. M. Webster is about Kungai, or Hector Barrabal, an English boy, son of John and Janet Barrabal, missionaries in the Belgian Congo. Hector's parents were slain by the Leopard-Men Society; the Oriental nurse of the twins, Hector and Lysander, flees into the jungle. She takes refuge in a cave but is scared off and flees with Lysander, leaving Hector behind. Hector is adopted by a leopardess who names him Kungai. Webster's book is not as well-written or as realistically detailed as Stoneham's novels, but it is dramatic and colorful. It lacks, however, the satirical picture of civilization which Stoneham paints, using Kaspa as the Outsider. Kungai also did not encounter human language during the critical period of growth and so would have been retarded.

Jan of the Jungle by Otis Adelbert Kline first appeared in Argosy magazine (1931). It starts with a credible premise. Jan Trevor, an American infant, is kidnapped by Doctor Bracken shortly after birth. The doctor is a psychopath who hates Jan's mother because she has rejected him. Bracken raises Jan in Florida in a large cage with an old female chimpanzee. Bracken teaches the child only two words, "Mother!" and "Kill!" and conditions him to attack a dummy fashioned to resemble Jan's mother. He plans to release the boy at a suitable moment so he can enjoy Georgia Trevor's realization, just before her death, that it is her own son who is her killer.

So far, so good. But in this story, the chimpanzees have a language and Kline adds even more fantastic elements as the story speeds along. I don't recommend this for the reality-bound or those who insist on psychological insights in their fiction.

On the same literary, or subliterary, level as *Jan of the Jungle* is *Ka-Zar, King of Fang and Claw*, by Bob Byrd. Ka-Zar, or David Rand, is raised by lions in the Belgian Congo.

Tam, Son of the Tiger, by Otis Adelbert Kline, combines the feral man theme with science fiction and is for adventure-story lovers only.

Giles Goat-Boy by John Barth is about a boy who has been raised by goats. There is not much of the feral man theme in this except as a foil to the science fiction setting. It is, however, recommended, since Barth is one of the best writers in America and the novel is as savagely satirical as *Gulliver's Travels*.

A novelette I recommend, despite its rough English translation, is *The Death of an Apeman* by Josef Nesvadba, a Czech author. Nesvadba uses a man raised by chimpanzees to mirror the hypocrisies of civilization.

His hero is a German nobleman who is cheated out of his inheritance by his brother. Eventually, he commits suicide. I would have liked to have included this funny-sad tale, but the rights to it were too entangled in red tape.

One of the most interesting, though not very credible, feral man stories is *Dolphin Boy* by Roy Meyers. Its hero has been exposed to radiation while a fetus and so has become a mutation. His respiratory system is similar to that of a seal's and his skin glands excrete an oily film when he is in water. An explosion throws him into a school of dolphins and he is adopted by a female who has lost her own pup. The dolphin boy eventually encounters civilization and finds that it lacks the love and honesty of dolphin society. The book is convincingly and realistically detailed, though the reader may have difficulty accepting the mutation of John Averill.

Incident at Hawk's Hill by Allan W. Eckert is a book I highly recommend. Though not a story of true feralism, it does show that there is a solid basis for such stories. This is a slightly fictionalized version of an event which occurred in 1870 on a farm near Winnipeg, Manitoba, Canada. Ben MacDonald, six-years-old, runs away from home, makes friends with a female badger, and lives with her in her burrow for two months. When he is found and brought home, the badger tracks him to his house and becomes his pet. Strangely enough, the boy's stay with the beast makes a lasting change in his behavior. Where he has previously been very shy and alarmingly untalkative, he now becomes outward going and communicative.

Orme Sackville's *The Jungle Goddess* is one of those rare stories about a feral female. Miota is a girl about eighteen years old who has lived in the African jungle since she was four or five. Apparently, her parents were explorers; she doesn't remember her father, but she does remember that her mother was killed by a lion. The mystery of her parents' identity, however, is never cleared up. She is more or less adopted by a pack of jackals. At least, they protect and feed her until she is able to fend for herself, and they maintain a loose connection with her thereafter. She is as ferally strong and as arboreal as Tarzan and talks with the monkeys. She has invented a unique weapon, a noose made of poisoned thorns. She falls in love with a member of a film company lost in the jungle, Garth Haversham; but when he leaves, she prefers to stay in the jungle. However, the implications are that Haversham will one day return and either live with her in the wilds or convince her to go with him to civilization.

The novel is adequately written, the story is nothing new, but Sackville does a realistic job of portraying an amoral feral girl. Her amoralism is, however, innocent and blameless. Deprived of human ethical guidance, she can only follow the dictates of her emotions. If she likes you, she'll help you; if she doesn't, she is likely to kill you.

The second main category, that which deals with the feral man in a rigorously realistic fashion, is represented solely by Eyton's *Jungle-Born*. Its protagonist is an Asiatic Indian infant whose peasant parents have been killed by a tiger. He is adopted by a monkey who has lost her own infant. The author calls him Nanga, meaning the Naked One, though this is only an auctorial label. Nanga and a native girl he meets go to live in the jungle and will apparently be happy together. However, the reader can draw his own conclusions about this. Since Nanga cannot communicate with Parmala except by signs and grunts, how is he going to keep her happy?

Some might doubt that it is realistic to suppose an infant could be raised by monkeys. Probably, very few would survive, but the record of authentic cases shows that some have lived through even more severe conditions. Also, the members of a monkey tribe take a tender and solicitous attitude toward the infants.

The final feral story to be described is in a class by itself. It could be classified as realistic, along with *Jungle-Born*, but it can't be said to have been influenced by Mowgli or Tarzan. It is also the only feral human story I know of which was written by a woman. This is *Karhun*

Tytär (translation: *The Bear's Daughter*) by Liisa Jalava.
A copy of this short novel was sent to me recently by a
friend who was touring Finland. He got his copy from a
Finnish friend who had inherited it from his grandfather.
I'd never heard of it, which isn't surprising, since it's
never been translated. It has no publication date, but the
preface by the authoress indicates that it was written in
1887. She was married, the mother of three children, and
forty-five years old. Apparently, it was her first and only
book. My friend's investigations revealed that the publisher had gone out of business about 1906.

My ability to read Finnish is far from fluent, but fre-
quent references to a Finnish-English dictionary have
enabled me to grasp its spirit.

Karhun Tytär should be translated into English and
published. It is a realistically and yet poetically told narrative, free of Victorian turgidity and moralism, sparing
of adjective. Eeva Kivi, the heroine, is five-years-old and
lives with her father, a trapper, and her stepmother in the
far north of Finland, near the Swedish border. She
escapes a cabin fire which kills her parents. After wandering around in the summer night, she meets a bear who
has lost her cubs. In a scene reminiscent of Ben's encounter with the female badger in *Incident at Hawk's Hill*, she
is accepted by the bear and lives with her until the she-
bear dies. The account of Eeva's physical and mental
survival is convincingly detailed and indicates that Mrs.
Jalava must have lived in the northern woods herself.
Eeva talks to herself, the bears, and a number of animals
with whom she becomes friends or at least establishes a
peaceful relationship.

Eeva's use of grammar stays throughout her childhood
and adolescence at the five-year level. But she adds to her
limited vocabulary by making up names for objects and
feelings as she first encounters them. These are based on
words she knew at the age of five or consist of nonsense
syllables which follow the Finnish pattern of morphology
and syntax. By this device, Mrs. Jalava enables her hero-

ine to pass successfully through the critical period of language development. Unlike the authentic feral humans studied, Eeva is not linguistically retarded. It's doubtful that Mrs. Jalava was aware of this critical stage in language learning. It was inspiration from her unconscious that let her hit upon this ingenious and necessary device. It is, however, possible that Jalava may have reasoned that a child cut off from human society for many years would forget her language unless she used herself as both speaker and auditor.

The words invented by Eeva caused me some trouble because they were not in the dictionary. When I caught on to what she was doing, I reread the portions I hadn't understood. Then I discovered that Jalava had clearly indicated the referents for the invented words.

Jalava's novel was ahead of its time in its portrayal of the psychology of the feral child and of the human female. Her frankness and unconventional observations must have shocked her Victorian Lutheran contemporaries, though a modern reader would find her unoffensive. She also seems to have been well acquainted with Laplander culture. Her heroine falls in love with a Lapland hunter but is unable to adjust to his culture. Pregnant, she flees back into the dark forest.

The modern novels I've described have heroes or heroines whose foster parents are wolves, jackals, bears, lions, tigers, leopards, elephants, chimpanzees, monkeys, or dolphins.

Could any of these beasts actually raise a human child to maturity? Dolphins and elephants can be dismissed at once for obvious reasons. If the well-known case of Lukas, the baboon-boy of South Africa, is authentic, then it can be assumed that chimpanzees could also rear an infant. Or, for that matter, since cases of wolf-boys seem authentic, a chimpanzee-boy seems even more possible. It is even possible that the monkeys of *Jungle-Born*, who were of a very large species, could successfully raise an infant.

Stoneham tells of a supposedly true case of a black

male, exiled from his tribe, who lived and hunted with a lioness for several years. His account of Kaspa's adoption and how he managed to survive is based on the case of the black. But the black was an adult and the lioness was his partner, not a foster mother. Cub mortality is so high in prides that it seems unlikely that Kaspa could have lived to manhood.

The same can be said for the children raised by tigers and leopards in Kline's and Webster's novels. The odds would be a thousand to one against survival. But then there is Victor of Aveyron, who lived through even more natural vicissitudes than Kaspa and Kungai.

In my own judgment, it is extremely unlikely that an infant would last long in a big-cat society. He might be adopted, provided that he encountered a nursing mother who had just lost her cubs. The mothering instinct seems to be strong in many animals, as witness the validated cases of dogs who nurse kittens and rabbits and reports of wild lionesses who have nursed puppies. Most probably, however, the big cat would eat the infant. In any event, there is no authenticated case of any big cat having adopted an infant.

A nursing chimpanzee or baboon might suckle an infant. But wild chimpanzees are very shy and would probably not go near a human stranger, infant or not. Baboons are a favorite prey of leopards and a fleeing mother would be much hampered by the weight of a human baby. Moreover, when the infant had grown to a large size, he would be regarded as a competitor by the very jealous males.

On reflection, I would say that wolves and bears make the best candidates for foster parents. The accounts of authentic cases of wolf-reared children indicate that *Canis lupus* is the favorite candidate. Bears as foster parents figure frequently in folktales and legends, and it is possible that they have actually adopted infants. Still, granting that a bear might make a good mother, it does hibernate. How would a child get food in the winter?

The counterquestion to this is, How did Victor of Aveyron get food in the winters of eighteenth-century France? The climate was even colder then and he didn't steal it from humans. But he did get it and he flourished, though at the cost of loss of speech.

If Victor could survive all alone, a child with animals as companions, protectors, and mentors would have an even better chance of survival.

Bibliography

BAKER, OLAF. *Shasta of the Wolves.* New York: Dodd, Mead and Company, 1928.

BARTH, JOHN. *Giles Goat-Boy, Or the Revised New Syllabus.* New York: Doubleday, 1966.

BRUCE, GEORGE. *Scream of the Condor,* in George Bruce's Sky Fighters. Langley House, Inc. (n. d.).

BURROUGHS, EDGAR RICE. *Jungle Tales of Tarzan.* New York: Ballantine, 1973.

BYRD, BOB. *Ka-Zar, King of Fang and Claw.* Chicago: Manvis Publications, 1936.

CHESTER, WILLIAM L. "Hawk of the Wilderness." *Blue Book* Magazine, April-October, 1935.

———. "Kioga of the Unknown Land." *Blue Book* Magazine, March-August 1938.

———. "Kioga of the Wilderness." *Blue Book* Magazine, April-October 1936.

———. "One Against a Wilderness." *Blue Book* Magazine, March-August 1937.

ECKERT, ALLAN W. *Incident at Hawk's Hill.* Boston: Little, Brown, 1971.

EYTON, JOHN. *Jungle-Born.* New York: The Century Company, 1925.

GARRON, MARCO. *Azan the Ape Man.* London: Curtis Warren Ltd. (n. d.).

GRAVES, ROBERT. *The Greek Myths.* Maryland: Penguin Books, 1966.
244

HEUVELMANS, BERNARD. *On the Track of Unknown Animals.* New York: Hill and Wang, 1959.

JALAVA, LIISA. *Karhun Tytär.* Menninkäinen, Turku (preface indicates ca. 1887).

JONES, THOMAS LLEWELLAN. "The Man Who Really Was . . . Tarzan." *Man's Adventure,* New York: Stanley, March, 1959.

KIPLING, RUDYARD. *The Jungle Book.* New York: Grosset and Dunlap, 1950.

KLINE, OTIS ADELBERT. "Jan of the Jungle," *Argosy,* April 18, 25, 1931; May 2, 9, 1931.

———. *Tam, Son of the Tiger.* New York: Avalon Books, 1962.

"Kwa of the Jungle." *Thrilling Adventures.* August 1932.

LUPOFF, RICHARD A. *Edgar Rice Burroughs: Master of Adventure.* New York: Ace Books, 1968.

MEYERS, ROY. *Dolphin Boy.* New York: Ballantine Books, 1967.

NESVADBA, JOSEF. *The Lost Face; Best Science Fiction from Czechoslovakia.* New York: Taplinger Publishing Company, 1971.

PRENTICE, HARRY. *Captured by Apes.* New York: A. L. Burt, 1892.

REYNOLDS, JOHN MURRAY. "Ki-Gor, King of the Jungle," in *Jungle Stories.* New York: Fiction House Publication, 1938.

REYNOLDS, VERNON. *The Apes.* New York: E. P. Dutton, 1967.

RUSSELL, WHITWORTH. *Survivors.* London: Rackham, 1887.

SACKVILLE, ORME. *The Jungle Goddess.* London: The Modern Publishing Company.

SHAKESPEARE, WILLIAM. *The Winter's Tale.* New York: Signet Classics, 1963.

Standard Dictionary of Folklore, Mythology, and Legend. New York: Funk & Wagnalls, 1949.

STONEHAM, C. T. *From Hobo to Hunter, The Autobiography of C. T. Stoneham.* London: John Long Ltd., 1956.

————. *Kaspa, the Lion Man.* London: Methuen & Co., Ltd., 1933.

————. *The Lion's Way.* London: Hutchinson & Co., ca. 1931.

TRUFFAUT, FRANÇOIS, and GRUAULT, JEAN. *The Wild Child.* New York: Washington Square Press, 1973.

WEBSTER, F. A. M. *The Curse of the Lion.* London: United Press Ltd. (foreword is dated 1922).

————. *Lord of the Leopards.* London: Hutchinson & Co.

WHEELER, POST. *Hathoo of the Elephants.* New York: The Viking Press, 1943.